MURDER IN THE CROOKED HOUSE

Born in 1948 in Hiroshima prefecture, Soji Shimada has been dubbed the "God of Mystery" by Japanese crime fans. A novelist, essayist and short-story writer, he made his literary debut in 1981 with *The Tokyo Zodiac Murders*, which was shortlisted for the Edogawa Rampo Prize. Blending classical detective fiction with grisly violence and elements of the occult, he has gone on to publish several highly acclaimed series of mystery fiction, totalling more than 100 books. In 2009 Shimada received the prestigious Japan Mystery Literature Award in recognition of his life's work.

Louise Heal Kawai grew up in Manchester, England, but Japan has been her home since 1990. She has translated a variety of novels and short stories from Japanese, including Mieko Kawakami's novella *Ms Ice Sandwich* for Pushkin Press, Seicho Matsumoto's *A Quiet Place*, and *Seventeen* by Hideo Yokoyama.

SOJI SHIMADA

TRANSLATED BY LOUISE HEAL KAWAI

PUSHKIN VERTIGO

MURDER IN THE CROOKED HOUSE

Pushkin Press
65-69 Shelton Street
London WC2H 9HE

Naname Yashiki no Hanzai © 2016 Soji Shimada
First published in 1982 in Japan by Kodansha Ltd., Tokyo
Publication rights for this edition arranged through Kodansha Ltd.

English translation © Louise Heal Kawai 2019

First published by Pushkin Press in 2019

7 9 8 6

ISBN 13: 978-1-78227-456-8

Although this translation is of the 2016 revised Japanese edition of *Murder in the Crooked House*, the novel was originally published in 1982, and all details, such as the angle of the Leaning Tower of Pisa, are correct as of that date. The translator has attempted to stay faithful to place and time.

Designed and typeset by Tetragon, London
Printed and bound by Clays Ltd, Elcograf S.p.A.

www.pushkinpress.com

CONTENTS

Dramatis Personae   7

Prologue   9

ACT ONE

Scene 1 · The Entrance of the Ice Floe Mansion   23

Scene 2 · The Salon of the Ice Floe Mansion   29

Scene 3 · The Tower   45

Scene 4 · Room 1   53

Scene 5 · The Salon   59

Scene 6 · The Library   90

ACT TWO

Scene 1 · The Salon   123

Scene 2 · Room 14, Eikichi Kikuoka's Bedroom   132

Scene 3 · Room 9, Mr and Mrs Kanai's Bedroom   138

Scene 4 · Back in the Salon   147

Scene 5 · Kozaburo's Room in the Tower   153

Scene 6 · The Salon   161

Scene 7 · The Library   175

Scene 8 · The Salon   205

Scene 9 · The Tengu Room   209

Scene 10 · The Salon   225

ACT THREE

Scene 1 · The Salon   235

Scene 2 · The Tengu Room   242

Scene 3 · Room 15, The Detectives' Bedroom   247

Scene 4 · The Salon   249
Scene 5 · The Library   260
Scene 6 · The Salon   272

Entr'acte   277
Challenge to the Reader   285

FINAL ACT
Scene 1 · The Ground Floor Landing of the West Wing
     Staircase, or By the Door of Room 12   289
Scene 2 · Room 14   297
Scene 3 · The Tengu Room   302
Scene 4 · The Salon   305
Scene 5 · The Hill   343

Epilogue   347

DRAMATIS PERSONAE

The Residents of the Ice Floe Mansion

Kozaburo Hamamoto (68)	*owner of the Ice Floe Mansion and President of Hama Diesel*
Eiko Hamamoto (23)	*Kozaburo's daughter*
Kohei Hayakawa (50)	*live-in butler and chauffeur*
Chikako Hayakawa (44)	*Kohei's wife, live-in housekeeper*
Haruo Kajiwara (27)	*live-in chef*

The Guests

Eikichi Kikuoka (65)	*President of Kikuoka Bearings*
Kumi Aikura (22)	*Mr Kikuoka's secretary and mistress*
Kazuya Ueda (30)	*Mr Kikuoka's chauffeur*
Michio Kanai (47)	*executive at Kikuoka Bearings*
Hatsue Kanai (38)	*Michio's wife*
Shun Sasaki (26)	*student at Jikei University School of Medicine*
Masaki Togai (24)	*Tokyo University student*
Yoshihiko Hamamoto (19)	*Keio University student, grandson of Kozaburo Hamamoto's brother*

The Investigators

Saburo Ushikoshi	*Detective Chief Inspector, Sapporo City Police Headquarters*
Ozaki	*Detective Sergeant, Sapporo City Police Headquarters*
Okuma	*Detective Inspector, Wakkanai Police Station*
Anan	*Constable, Wakkanai Police Station*
Kiyoshi Mitarai	*fortune teller, psychic and self-styled detective*
Kazumi Ishioka	*Mitarai's friend*

PROLOGUE

I am like the king of a rainy land
Wealthy but powerless, young and yet very old
Who condemns the fawning manners of his tutors
And is bored with his dogs and other animals.
Nothing can cheer him, neither the chase nor falcons
Nor his people dying before his balcony.

CHARLES BAUDELAIRE,
Spleen

In the village of Hauterives in the south of France, there's a curious building known as Cheval's Palais Idéal. For thirty-three years, a humble postman by the name of Ferdinand Cheval laboured completely alone to create his dream palace, finally completing his task in 1912.

The structure is part Arabian palace, part Hindu temple; its entrance is like the gateway to a medieval European castle, with a Swiss-style shepherd's hut sitting next to it. The whole effect lacks unity, but there is no doubt that this is a perfect rendition of a child's fantasy castle. Here in Tokyo people worry too much about style, economy, or how they will be judged by others, and that is how they end up with characterless rows of rabbit hutches crammed in together.

Cheval was barely literate. The notes he left behind were full of spelling mistakes. But they were also alight with his burning belief that it was his life's mission to build this unique place of worship.

According to these notes, he embarked on his project while delivering the mail. He began by picking up any interesting or unusually shaped rocks or pebbles he found while out on his rounds, and putting them in his pockets. He was already forty-three years old at this point. After a while, along with his postbag he began to carry a large basket over his shoulder for the rocks. And then it wasn't long before he was taking a wheelbarrow out on his rounds.

One can only imagine how this eccentric postman was treated in his dull country village. Every day he took his collection of rocks and worked on building the foundation for his palace.

Twenty-six metres long, fourteen metres wide and twelve metres high—the construction of the palace building itself took three years. And then, slowly and steadily, all kinds of cement statues were added to its walls: cranes, leopards, ostriches, elephants, crocodiles. They would eventually cover all the surfaces of the building. Next, Cheval made a waterfall and three giant statues for the front wall.

He was seventy-six when he finally completed his great oeuvre. He enshrined his number one assistant—his trusty wheelbarrow—in the place of honour inside the palace, and built himself a modest house by the front entrance. After retiring from his job at the post office, he took up residence in the house with its excellent view of his palace. Apparently he had never intended the palace to be lived in.

In photos of Cheval's palace, the materials used to construct it seem to have the soft texture of rubber. The ornamental statues that adorn its whole surface are more intricate than those of Angkor Wat, but the overall form and appearance of the walls are not fixed or uniform. There seems to be no order or balance—everything seems to be in a kind of warped confusion. If you weren't interested in this kind of thing, you might just see the work of art to which Cheval dedicated the latter half of his life as a worthless antique or maybe even the equivalent of a pile of scrap metal.

It was easy for his fellow villagers to call Cheval a madman, but there was a clear commonality between the concept behind his palace and the work of the celebrated Spanish architect

Antonio Gaudí. Cheval's Palais Idéal is to this day the only tourist attraction in the otherwise unremarkable village of Hauterives.

If we're talking oddballs with a mania for architecture, then there is one character who cannot be ignored: King Ludwig II of Bavaria. He is also famous for being the patron of the composer Richard Wagner. His two lifelong passions seem to have been the reverence he had for Wagner, and the construction of his castles.

The Linderhof Palace was one of his architectural master-pieces. Many complained that it was a blatant rip-off of the style of the French House of Bourbon, but after pushing open the revolving stone door in the hill behind the castle and entering the high-roofed tunnel, you realize that the space you find yourself in is one of a kind.

The tunnel leads into a magnificent man-made cave with a wide, dark lake. In the middle of the lake sits a boat fashioned in the shape of a pearl oyster. The multicoloured lighting flickers, and at the water's edge there is a table made from branches of imitation coral. The cave walls are painted with fantastic scenes of angels and cherubs. There is no human being who wouldn't look at this scene and find their imagination piqued.

It is said that when his beloved Wagner passed away, King Ludwig II buried himself away in this gloomy underground burrow, and took all his meals at that fake coral table while reminiscing about his dear friend.

In the West, there are all kinds of buildings with surprises built in: sliding walls, secret tunnels, hidden passageways. By comparison, Japan has relatively few.

There are a few ninja houses with their secret entrances and exits, but everything in those is designed with a practical purpose.

But there is one, the Nijotei, a strange residence built in Fukagawa in Tokyo after the Great Kanto Earthquake. It seems to have been fairly well known. There were ladders that went right up to the ceiling, glass peepholes in the doors, a pentagon-shaped window in the entrance way.

Maybe the equivalent of Cheval's Palais Idéal exists somewhere in Japan, but I've never heard of one. There is, however, one place I ought to tell you about—the Crooked House in Hokkaido.

At the top of Japan's northernmost island, Hokkaido, on the very tip of Cape Soya, there's a high plain that overlooks the Okhotsk Sea. On this plain stands a peculiar-looking structure known by the locals as "The Crooked House".

It looks somewhat Elizabethan with its three-storey main building complete with pillars and white-painted walls. To the east of this is a cylindrical tower the spitting image of the Leaning Tower of Pisa.

The major difference between this tower and the one in Pisa is that all its surfaces are made from glass. And on this glass is a thin layer of aluminium, deposited by vacuum, or what is known as aluminium mirror-coating. Consequently, when the sun shines, everything that surrounds this tower is reflected in this glass cylinder.

On the edge of the high plain is a hill. Viewed from the summit of this hill, the giant cylindrical glass... or perhaps I should say mirror... anyway, this glass tower and Western-style house look like some kind of fairy-tale castle.

There's not another house in any direction as far as the eye can see. Nothing but a vast plain of grass the colour of dead leaves, stirred up by the wind. The nearest settlement is a small village situated way past the mansion and down the slope from the plain, at least ten minutes by foot.

When the sun goes down, the north wind roars across the plain, and the glass tower turns golden in the sunset. Behind it stretches the northern sea.

Here, the cold north sea is a deep shade of indigo blue. If you were to run down the hill and dip your hand into its water, you'd expect to see your fingers emerge blue with dye. In front of this sea, the gold-tinted glass tower looks as solemn and imposing as any place of religious worship.

Just in front of the main, Western-style house is a large stone patio, dotted with sculptures, a small pond and a flight of stone steps. At the base of the tower is what appears to be a flower bed in the shape of a fan. I say "what appears to be" because it is quite overgrown, and clearly hasn't been tended for a long while.

Neither the main house nor the tower is currently occupied. It's been for sale for many years, but it will probably stay that way. It's less the fault of the remote location; it's far more likely the murder that keeps buyers away.

This particular murder case was a very mysterious one. It caused quite a stir among the crime buffs and murder enthusiasts of the day. So for all of you who have not yet heard it, I am going to tell you the tale of "Murder in the Crooked House". I believe I've done all that's necessary to set the scene for this strange mystery. The setting is of course a bleak, wintry plain, and that crooked house.

*

The history of the main building and tower that make up the Crooked House is rather less like that of Cheval's palace, and a lot closer to Ludwig's castle, in the sense that the man who built them was a kind of modern-day king—a millionaire with both fortune and influence. His name was Kozaburo Hamamoto, and he was the president of Hama Diesel Corporation. But unlike either Cheval or Ludwig, he didn't have any crazy tendencies. He was simply a man of very particular tastes, and having money, he was able to indulge those tastes.

The boredom or the depression that plagued such a man who had reached the peak of his career might have been what turned him into something of a recluse. In a familiar story that we might hear from any corner of the world, it seemed that all the gold he had amassed weighed heavily on his mind.

There was nothing really unusual about the structure of the house and the tower. The interior resembled a maze in some ways, but it was nothing too complicated, and once you got your bearings it wasn't likely that you would get lost more than a couple of times at most. There were no revolving wall panels, underground caves or descending ceilings. The feature that caught the attention was exactly what gave it its local nickname: that from the very beginning it had been built crooked, or rather, leaning at an angle. Thus the glass tower was literally a "Leaning Tower".

The main house leans at an angle of about five or six degrees off the vertical, not really enough to be obvious from the outside. On the other hand, the inside is quite bewildering.

The building leans towards the south. The windows on the north and south sides are the perfectly normal kind that you'd find in any house, but the ones on the east and west sides are

16

problematic. On these walls, the windows and their frames have been constructed to run parallel with the ground outside. Once your vision adjusts to the strange appearance of the rooms, you feel like a hard-boiled egg that has been dropped on the floor and is trying to roll uphill. It's a feeling that's difficult to imagine without having stayed at the mansion. The longer you stay, the more confused your mind becomes.

The lord of the manor, Kozaburo Hamamoto, was reputed to have had a lot of fun at his guests' expense, watching them try to navigate his twisted home. Quite an expensive way to get some childish laughs.

I think that should be enough information for you to get an idea of the man behind the mansion and to set the scene for this tale.

My story begins when Kozaburo Hamamoto was almost seventy years old. His wife had already passed away, and he had left fame and reputation behind, retiring up here in the far north of Japan.

He would listen to his favourite classical music and loved reading mystery novels. His hobby was studying and collecting mechanical toys and dolls, particularly Western automata, or clockwork dolls. He had amassed a lot of capital through acquiring the stock of various small- and medium-sized companies, and he used the money to build up his collection. He stored his precious dolls and other toys in a room in the mansion known as the "Tengu Room", so named because its walls were entirely covered with masks of that famous long-nosed demon of Japanese folklore.

This same room was also home to a certain life-sized doll known as either Golem or Jack. According to ancient European folklore, on a stormy night, this doll had the power to get up and walk around by itself. It ended up playing a leading role in the inexplicable events that unfolded that winter.

Despite having such eclectic tastes and hobbies, Kozaburo Hamamoto was not really eccentric at all. In order to offer a glimpse of the natural beauty of the different seasons of northern Hokkaido, he would invite guests to stay at his home – and he loved to talk. Probably he was searching for a kindred spirit; sadly, he never seemed to find one. The reason for this will be revealed as soon as the curtain rises on our story.

The incident took place at Christmas in 1983. Back then, the Crooked House—or to give it its proper name, the Ice Floe Mansion—was scrupulously cared for by its live-in staff, Kohei and Chikako Hayakawa. The garden and stone patio were carefully tended, and at that time of year covered by a thick layer of snow.

On that particular day, it was hard to imagine that a raging blizzard had left behind such a gentle coating of snow, with the dry brown grass sleeping peacefully beneath. The snow-dusted crooked house stood majestic on its carpet of pure white.

Night fell, and the Okhotsk Sea was full of drift ice, ice floes that jostled each other daily, as if trying to take over the whole surface. The sky turned a gloomy shade of grey, and the high and low moans of the northerly wind were a permanent soundtrack.

Presently, lights came on in the mansion, and soft flakes of snow began to fall. The scene was set, the mood slightly bittersweet.

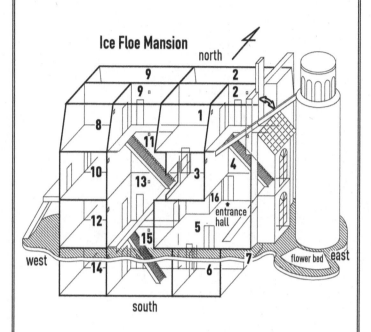

Fig. 1

Ice Floe Mansion

north

Room Allocation on December 25th—Key to Fig. 1

Room 1: Kumi Aikura
Room 2: Eiko Hamamoto
Room 3: Display / Tengu Room
Room 4: Library
Room 5: Salon
Room 6: Haruo Kajiwara
Room 7: Kohei and Chikako Hayakawa
Room 8: Yoshihiko Hamamoto
Room 9: Michio and Hatsue Kanai

Room 10: Kazuya Ueda
          (sports equipment storeroom)
Room 11: Table tennis room
Room 12: Masaki Togai
Room 13: Shun Sasaki
Room 14: Eikichi Kikuoka (study)
Room 15: Unoccupied
Room 16: Kitchen
The Tower: Kozaburo Hamamoto

ACT ONE

*If any dance could distract us from the boredom of living,
it would be the dance of the dead.*

The Entrance of the Ice Floe Mansion

The cheerful notes of "White Christmas" and the sounds of merrymaking spilt out from the salon behind them.

From down the hill came the grinding of tyre chains, and a black Mercedes-Benz appeared out of the swirling snow—more party guests arriving.

Kozaburo Hamamoto stood in front of the open double doors, smoking a pipe, a brightly coloured ascot tied at his neck. Although his hair had turned completely silver, he was in excellent shape with no hint of excess flab, making his age difficult to estimate from his appearance. He lowered his pipe to exhale a plume of white smoke, then turned to smile at the woman by his side.

His daughter, Eiko, was wearing an elegantly expensive cocktail dress. Her hair was up, exposing her shoulders to the evening chill. She'd inherited her father's aquiline nose and rather prominent chin, but was nevertheless something of a beauty. She was tall; in heels she stood slightly taller than her father. Her make-up was carefully done, but on the heavy side, as you would expect for an occasion like this evening. Her tight-lipped expression was that of a company president listening wordlessly to the demands of her union members.

The porch was illuminated in a yellow glow as the car pulled in. The instant it stopped in front of the Hamamotos, the door was flung open with great force and a tall, rather heavily built man with thinning hair leapt out into the snow.

"Well, what have we here? My own personal welcoming committee!" he bellowed, rather louder than necessary, his words forming white clouds in the air around him. Eikichi Kikuoka was the kind of man who had probably never spoken softly in his life; the extroverted company president was forever out and about attending social events. Perhaps that was why his voice always sounded a little raspy.

The lord of the manor nodded graciously, and his daughter formally welcomed the guest to their home.

A petite woman emerged from the car behind Kikuoka. She wore a black dress with a leopard-skin coat thrown over her shoulders and her movements were graceful and catlike. Her presence seemed to make the two inhabitants of the manor— or at least the younger—uneasy. Neither of the Hamamotos had set eyes on her before this evening. Her face was kittenish too—tiny, cute.

"Allow me to introduce you to my new secretary, Kumi Aikura. Kumi, this is Mr Hamamoto."

It was clear that Kikuoka was doing his best to suppress it, but a hint of pride had crept into his voice.

Kumi Aikura smiled sweetly.

"I'm very pleased to meet you," she said. Her voice was astonishingly high-pitched.

Unable to stand the sound of that voice, Eiko quickly stepped up to the driver's window and gave the chauffeur parking directions.

As soon as the butler, Kohei Hayakawa, who'd been waiting politely in the entrance way, showed the two new guests into the salon, a grin of amusement appeared on Kozaburo Hamamoto's face. How many secretaries had Kikuoka gone through now? It was getting difficult to keep count. This Kumi Aikura would be doing her utmost to perform those all-important duties of sitting on her boss's lap and walking arm and arm with him through the streets of Ginza, no doubt earning a small fortune in the process.

"Daddy?"

"What is it?" Hamamoto replied without taking his pipe from his mouth.

"Why don't you go inside now? There's only Togai and the Kanais still to come. There's no need for you to welcome them personally. Kohei and I will be fine by ourselves. Go and keep Mr Kikuoka company."

"Hmm. I suppose you're right… But aren't you going to catch cold dressed like that?"

"Could you ask Auntie to fetch me a mink? Any of them will do. See if she can get Sasaki to bring it out to me. It'd be nice if he could be out here too to greet Togai when he arrives."

"Will do. Kohei, where's Chikako right now?"

"She was in the kitchen last time I saw her…" replied the butler from his post inside the doorway.

The two men disappeared into the house.

Left alone, Eiko hugged her exposed arms as she listened to the music of Cole Porter drifting out from the salon. And then suddenly she felt the soft brush of fur around her shoulders. She turned her head to see Shun Sasaki.

"Thanks," she said curtly.

"Togai's late," Sasaki remarked. He was a young man, fair-skinned and handsome.

"He'll be stuck in the snow somewhere. You know what a terrible driver he is."

"You're probably right."

"I want you to stay until he gets here."

"Sure."

They stood there quietly for a while, until Eiko abruptly broke the silence.

"Did you see Kikuoka's secretary?"

"Yes, er... Well... Yes, I saw her."

"What taste!"

Sasaki looked confused.

"Vulgar and ill-bred."

Eiko frowned. Normally when she spoke, she took the greatest care to conceal her true emotions. It made her something of an enigma to all the young men who moved in her circle.

A Japanese-made mid-size saloon came struggling up the hill.

"Looks like he made it."

The car pulled up in front of them and the window was wound down. The driver's plump face with its silver-framed glasses appeared. Despite the wintry weather, Togai was covered in sweat. He opened the door slightly, but stayed in his seat.

"Thank you for inviting me, Eiko."

"You're late!"

"The roads were thick with snow. It was terrible. Whoa! You're more beautiful than ever tonight. Here, I've got a Christmas present for you."

He handed her a wrapped gift.

"Thanks."

"Hey, Sasaki. What are you doing out here?"

"Been waiting for you. Just about to freeze to death, too. Hurry up and come inside."

"Right. Will do."

The two men knew each other and would sometimes get together in Tokyo for a drink.

26

"Go and park. You know where, right? The usual place."

"Yeah, I know."

The saloon puttered off through the snow and disappeared around the back of the mansion. Sasaki hurried after it.

Right away, a taxi pulled up in its place. The back door opened and a tall and extremely skinny man stepped out into the snow. It was one of Kikuoka's employees, Michio Kanai. He turned and reached back into the taxi, his silhouette like a solitary winter crane in the middle of a snowbound field. It appeared to take all his physical strength to extract his wife, Hatsue, from the narrow back seat. The woman who eventually emerged was his exact physical opposite.

The husband turned to Eiko.

"It's so lovely to see you, Ms Hamamoto. How kind of you to invite us again."

It might be a little unkind to say, but Kanai was the master of the ingratiating smile—so much so that the muscles of his face seemed to be permanently fixed in that one expression. You could call it an occupational hazard. With only the slightest flexing of these muscles, he was able to create a smile, even when his real emotion was something quite different. Or maybe it was every other expression besides this smile that required special muscle power. It was hard to say.

It was impossible to recall this man's regular facial expression, Eiko always thought. In fact, whenever she tried to picture Kanai he was wrinkling up the outer corners of his eyes and showing his teeth. Eiko frequently wondered whether he had been born that way.

"We've been looking forward to seeing you. Thanks for making the journey."

"Not at all. Not at all. Has the boss arrived yet?"

"Yes, he's here already."

"Oh, dear. We're late!"

Hatsue Kanai stood patiently waiting in the snow. At first glance, she appeared pleasant and laid-back, but her eyes were surprisingly sharp, and now her gaze was hastily checking out Eiko, sweeping her over from head to toe. In the next instant, her face broke into a smile.

"What a simply gorgeous outfit!" she announced. Her praise didn't extend beyond her hostess's dress.

With the arrival of the Kanais, all the guests were assembled.

The last of them safely inside the mansion, Eiko primly turned on her heel and headed in towards the salon. Cole Porter became louder. She strode like a stage actress passing from her dressing room, through the wings and out to her audience, with just the appropriate mix of apprehension and confidence.

The Salon of the Ice Floe Mansion

A gorgeous chandelier hung from the ceiling of the salon. Her father had protested that such a grandiose item didn't suit the style of the house, but Eiko had insisted and won.

In the west corner of this oversized living-dining room, there was a circular fireplace, next to it a pile of branches and logs. Above the fireplace was a giant inverted funnel that served as a chimney. On the brick surround of the fireplace, a single metal coffee cup sat forgotten by the side of Kozaburo Hamamoto's favourite rocking chair.

All of the guests were seated around a long, narrow table beneath the electric candles of the chandelier. The effect was of a tiny floating forest of lights. The music had changed from Cole Porter to a Christmas medley.

Because the floor of the salon was on a slope, the legs of the table and surrounding chairs had been cut just the right amount to keep the dining arrangements perfectly horizontal.

The eyes of each guest were on the glass of wine and a candle in front of them, as they politely waited for Eiko to begin her speech. Presently, the music faded out and all eyes turned to the mistress of the mansion.

"Thank you, everyone, for making the long journey to be here this evening."

Her shrill voice carried clearly through the large space.

"We have both young guests, and older. You must be exhausted, but I'm sure it's going to be worth your while having made the trip as there is something very special about tonight. It's Christmas Day, and Christmas means snow. And by snow I don't mean a bit of decorative cotton wool or shredded paper. I'm talking about the real thing. Our Hokkaido home is the best place for the authentic experience. Tonight, for your delight, we have prepared a very special Christmas tree."

The moment the words were out of her mouth, the lights of the chandelier faded to darkness. Somewhere at the back of the room the chef, Kajiwara, had hit the switch. The music changed to a more solemn, traditional carol.

This part of the programme had been rehearsed what felt like a thousand times over. The military precision of her preparations would have put an army to shame.

"Please take a look through the window."

There were gasps and exclamations of wonder. A real fir tree had been planted in the back garden and decorated with hundreds of multicoloured light bulbs which suddenly began to twinkle in every colour. The snow that dusted its branches sparkled with the lights.

"Lights!"

At Eiko's command, the room lighting snapped back on, and the music changed back to upbeat Christmas songs.

"You will all have plenty of chances to enjoy the tree. If you don't mind the cold, I recommend standing under its branches and listening to the creaking sound of the ice floes rubbing together out in the Okhotsk Sea. Christmas here is the real thing—like nothing you can experience in Tokyo.

"And now, lend an ear to the man who has made this fantastic Christmas experience possible for all of us. My dear father, of whom I am incredibly proud, will now address everyone."

As she spoke, Eiko began to applaud vigorously. The assembled guests scrambled to follow suit.

Kozaburo Hamamoto got to his feet, his pipe clasped in his left hand as always.

"Eiko, please don't flatter me so much. You're embarrassing me in front of our guests."

There was general laughter.

"Not at all! Everyone here is proud to be a friend of yours, Daddy. Aren't you?"

This last part was addressed to the assembled guests, and like a flock of sheep they all began nodding as one. The most emphatic of all was Eikichi Kikuoka. It was well known that the fortunes of his company were entirely tied up with the Hama Diesel Company.

"Dear friends, this is the second time most of you have been invited to this old man's whimsical mansion, and I'm sure it won't be the last. I hope you have got used to our sloping floors, and that no one will lose their footing and take a tumble. But don't get too comfortable. I do rather enjoy watching you all stagger around."

The guests laughed.

"Here in Japan, Christmas is just an excuse for bars and restaurants to make a bit of money. It was very wise of you all to come and spend it here instead.

"And now let's enjoy our champagne before it gets warm. Well, I don't suppose it matters if it does. You only need to put it outside for five minutes and it'll be perfectly chilled again. Anyway, I'd like to lead you all in a toast…"

Kozaburo picked up his glass. Everyone reached immediately for theirs and held them up. As Kozaburo toasted Christmas, everyone else in the room murmured something like "Thank you for everything and all the best for the next year" or other choice phrases that they hoped would help to improve their business relationship with their host.

Kozaburo put down his glass.

"Many of you will be meeting for the first time this evening. Young, silver-haired alike, I'll make the introductions right now. And lest I forget, there are several people among us who also make this mansion their home and are of the greatest help to my family. I really ought to include them in my introductions. Eiko, I'd like to introduce Kohei and Chikako to everyone."

Eiko raised her right hand and spoke briskly.

"I'll take care of that. You don't need to make the introductions yourself. Sasaki, go and fetch Mr Kajiwara, Kohei and Auntie."

The mansion's staff arrived in the salon and followed the mistress's directions to line up by the side wall.

"Mr Kikuoka and Mr Kanai already visited us back in the summer, and so you'll both probably remember the faces of our staff, but I think it's the first time for many of you to meet them, or each other. So let me introduce everyone, beginning with our guest of honour. Please listen carefully and remember everyone's name. No mistakes later, please.

"First of all, this fine figure of a gentleman. I think you are all familiar with Mr Eikichi Kikuoka, President of Kikuoka Bearings? Some of you may have seen his photo in the magazines, but now you have the opportunity to see the real thing."

Kikuoka had twice been the subject of a big scandal in the weekly gossip magazines. One time he'd got himself into a mess over payments to a mistress at the end of an affair, and ended up in court. The second time was after he'd been dumped by a famous actress.

His nickname had long been "the Chrysanthemum" (the Japanese characters for "Kikuoka" mean "chrysanthemum hill" and he used to have a rather impressive mop of lightish hair). But now as he bowed to everyone, he revealed a rapidly growing bald spot. He turned to Kozaburo and bowed once again.

"Would you mind giving us a word?"

"Sure. Sorry to go first, folks. So every time I come, wonderful house. Amazing location too. It's a real honour to be able to sit by Mr Hamamoto and share a glass of wine in a place like this."

"And next to Mr Kikuoka, in the gorgeous outfit, is his secretary, Ms Aikura. I'm sorry, what was your given name again?"

Of course, Eiko remembered perfectly well that the woman's name was Kumi, but this way she could imply that she didn't quite believe it was her real one. However, Kumi Aikura wasn't fazed by this in the least. In her sugar-sprinkled voice, she replied with perfect dignity,

"I'm Kumi. So nice to meet you all."

This woman is a tough customer, Eiko decided on the spot. For sure, she must have worked in a hostess bar.

"What a lovely name! Not at all ordinary." Eiko paused for a moment. "It makes you sound like a TV star or something."

"I'm always afraid I'll fail to live up my name."

The high-pitched, girlish tone didn't falter for a second.

"I'm so short. If I were taller and more glamorous, I might be able to live up to a name like that. I envy you, Eiko."

Eiko was five feet eight. For that reason she always wore flat slipper-like shoes. If she wore heels she'd be getting up towards six feet. Right now, she was momentarily at a loss for words. She moved on quickly.

"And next to Kumi, we have the president of Kikuoka Bearings, Mr Michio Kanai."

She'd been thrown, and the words had just slipped out. But even though she heard Kikuoka tease his employee—*Hey, when were you made president?*—she still didn't recognize her mistake right away.

Kanai got to his feet, and with his usual fixed smile, began to shower Kozaburo Hamamoto with praise. He didn't forget his own boss either. The skilful speech went on for quite a while. This was exactly the kind of performance that had got him to where he was in the world.

"And the voluptuous lady next to him is his wife, Hatsue."

Eiko realized this blunder immediately. *Voluptuous…* Sure enough, Hatsue had a comeback.

"I had to miss my exercise class to come today."

From the other side of the table, Kumi gave her a quick once-over and looked very obviously self-satisfied.

"I'm hoping a breath of this pure air will be a boost to my diet."

She seemed to have been quite put out by Eiko's comment, and didn't add anything else.

Returning to the male guests, Eiko quickly regained her usual composure.

"This handsome young man is Shun Sasaki, in his sixth year at Jikei University School of Medicine. He'll soon be taking the National Medical Examination. For now, he's keeping an eye on my father's health, and staying with us through the winter holidays."

How easy it was to introduce the men, Eiko thought, as Sasaki spoke.

"The food is delicious, the air is pure, no noisy telephones ringing; as a medical student I'd really like to meet the person who could fall ill in a place like this."

Kozaburo Hamamoto was famous for his dislike of telephones. There was not a single one anywhere in the Ice Floe Mansion.

"Next to Sasaki is his friend, Masaki Togai, a Tokyo University student with a promising future. I think you have probably heard of his father, Shunsaku Togai, member of the House of Councillors?"

There was a slight murmur of appreciation among the guests, naïve excitement at being in the presence of political royalty…

"A real thoroughbred, if you will. Please, Mr Thoroughbred…"

Togai stood up, his face pale, and fiddled momentarily with his silver-framed glasses.

"I'm honoured to be here this evening. When I told my father about the invitation, he was delighted."

And with that, he took his seat again.

"And next we have a boy who seems to have caught the sun out on the ski slopes, my nephew—well, technically Daddy's older brother's grandson—Yoshihiko. He's rather good-looking, don't you think? Still only nineteen, and a first-year student at Keio University. He's staying with us for the winter break."

The suntanned boy in the white sweater got to his feet, shyly said hello and sat straight back down.

"Is that it? Sorry, Yoshihiko, you have to speak properly."

"But I haven't got anything to say."

"Of course you have. You're too shy. Your hobbies or something about your university, there are plenty of things you could talk about. Come on, speak up!"

But there was no reaction.

"Well, I believe I've covered all of our dear guests. Now I'd like to introduce our staff to you. First of all, the gentleman standing over there, Kohei Hayakawa. He's been with our family ever since we lived in Kamakura—about twenty years. He's our butler and our chauffeur and general odd-jobs man.

"Next to him is his wife, Chikako. She's our housekeeper and is an invaluable help to us all. Please feel free to ask her for whatever you need.

"The man standing closest to us is our wonderful chef, Haruo Kajiwara. As you can see, he is still in his twenties, but his skills are world class. We managed to lure him away from the Hotel Okura, which didn't want to let him go. Very soon, everyone will be able to taste for themselves how skilled he is."

She turned to the three members of the staff.

"Thank you, everyone. That will do. Please get back to what you need to do.

"So that completes the introductions," she continued, addressing her guests once more. "I'm confident you are all excellent at remembering names and faces.

"And now, while dinner is being served, and you enjoy the view of our Christmas tree, I'm sure you have much to discuss. So without further ado, Yoshihiko, Sasaki, Togai, would you light the candles for us? As soon as that's done, we'll lower the salon lights. I wish you all a very enjoyable evening."

The middle-aged contingent immediately flocked around Kozaburo Hamamoto and began to chat, but it was noticeable that the loudest laughter was from the president of Kikuoka Bearings. Kozaburo's pipe remained firmly in place.

Eiko realized that thanks to the business with Kumi Aikawa and Hatsue Kanai, she had been guilty of one more blunder. She had forgotten to introduce Ueda, Kikuoka's chauffeur, probably because he had been blocked from view by the large-set figure of Togai. But she soon shrugged it off: *He's just a driver, after all.*

Dinner was served. The guests were treated to roast turkey with all the trimmings. As Eiko had promised, here at the very northern tip of Japan they were able to enjoy the flavours of a top-class Tokyo hotel.

While the other guests were finishing their after-dinner cup of tea, Sasaki got up and went to the window to take a closer look at the Christmas tree. It continued its lonely blinking from beneath its layer of snow.

Sasaki watched the tree for a while, but then noticed something strange. Near the French windows that led from the salon out into the garden, there was a thin stake or pole of some kind sticking out of the snow, about two metres out from the wall of the house. Somebody must have stuck it there. The section visible above the snow was about a metre. The stake itself resembled a piece of the wood that was piled up by the salon fireplace. Except that whoever had done this had apparently selected a particularly straight piece. Earlier that day, when he had been helping Eiko with the tree decorations, the stake hadn't been there.

What on earth? thought Sasaki, wiping the condensation from the window pane to get a better look. He peered out into the night and as he did so he noticed that over towards the west corner of the house, only vaguely visible through the whirling snowflakes, there was a second stake. Because of the distance it was hard to be certain but it seemed as if this too was another thin branch of firewood, protruding about a metre from the snow. As far as he could tell, there were no other stakes visible – at least from the salon window. Just these two.

Sasaki wanted to call Togai over and ask him what he thought they might be, but he was deep in conversation with Eiko. Yoshihiko was in the circle of older guests including Kozaburo,

Kikuoka and Kanai, and Sasaki didn't want to disturb their conversation, although whether it was business talk or idle chat wasn't clear. Kajiwara and the Hayakawas were nowhere to be seen—probably back in the kitchen.

Suddenly Kozaburo raised his voice above the chit-chat.

"All you youngsters, haven't you had enough of listening to old people prattling on? Come on, let's hear something amusing."

Sasaki took this cue to sit back down at the table, and with that, the mysterious stakes in the snow were forgotten.

To tell the truth, Kozaburo Hamamoto was fed up with listening to the empty flattery from tonight's guests. In fact, his mood was turning sour. The very reason he had built this eccentric home up here in the far north was to escape the clutches of suck-ups like this.

And yet, like a herd of wild animals they came stampeding after him across hundreds of kilometres. However weird the sloping floor, however eccentric his collection of antiques, they just blindly praised everything in sight. As long as he still had the scent of money, they would hunt him down to the ends of the earth.

His hopes were with the younger generation, and he addressed them now.

"All right, do you like mysteries? I'm very fond of them myself. I'm going to set you a puzzle to solve. Everyone here is attending, or has attended, a top university, so I'm sure you have some of the smartest minds in the country.

"How about this one? In the gold-panning region of Mexico, right by the US border, there was a young boy who piled up bags of sand on his bicycle and crossed the border from Mexico into the United States every single day. The US customs officials assumed that he was a smuggler and would open and search the suspicious sandbags. However, all they ever found inside was plain old sand, and not a single nugget of gold. So what was the boy up to? Here is your quiz: What was he smuggling, and how was he doing it? How about it, Mr Kikuoka? Can you solve it?"

"Let's see… No, I can't."

Kanai immediately echoed his boss.

"I can't get it either."

Neither man looked as if he were giving the problem any thought whatsoever.

"Yoshihiko, how about you?"

The boy silently shook his head.

"Do you all give up? This one wasn't difficult at all. The boy was smuggling bicycles."

The loudest laughter came from Kikuoka. Kanai also offered his own fawning reaction,

"It was bicycles! I see. Very good."

"Now that puzzle was one thought up by Perry Mason's friend Drake and his secretary, Della. Pretty good, wasn't it? If you want to smuggle bicycles, the way to do it is to base your operation right in a gold-panning region.

"Okay, let's think of another one… This time I'm not going to give you the answer. Let's see… What would be a good one…? All right, here we go. This one is a true story—something that a friend of mine used to boast about long ago. I've told it many times in my speech to the new recruits at the company. The story is set in the 1950s.

"These days, all the railway companies in Japan, both public and private, have what look like little burners on the rails to prevent a thick layer of snow from building up on the tracks

39

or the rails freezing. But back in the fifties, Japan was still a poor country, and no railway companies had anything like that.

"One winter, maybe 1955, Tokyo had a very heavy snowfall. Fifty centimetres fell in one night. Of course, all the private and public railway companies were forced to suspend operations. I'm not sure what would happen these days, but in Tokyo where they weren't used to so much snow, they didn't have snow ploughs. Back then, all the railway company employees used to be put to work shovelling the snow by hand. It was a terrible task and took hours. It was impossible to get the tracks clear by the morning rush hour.

"However, Hamakyu Railways, whose current president is that good friend I mentioned at the start, managed to get their trains running after only the shortest of delays. And by rush hour, all their trains were running on time. So how do you think they did it?

"My friend used a method; I suppose we could call it a trick. However, I must stress that he wasn't the president back then, and was in no position to mobilize a whole army of employees to help deal with the snow. Nor did he have access to any specialized equipment. He had to rely on his own brilliance. He rose to fame overnight within the company."

"That really happened? Sounds like a miracle," said Kikuoka. Kanai had to chime in too.

"Yes, you're right. A true miracle…"

"Yes, I know it was a miracle! But I'd like to hear the answer," said Kozaburo, a little frustrated.

"Yes, yes, of course. I'm going to say that the first train of the day had a snow plough attached to the front."

"No, they didn't have anything like that back then. Besides it would have been impossible—the snow was too deep. And if that kind of equipment had been available, then for sure all the other train companies would have owned the same thing. No, he used nothing like that. Just what was already available."

"Mr Hamamoto, all of your friends are really amazing people."

Kozaburo paid no attention to Kanai's gratuitous flattery.

"I've got it."

It was Sasaki who spoke. Next to him, Togai's expression was inscrutable.

"They kept the empty trains running all through the night."

"Well done! You got it. As soon as it began to snow and looked like it was going to stick, my friend got the trains to run at ten-minute intervals throughout the night. And back then it took a lot of determination on his part to get something like that done. There are hard-headed bosses who resist new ideas everywhere. But thanks to that level of resolve, he now sits in the president's chair. What do you think? Are you ready to try another one?"

Togai, eager to recover from his slow start, nodded energetically.

Unfortunately for him, all of the puzzles that Kozaburo came up with were successfully solved by Shun Sasaki. Every time Sasaki opened his mouth and came out with the next impressive correct answer, Togai's face would turn steadily more crimson, until it matched the lights on the Christmas tree.

Kozaburo glanced at the young man's expression. He realized what his eccentric quiz had become. A chance to win the ultimate prize.

Both young men, or Togai at least, were treating this quiz as a way to win Eiko's favour. If he succeeded in coming first, Togai believed that his prize would be a ticket for that most

41

romantic trip around the world—a honeymoon. And then on his return, the rest of his prize money would be the legacy of a lifetime in this mansion.

Kozaburo had predicted this might happen, and with a level of cynicism that had been perfected over many years, he had prepared these puzzles purposely to get this reaction.

"Mr Sasaki, you seem very good at this. Would you like a more challenging problem?"

"If possible," Sasaki replied, clearly emboldened by his success.

And then Kozaburo said something that made everybody assembled think they'd lost their hearing for a moment.

"Eiko, have you decided yet who you're going to marry?"

Naturally, Eiko looked horrified.

"What are you talking about, Daddy? Where did that come from all of a sudden?"

"If you haven't made your decision yet, how about one of these young men sitting here tonight? How about whoever is able to answer the question I'm about to set them?"

"Daddy, stop joking around!"

"Actually, I'm not joking at all. I'm perfectly serious. This eccentric house, the ridiculous pile of junk I've collected that sits in Room 3, that can all be called a joke. But this, right now, is me being serious. Here before you are two fine young men. I would have absolutely no objections to you choosing either one of them. To be honest, I don't have the energy to object. And if you don't know which to choose, you have nothing to worry about. Leave it to me. I can choose for you—with a puzzle. I've come prepared with a question for that very purpose."

That'll do it, thought Kozaburo. Now we'll see their true colours.

"Of course this is no longer the olden days when the man who solves the riddle gets a reward of the daughter's hand in marriage. Instead I'll say that the kind of man who can solve a puzzle like this one will get no objection from me. Apart from that it's up to my daughter to choose."

The two young men's eyes gleamed, possibly reflecting the mountain of gold coins that they had in their sight. In contrast, Kozaburo was inwardly grinning. His full intentions wouldn't be clear until the puzzle was solved.

"The matter of Eiko aside, I'm very interested in tackling another puzzle," said Sasaki.

"Not to mention a chance for Mr Togai here to redeem himself... Anyway, this man you see before you both has spent a long life in a forest being buffeted over and over by the wind, and now I'm just a dead tree that has dropped all its leaves. I've had enough of all the manoeuvring and haggling that my life requires. I no longer recognize nor care for the marks of what we call 'good birth' or 'pedigree'. It's what inside that matters. I've said it repeatedly, but as you get older, or as your status in society rises, you start to forget about, or cease to care for, the things that others are obsessed with. And so, this quiz I offer not only to Togai and to Sasaki, but also to Mr Ueda and Mr Kajiwara."

"It makes no difference to me whether a man can solve some puzzle or not," interrupted Eiko. "If I can't stand him, I can't stand him."

"Well, obviously, my dear. I know you're not the type to quietly acquiesce if I tell you to marry one of these men."

"I do what you tell me on other matters, but not this."

"You're from a good family, so I know you're much more discerning than I am. So on that matter I'm completely confident."

43

"If I solve the puzzle, may I marry your daughter?"

This last question was from Kikuoka.

"If the young lady is agreeable, then I suppose you may," said Kozaburo generously. Kikuoka laughed.

And then Kozaburo had one more surprise announcement.

"So please go and call Mr Kajiwara. I'm going to show everyone my room at the top of the tower."

"What did you say?" Eiko couldn't believe her ears. "Why are we going up there?"

"Because that's where the puzzle is."

Kozaburo got to his feet.

"At any rate," he added, as if an afterthought, "I've got a special trick up my sleeve."

SCENE 3

The Tower

Kozaburo set off up the stairs from the salon, his guests filing after him. He called back over his shoulder as he climbed.

"My puzzle is a bit of a silly, self-indulgent thing, but it's something that I was thinking about when I built this house, and I always hoped this day would come. Ladies and gentlemen, next to this building is a tower, which houses my bedroom. At the base of the tower there's a rather strangely shaped flower bed. Have you ever wondered about its layout? The mystery that I'm challenging you to solve is, One, What is the significance of its design? And Two, Why is it there? That's all."

The higher they climbed, the narrower the staircase became, until eventually it came to a dead end. An imposing black door made of iron blocked their way, feeling rather like an exit from this world to the next. The metal had broad horizontal folds over its whole surface, giving the impression of some kind of avant-garde sculpture—a hulking, graceless monument.

Everyone watched as Kozaburo reached for a looped chain that hung from the wall and pulled on it. There was a great rattling sound that seemed to come from a long-gone era, and then something unexpected happened. The assembled guests had expected the door to swing open towards them, hinged on the left or the right, but instead it began to fall slowly away from them—downwards and outwards.

Everyone stayed frozen in one line on the narrow stairs. The staircase was lower on the right side than the left and the roof sloped down over their heads, making the wall appear to lean towards them. Right now everything was disorientating.

Like the second hand of a giant clock, the door very slowly moved from its number twelve position, and continued to revolve downwards. Now there was a second surprise in store for the observers.

What had been visible of the door from the inside—well, if you could call it a door—had been no more than one small section of the whole. As it continued to fall, it became clear that they had been looking at just the lower extremity of a massively tall metal slab. The top reached way up into the heavy black sky and was swallowed up in the darkness. As it fell away from the wall and the gap opened up farther, the noise of the wind was added to the loud rattling of the chain, and a few snowflakes fluttered in. The waiting guests finally began to understand why the operation was taking so long.

The structure was in fact a sort of drawbridge, which led across to the tower. The horizontal folds in the welding weren't decorative after all; they served a very practical purpose—that of steps in a massive outdoor staircase. The party had climbed the regular stairs from the salon to the top of the main building, but the summit of the neighbouring tower was farther up yet.

The bridge was about to reach its target, and now through the newly exposed rectangular opening, the assembled guests were treated to a view of the night sky. Beyond the madly whirling snowflakes, the turret of the tower loomed out of the darkness, majestic as a religious painting.

The circular tip of the tower looked rather like the highest turret of the Leaning Tower of Pisa. Around the outside was a kind of covered walkway with a fenced handrail. From the eaves above the walkway hung several giant icicles, looking disturbingly like vicious fangs in the midst of the furiously whirling powder snow.

With its stunning backdrop, the scene could have been straight out of a hitherto unknown Wagner opera. Behind the tower hung a great black curtain, concealing backstage the northern sea buried in drift ice. The audience was transported to a different time and place—to nineteenth-century northern Europe. Everyone's attention was on this performance of winter hell playing out beyond the proscenium arch.

Finally, there was a loud clang as the giant bridge made contact with the tower and rested on its parapet.

"Right, the bridge is in place," Kozaburo called over his shoulder as he set out. "It's a little steep, so be careful as you climb."

There was no need for the warning. The guests gripped the handrail as if their lives depended on it, as they inched their way out into the freezing air. The stairway, which led upwards like a ladder placed on a slant, gave the illusion that with so many people climbing at once, it might suddenly lurch sideways and turn upside down. Fearing such a disaster, everyone instinctively clung to the handrail, hoping this would be the one thing that saved them from tumbling to the ground. Glancing down, they saw that they were more than three storeys up, and they became even more terrified. It didn't deter anyone that the handrail was as cold as ice.

Arriving at the tower ahead of the rest, Kozaburo locked the end of the drawbridge firmly in place. The walkway at the top of the tower was maybe a little over a metre wide, and circled the whole tower; the eaves didn't completely protect it from the snow, which had piled up all around.

Right at the point where the drawbridge made contact with the tower there was a window, and about two metres to the right, a doorway. There was no light coming from inside, so Kozaburo slipped in through the door to turn on the room lamp, and came back out. The glow that shone from the window onto the walkway was enough for everyone to see where to put their feet. Kozaburo began to move in an anti-clockwise direction around the windswept walkway, past the window and the door. The guests filed along behind him, taking care not to tread in the heaps of snow.

"My challenge is for you to tell me the significance of the design of the flower bed at the foot of this tower. That's really all there is to it. Because of its size, when you're down on the ground, standing in the middle of the plants, its shape is impossible to make out. And so I've brought you up here for a bird's-eye view."

Kozaburo stopped walking and leant over the railing.

"This is the perfect spot to get the full effect," he announced, tapping the railing. The rest of the party lined up next to him and looked gingerly down in the direction of their own feet. Around three floors below them there was indeed a flower bed. It wasn't difficult to make out, illuminated as it was by three sources of light—the regular garden lighting, the bulbs on the Christmas tree, and what spilt out from the salon window. As Kozaburo had promised, the full effect was clearly visible from where they stood. Covered in a layer of white snow, it looked like a decorated Christmas cake. The raised pattern stood out in clear relief against the darker shadows. (See Fig. 2.)

48

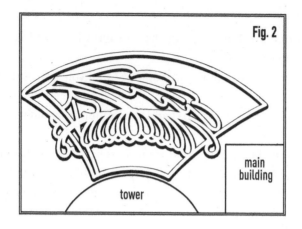

Fig. 2

main building

tower

Sasaki clung to the railing as he leant out for a better look. "Oh, that's what it looks like!"

His voice shivered from the cold and its battle with the noise of the wind.

"Whoa! Splendid!" cried Kikuoka in his usual booming voice.

"Right now, it's covered in snow so we can't enjoy the colourful leaves and flowers, but the parts where they're planted are raised above the ground, so actually the basic design is much easier to make out than usual. There aren't any distracting features to detract from the lines."

"It's a fan," declared Kikuoka.

"Yes. It's shaped a bit like a folding fan. But I don't think it's enough to say it's fan-shaped," said Sasaki.

"Right. It's not supposed to be a fan," said Kozaburo.

"You designed it to surround the tower, and so it ended up being that general shape," said Sasaki.

"You're exactly right."

"There aren't any straight lines."

"Hmm. Yet again, Mr Sasaki, you're on the right track. There's an important point in there."

Kozaburo looked along the row until he found Haruo Kajiwara, the chef.

"What do you think, Mr Kajiwara? Can you solve a riddle like this one?"

Kajiwara looked as if he hadn't really thought about it at all.

"No, I can't. I'm sorry."

"Well, then... What kind of object is it? What are its properties? Any ideas? But there is one more thing I need to tell you. The location of this strange and unusual flower bed within the Ice Floe Mansion is of great significance. It has to be in that exact spot. I want you to think of it as part of the mansion itself. The reason this building is leaning slightly is because of the design of that flower bed. I want you to think hard about the connection."

Sasaki looked astonished.

"It's because of that flower bed that this building leans?"

Kozaburo nodded.

That strange flower bed and the slant of this building... pondered Sasaki, as he watched the falling snow that seemed to be sucked down by the flower bed below. As he stared down at the white walls that showed the strange design in relief, he thought how the snow was like a multitude of little darts flying towards their target. And slowly he began to lose his sense of balance, and fear that he too was going to fall. He guessed it was probably because the main building, as well as this tower, both leant in the direction of the flower bed as if they were about to topple right into it.

Just a minute... Sasaki thought. He believed he had just made a connection. *Was that it?* The slant of the tower and the feeling you were about to fall, the unease, all those kinds of sensations, did they have something to do with the puzzle?

Human emotions? But if that were the case this was a supremely difficult puzzle to solve. Vague, abstract ideas, but how did they connect? It was like some kind of Zen-style conundrum.

A fan... a classic Japanese symbol. One that when you look down at it from a tall tower, you get the weird sensation you're falling. That's because the tower leans... Now what school of thought does a tower represent...? Was it that kind of a riddle, perhaps...?

No, probably not after all, Sasaki decided. Kozaburo Hamamoto was more Western in his style and way of thinking. This wasn't going to be a spiritual or philosophical problem. He definitely preferred the kind of puzzle that had a clear-cut answer, which when revealed, would be immensely satisfying and cause everyone to say, "Of course!" Which meant that there was a more concrete solution. It was a clever puzzle for sure.

Sasaki continued to ponder.

Togai, however, was even more enthusiastic than his friend.

"I'd like to sketch the shape of the flower bed," he said.

"Of course you may," replied Kozaburo. "But you don't have a pen and paper with you right now, I'm sure."

"It's cold."

Eiko spoke on behalf of the rest of the guests who were all starting to shiver.

"All right, ladies and gentlemen, if we stay out here much longer we're all going to catch cold. Mr Togai, I'm going to leave the bridge in place, so feel free to come up here and draw your sketch whenever you'd like. I'd love to invite you all to visit my room here in the tower, but with so many people it'd be terribly cramped. Let's go back to the salon and ask Mr Kajiwara to serve us a cup of steaming hot coffee."

There were no objections to that plan. Kicking the snow out of their path as they walked, they set off to finish their tour of the walkway, back to where the drawbridge waited.

As they made their way back across towards the main building, it was as if they were re-entering the real world, and there was a general sense of relief. Outside, at least for now, the snow continued to fall.

SCENE 4

Room 1

The snow had finally stopped falling and the moon was out. There'd been no sign of it when they'd been up on the tower, but now its pale whitish glow shone through the curtains. The whole world was silent.

Kumi Aikawa had been lying in bed for what seemed like hours, but she couldn't sleep. One of the main reasons was that she couldn't stop thinking about Eiko Hamamoto. And when she thought about that woman her stomach lurched. She felt like a jouster waiting for tomorrow's tournament.

Outside it was utterly still, and to Kumi's mind way too much so. She began to feel uneasy. Room No. 1, to which she'd been assigned, was on the top floor of the main building. It had a great view, but Room No. 2, next door, which belonged to Eiko had a far better view of the sea. Frankly, though, she'd have been more comfortable in a room on the ground floor, where she thought perhaps there'd have been more reassuring noise.

To city dwellers, complete silence was as disturbing to their sleep as a construction site. In Tokyo, there was always some kind of din, even in the middle of the night.

Kumi was reminded of blotting paper. The thick layer of snow that shrouded everything outside had that effect. She was sure that it was maliciously absorbing all the sounds. She couldn't even hear the wind any more. What a horrid night!

But then she did hear something. A strange noise, very faint, but surprisingly close by. It seemed to be coming from above the ceiling. It was like nails scratching a rough surface—not a pleasant sound. Kumi's body stiffened and she strained to listen. But that was it. The noise had stopped.

What could it have been? She quickly turned and fumbled for the watch on the bedside table. It was a classic ladies' watch with a tiny face so it was difficult to make out the dial, but it appeared to be after 1 a.m.

Suddenly the noise was back. It made her think of a crab struggling to get out of an earthenware pot. She instinctively braced herself. It was above her. There was something there on the other side of the ceiling!

The next sound was far louder. Kumi's heart leapt into her throat and she almost screamed. But no, it was coming from outside. She couldn't guess what was really making the noise, but... She pictured a giant crab stuck to the wall of the building. Step by step it was making its way up towards her upper-floor window. Now she was finding it hard not to scream.

The sound came again. Two hard objects scraping against each other... over and over. It appeared to be getting closer. *Help me, help me*, she mumbled over and over to herself.

Gradually, her whole body was overcome with acute terror. It felt as if an unseen hand was around her throat, suffocating her, and she began to silently pray.

Please, no! I don't know what you are but please go away! If you're climbing up the wall, please turn around, and go back down. Go to someone else's window!

Suddenly there was a metallic sound. Just once, like a small bell... But no, not a bell at all. It was the window. Something was on the glass.

Almost against her will, Kumi's head spun around to look in the direction of the window. And it was now that she finally let out a scream, so loud that she surprised even herself. So loud that her voice filled the room, bouncing off the walls and ceiling and back to her own ears. Her hands and feet turned to jelly. When was it that she had started crying? She hadn't even noticed.

How could it be? This was supposed to be the top floor. There was no kind of balcony or overhang of any kind under the window. It was a completely flat wall like a vertical rock face. And yet, through the gap in the curtains, she saw a face peering into the room.

That face… It was no normal human face. The crazy eyes— wide, staring eyes that didn't blink. The skin charred to a deep bluish-black. The tip of the nose white with frostbite, the scraggly moustache and beard beneath. The cheeks were scarred—were they burn scars? Despite all of this, there was a faint smile of amusement on his lips. This face, bathed in the icy moonlight, stared at Kumi like some kind of crazed sleepwalker as she wept in terror.

Kumi's hair began to stand on end. The moment seemed so long that she felt as if she were going to faint, but it was in reality only a few seconds. Before she knew it, the face had disappeared.

But it didn't matter that it was gone, Kumi now summoned all her strength and let out a new, more piercing shriek. She immediately heard a man's voice roar in the distance. It was coming from somewhere beyond the window, but Kumi couldn't tell where for sure. It felt as if the whole house was shuddering with the sound. Kumi broke off screaming for a moment to listen. The roar had only lasted a few seconds at the most, but it echoed in her ears still.

As soon as all was quiet again, Kumi resumed her screaming. She had no idea what she was doing or why exactly she was doing it. It just felt that if she continued to scream, somehow she would be rescued from the terror of being alone.

Right away there was a loud banging at her door, and she heard a shrill female voice.

"Ms Aikura! Ms Aikura! What's the matter? Open up! Are you okay?"

Kumi immediately stopped screaming. Sluggishly, she sat up in bed and, blinking several times, managed to drag herself up and over to the door. She unlocked it to reveal Eiko standing there in a robe.

"What's going on?" Eiko asked.

"There was a… There was a man looking in my window."

"Looking in? This is the top floor!"

"Yes, I know. But he was there, looking in."

Eiko marched into the room and walked determinedly over to the offending window. Taking hold of the gaping curtains, she briskly pulled them apart, then made to open up the casement windows beyond.

In order to protect against the cold, there were double windows throughout the building. Each window layer had to be unlocked separately, which was a bit of a chore. Eventually, chilled air poured in and caused the curtains to sway.

Eiko leant out and looked up and down, left and right, then pulled her head back in.

"There's nothing there. Look for yourself," she said.

Kumi was already back in her bed. Her body began to tremble, but not from the cold. Eiko closed the window again.

"I really saw him."

"What did he look like? Did you see his face?"

"It was a man. He had a totally creepy face. It wasn't normal at all. He had crazy eyes. His skin was really dark, and he had what looked like bruises and burn scars all over his cheeks. He had a beard too—"

At that moment there was such a loud clattering noise that they both jumped. Kumi froze. If Eiko hadn't been right there in front of her, she was sure to have started screaming again.

"Daddy's coming to see what's going on."

Kumi realized that the noise was Kozaburo lowering the drawbridge from the tower.

"You must have been dreaming," said Eiko, looking faintly amused.

"No way! I definitely saw him. Someone was there."

"Look, this is the top floor. The middle-floor windows don't even have an overhang, and there are no footprints in the snow. Look for yourself!"

"I saw him!"

"And there's no one in this house with burn scars on their face. Nobody who looks frightening. I think you had a nightmare. There's no other explanation. They say if you sleep in a different bed from your usual one, you often don't get a good night's sleep."

"That's not what happened. I can tell the difference between a dream and real life! And that was real."

"Are you sure?"

"Yes! I heard a noise too. Didn't you hear it?"

"What noise?"

"A kind of scraping sound."

"Nope."

"Then did you hear him yell?"

"I heard you screaming plenty."

"Not me. A man's voice. It sounded like a roar."

"What's going on?"

Eiko turned to see her father standing in the open doorway. Over his pyjamas he was wearing his usual jacket and trousers, with the addition of a sweater under the jacket. It was cold out on the drawbridge.

"Ms Aikura has had a visit from a molester."

"It wasn't a molester!" Kumi blubbered. "Somebody was looking in my window."

She wiped her eyes.

"The window?" said Kozaburo in amazement. "This one here?"

Everyone seems so surprised, thought Kumi. *But I'm the one who had the biggest shock of all.*

"But this is the top floor."

"I told her that already, but she insists that she saw him."

"Because I did see him."

"Are you sure it wasn't a dream?"

"No, it wasn't!"

"Then he must have been an incredibly tall man. We're pretty high up."

There was a rapping noise. Michio Kanai was there, knocking on the already open door.

"What's happening?"

"This young lady seems to have suffered a nightmare."

"It wasn't a nightmare! Mr Kanai, did you hear a man yell?"

"Yes, I believe I did hear something."

"Actually, so did I. I thought it was just a dream," said Kozaburo. "That's why I got up in the first place."

SCENE 5

The Salon

The next day was bright and sunny, but winter mornings in the far north of Hokkaido are always cold, even with the heating on. The guests were grateful for the crackling fire in the living room. It didn't matter how many kinds of home heating systems that human beings came up with, nothing could beat a simple fire with an open flame. Right now, as if in proof of this fact, each guest as he or she came down was drawn instinctively towards the fire, and soon everyone had gathered around the curved brick fireplace.

To Kumi's disbelief there were many guests who knew absolutely nothing of the mysterious bearded stranger, nor the blood-curdling roar, or even her own screams. Eiko wasn't down yet, so Kumi decided to treat everyone to a passionate retelling of last night's events. Her audience consisted of Mr and Mrs Kanai, Sasaki, and Yoshihiko Hamamoto, but they all seemed a little dubious about her story. Kumi felt frustrated that she didn't seem to be able to communicate her terror sufficiently.

On the other hand, she reflected, it wasn't all that surprising. Even Kumi herself was finding it difficult to reimagine last night's events in the cheerful morning light. The terror she had experienced now felt as if it had been a dream after all. The Kanais were outright smirking.

"So you think the roaring man and the one with the strange face at your window were one and the same?" Yoshihiko asked.

"Yes... Well, probably."

To be honest, this was the first time Kumi had really made the connection.

"But there are no footprints in the snow."

Sasaki's voice came from a little way off. Everyone turned to look. He'd opened the window and was leaning out observing the back garden.

"That area over there would be right under your bedroom window, but there's not a single footprint. The snow is pristine."

Hearing this, Kumi felt as if she were in another dream right now. She went silent. What could that have been last night? That horrifying face that wasn't quite human?

Togai, who had spent the rest of the previous evening by himself, drawing a diagram of the flower bed, was the next to appear in the salon, followed closely by Kozaburo Hamamoto.

"Hey! Weather's really cleared up, hasn't it?"

Kikuoka was preceded by his usual bellow. Everyone was now awake and gathered in the salon.

The morning sun was indeed radiant. Now that it had risen sufficiently in the sky, the ground had turned into a giant reflecting plate and was almost painfully dazzling to look at.

Kikuoka, too, was ignorant of all the uproar involving Kumi the previous night. He explained that he'd taken a sleeping pill. Knowing well already what his reaction would be, Kumi didn't mention it to him.

The familiar shrill tones of the mistress of the mansion suddenly filled the room.

"Hello, everyone! It's about time for breakfast. Shall we move to the table?"

The topic of conversation at the breakfast table was still Kumi's adventure. After a while, Kikuoka noticed that his chauffeur was missing.

"Looks like young Ueda's not up yet. Typical! He's always waltzing in late like he thinks he's the boss."

Eiko realized that Kikuoka was right. But she couldn't decide whether to go and call him or not.

"I'll go and get him," Sasaki offered. He opened the French windows, and stepping easily out into the snow, set off in the direction of Room 10, where Ueda was staying.

"Please, let's not wait for them, or the food'll be cold," Eiko urged the guests, and everyone began to eat.

Sasaki took rather longer than expected, but eventually he returned.

"Is he up?" Eiko asked.

"Well…" Sasaki hesitated. "It's a bit weird."

Everyone stopped eating to stare at him.

"There's no answer."

"Maybe he's just gone out somewhere?"

"No, I don't think so. The door's locked from the inside."

Eiko's chair made a loud scraping noise as she got swiftly to her feet. Togai got up too. Kikuoka and Kanai exchanged looks, and then the whole company got to their feet and followed Eiko out into the snow. They couldn't help noticing that there were only two sets of footprints in the soft snow—Sasaki's—going out and coming back.

"It was strange that he didn't reply but there's one more thing…"

Sasaki pointed towards the west corner of the main building where Room 10 was situated. There was a dark figure lying in the snow. The whole party recoiled in shock. If that body had been lying in the snow for a while, then it must surely be dead. A corpse. Was that Kazuya Ueda?

Their second reaction was to turn and stare at Sasaki.

How had he not mentioned this already? And why was he so composed right now?

Sasaki saw the way everyone was looking at him, but he apparently had nothing to say.

Still confused by Sasaki's demeanour, the guests began to make their way towards the corpse. The closer they got, the stranger the sight. Strewn around the figure in the snow was a whole array of objects, almost as if his possessions had been thrown there with him. But on closer examination they were not exactly his possessions.

Some members of the party, including the butler, Kohei Hayakawa, and Kumi Aikura were seized with a bad premonition and found their feet barely able to move any farther.

When they finally reached the scene, everyone, without exception, was utterly dumbfounded. But at least they finally understood Sasaki's strange nonchalance.

Kozaburo Hamamoto let out a great shout and fell to his knees, reaching out to touch the figure, half buried by the snow. It was one of his antiques, a life-sized puppet-like doll. Everyone was amazed of course that this doll, which should have been up in Room 3, the antiques and curios storeroom, was lying out here in the snow, but what was more shocking was the way its limbs had been pulled apart. There was only one leg left attached to the body; both arms and the other leg were scattered around in the snow. Why?

For Sasaki and Togai, Kikuoka and Kanai, and all of the house staff, this wasn't the first time they'd seen this doll. Even without looking too closely they knew at once what it was. It was an antique that Kozaburo had bought in the former Czechoslovakia, back when he'd lived in Europe. He had nicknamed it "Golem".

Right now it had been pulled apart at the arms and one leg joint, and the various wooden pieces lay partially buried in the snow. Kozaburo immediately began to gather them up, carefully brushing the snow off each piece.

Sasaki wanted to tell him to leave it alone, not to touch anything, but he couldn't quite bring himself to say it. Did something like this qualify as a crime scene?

"I can't find his head!"

Kozaburo sounded desperate. Everyone else immediately began to search for the doll's head, but it soon became clear that it wasn't anywhere around.

The imprints left after removing Golem's arms, legs and torso from the snow were rather deep, and so it could be assumed they had been scattered there while it was still snowing.

Kozaburo announced he was going to take Golem back to the salon and set off in that direction. To him, the doll was a precious collector's piece.

The rest of the group decided not to wait for the lord of the manor's return, and headed for the concrete steps that led up to the middle floor, right between the outward-facing doors of Rooms 10 and 11. There was snow on the steps, but again only Sasaki's footprints were visible.

After climbing the stairs up to Room 10, Kikuoka banged loudly on the door.

"Ueda! Hey, it's me! Ueda?"

But there was no reply.

Next they tried to look in through the window, but it was made of frosted glass with wire mesh running through it, and they could see nothing at all of the interior of the room. Not to mention that the curtains were apparently closed. On top of that, there were solid iron bars protecting the window on the outside. Kikuoka slid a hand through the bars and tried to open the window, but it was securely locked from the inside.

"Break in if you need to." They turned around to see Kozaburo standing behind them.

"That door opens outwards! You've gotta be kidding me!" boomed Kikuoka.

"It does, but it's not all that sturdy. Perhaps we could try to break it down."

Kikuoka threw his huge frame against the door several times, but it didn't budge.

"Hoy, Kanai, you give it a try."

Kanai shrunk back in fear.

"Me? I don't think I've got a chance. I'm just a lightweight."

Ironically, the man most suited to this kind of a challenge was the one on the other side of the door.

"Come on, boys," said Eiko firmly. "One of you give it a try!"

Realizing it was his moment to impress his queen, Togai hurled himself against the door with all his might, but the only thing that went flying was his glasses.

The next to try was Sasaki, then Kajiwara, the chef, but strangely not one of the men thought to pair up for the task. However, when Eiko and Hatsue simultaneously threw themselves against the door, there was a cracking sound and the top bent slightly inwards. After a few further shoves, it broke completely.

With Hatsue in the lead, the whole party rushed into the room, to be met by the very sight they had begun to dread. Kazuya Ueda lay there in his pyjamas, the handle of a hunting knife protruding from his chest, the dark stain on his pyjama top already partially dried.

Kumi screamed, and clung to Kikuoka. Eiko and Hatsue stood there in stunned silence. Kozaburo was the only one among the men to gasp out loud. It was the bizarre position-ing of Ueda's body...

Ueda wasn't in his bed. He was lying on his back on the linoleum flooring at the foot of the bed, his right wrist bound with white cord. The other end was tied around the nearest foot of the metal bed frame, so that he appeared to be raising his right arm over his head. The bed didn't look as if it had been moved from its normal position by the window.

Ueda's left hand was unbound, but it too was high above his head. In other words, one hand was tied up, the other not, but both stretched out above his head, almost like a gesture of victory.

But even stranger than the placing of his arms, was that of his legs. He lay twisted to the side at the waist, both legs straight out to his right side, almost as if he were dancing. To be more precise, while the right leg was bent at approximately 90 degrees to his body, the left was placed slightly behind it and lower, at what must be around 110 or 120 degrees.

Just behind his back—to his left, there was a dark reddish-brown spot about five centimetres in diameter, drawn on the linoleum. As all four fingers of his free left hand were smeared in blood and a layer of grey dust, presumably he had drawn it himself. Which would mean that after tracing the circle he had, of his own free will, raised his left hand above his head...

But the thing that caught everyone's attention was the hunting knife in Ueda's chest. Attached to its handle was a metre-long piece of white string. The part about ten centi-metres from the hilt was trailing slightly into the bloodstain on Ueda's pyjamas, and was tinged faintly brown. However, the blood had already stopped flowing. From the expression on his face, it was clear he was no longer in pain. (See Fig. 3.)

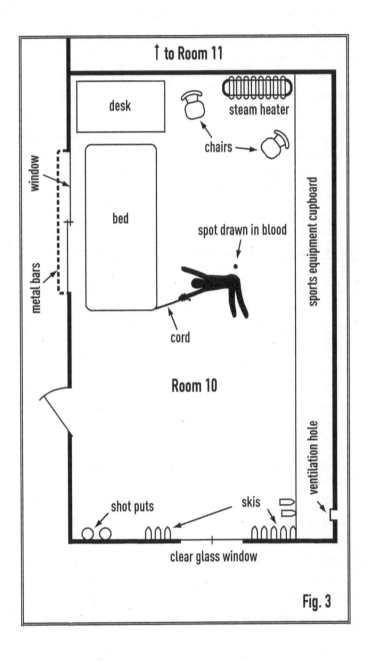

↑ to Room 11

desk

steam heater

chairs

window

metal bars

bed

spot drawn in blood

cord

Room 10

sports equipment cupboard

ventilation hole

shot puts

skis

clear glass window

Fig. 3

It was obvious that Ueda was dead; nevertheless Sasaki, the medical student, got down on the floor and checked the body.

"We'd better call the police."

Kohei Hayakawa, the butler, set off immediately by car for the general store in the village at the foot of the hill, where there would be a telephone.

It wasn't long before uniformed police turned up in full force, roping off Room 10 and drawing a chalk outline on the floor. The body of Ueda was long-since cold, but due perhaps to some misunderstanding, an ambulance also came tearing up the hill, snow chains around its tyres. The white clothing of the paramedics became jumbled in with the crowd of dark police uniforms, and what was once a peaceful hermit's retreat buzzed with activity.

Guests, staff, hosts alike were confined to the salon, listening anxiously to the disturbance that filled the Ice Floe Mansion. It was still early in the morning, and for most of the guests this was only the beginning of the second day of their stay. Kikuoka and the Kanais had arrived barely more than twelve hours ago. Already something like this happening—what on earth could be next? They'd enjoyed just one dinner and now it looked as if they were to spend the rest of their stay surrounded by police officers. Perhaps they would be released and allowed to go home as scheduled, but if they were unlucky, they couldn't help wondering whether they'd end up under house arrest indefinitely.

A plainclothes police officer appeared in the salon. He was ruddy-cheeked and well built, with an air of importance about him—most likely a homicide detective. In a superior tone he introduced himself as Detective Inspector Okuma from the nearby Wakkanai Police Station, seated himself at the table and proceeded to question everyone present. However, there didn't seem to be any obvious pattern to his questioning—he just seemed to be asking whatever occurred to him in the moment, and there was a lot of confusion.

When eventually he seemed to be done with his vague line of questioning, Okuma had one more.

"So where's this doll you're talking about?"

Kozaburo had put Golem back together again, minus his missing head, and he was still there with them in the salon.

"What the... Is this it? Huh! Where's it normally kept?"

Kozaburo picked up Golem and led Okuma up to the antiques display room, Room 3. When they returned, Okuma seemed amazed, chatting in simple layman's terms about all the precious items in Kozaburo's collection, but after a while he fell silent and seemed to be thinking something over. For a short while he managed to give off the air of a competent detective. Eventually, he brought his hand to his mouth and lowered his voice to a whisper.

"Would you agree that what we have here is a classic locked-room murder mystery?"

That had been pretty much obvious from the start.

Detective Inspector Okuma was such a bumbling yokel that nobody really felt that this was a serious murder investigation until around four o'clock that afternoon when Detective Chief Inspector Saburo Ushikoshi from the Sapporo City Police Headquarters turned up. He was accompanied by a younger detective named Ozaki.

The officers pulled up chairs to the dinner table, and introduced themselves. Then Chief Inspector Ushikoshi spoke.

"Bit of a weird place, this."

His tone was excessively casual. Although his younger colleague, Detective Sergeant Ozaki, seemed rather quick-witted, Ushikoshi came across as a more simple, matter-of-fact type. From first impressions, there didn't seem to be much difference between him and the Wakkanai police inspector, Okuma.

"It takes a while to get used to this floor," continued Ushikoshi. "You feel as if you're going to take a tumble."

Young Ozaki looked scornfully around the salon, but said nothing. His senior colleague turned to address the assembled residents of the Ice Floe Mansion and their guests. He didn't get up from his seat.

"All right then, everyone, we've introduced ourselves to you. Or rather, I should say that we are police officers and therefore some of the most boring people on this planet. Apart from our names, there's not much more to tell about us. That being the case, I think it's about time you all did us the honour of introducing yourselves. If possible, we would like to hear where you usually reside, what kind of work you are employed in and what brings you here to this mansion. Any more details, such as what your relationship was to the deceased man, I will be asking you later when I interview you all individually, so there's no need to cover that right now."

Just as Detective Chief Inspector Ushikoshi had said, there was nothing interesting at all about the three detectives. Not in their clothing, nor their manner of talking, which, although polite, suggested that no scene of carnage would ever perturb them in the slightest; their facial expressions slightly intimidated the assembled guests and left them a little tongue-tied. Each gave their own faltering self-introduction, which Ushikoshi occasionally interrupted with a politely phrased question, but he took no notes.

When everyone had finished, Ushikoshi addressed them all in a manner which suggested that now this was what he had really wanted to say all along.

"Right, I'm sorry to have to say this, but it has to be said sooner or later. From what I understand, the victim, Kazuya Ueda, is not from around here. Yesterday was only the second time in his life that he had visited this mansion, or had even set foot on the island of Hokkaido. Which means that it would be very difficult to imagine that he has friends or acquaintances in this area, and certainly, no one who might have paid him a visit last night.

"So was it a robbery? It doesn't look like it. His wallet containing 246,000 yen was in a relatively accessible spot in the inside pocket of his jacket, but it wasn't touched.

"The strangest aspect of this case is his bedroom door, which was locked from the inside. Let's imagine that a complete stranger knocked on his bedroom door: it's extremely unlikely that he would have opened it just like that. And even if he had opened it and let a stranger in, there would have been some sort of a struggle and voices would have been raised. But there was no evidence of a struggle in the room. What's more, Mr Ueda was ex-military, and therefore physically much stronger than the average person. There's no way he would have been overpowered so easily.

"Which leads me to suspect that the murderer must have been known to, or even close to, the victim. But as I said earlier, Mr Ueda had no friends living in this area.

"What we have been able to ascertain from talking to you, and from our own preliminary investigations, is that Kazuya Ueda was born in Okayama Prefecture and grew up in Osaka. At the age of twenty-five he enlisted in the Ground Self-Defence

Forces, was based in Tokyo and Gotemba for a while, but was discharged three years later. At the age of twenty-nine he joined Kikuoka Bearings, and was thirty years old when he died. Ever since his time in the Self-Defence Forces, he was the unsociable type, and doesn't appear to have any close friends. A man like Ueda is extremely unlikely to have friends or acquaintances up here in Hokkaido. We also believe it unlikely that someone from the Tokyo or Osaka areas would come all the way up here just to pay him a visit. In conclusion, there are no people in Kazuya Ueda's close circle besides the people in this room right now."

Everyone exchanged uneasy glances.

"Now it would be different if this were Sapporo or Tokyo, or another major city, but if a stranger were to turn up in this remote location, someone would be bound to notice him or her. Down in the village there's only one inn. And perhaps because of the season, last night they didn't have a single guest.

"And then there is one more huge problem with this case: the matter of the footprints. Normally, this isn't the kind of thing that police officers talk about with the average person, but on this occasion I think it's called for. I'm referring to the fact that Kazuya Ueda's time of death has been established: last night between midnight and half past. Sometime between 12 and 12.30, the killer stuck a knife in Ueda's heart. In other words, he or she must have been in Ueda's room somewhere in those thirty minutes. Unfortunately for this killer, the snow stopped around 11.30 last night. So it was no longer snowing when the murder was committed. And yet, there are no footprints in the snow belonging to the killer; neither arriving nor leaving the scene of the crime.

"I believe you already know that room can only be accessed from the outside of the mansion. If the killer had been there in that room—Room 10, is it?—at the time of Mr Ueda's death, then at the very least there should have been footprints leaving the room. If not, then Mr Ueda must have somehow stabbed himself in the heart, but there is nothing to suggest that this was a suicide. But it still remains that there were no footprints. And that's a huge problem.

"Allow me to amend that slightly. Don't imagine that we, the investigators, are stumped by the lack of footprints or the locked room. Footprints can be swept away by a broom, for example. There are many ways this trick could be pulled off. The locked room even more so. Crime fiction has already shown us a myriad of solutions.

"And yet, if there was an intruder from the outside, he would have had to continue erasing his footprints from the door of Room 10 all the way down the hill as far as the village. That's no simple task. And no matter how scrupulously he erased them, there would be some trace somewhere in the snow. Our expert went through the area with a fine-tooth comb, but came up with absolutely nothing. Since 11.30 last night, it hasn't snowed at all. And whether between Room 10 and the village at the foot of the hill or any other corner of the grounds, there is absolutely no sign of footprints, or a clever attempt to cover some up.

"I think you understand what I'm trying to say. I hate to put it so bluntly, but with the exception of the windows for now, access to Room 10 can only have been gained from the three doors on the ground floor of this building: the front entrance, the French windows from the salon or the service entrance from the kitchen."

Everyone in the room took this as a declaration of war.

"But on the other hand…"

It was Sasaki who had made himself spokesman to try to disprove the police's theory.

"Did you find any evidence of footprints being erased between any of those three entrances and Room 10?"

It was a good question.

"Well, for a start, between the salon door and Room 10, there was a whole jumble of footprints, so it was impossible to tell. I can say that the chances that footprints had been erased from either of the other two entrances, or from under any of the windows is very slim. We investigated, and the snow appears to be undisturbed."

"So what you're saying is, there's just as little evidence it was one of us as it was an outside intruder?"

Sasaki's rebuttal was logical.

"But as I already told you," Ushikoshi went on, "the footprints are not the only aspect. There's everything else that I explained to you just now."

"But there's no broom of any kind here in the main building," said Eiko.

"You're quite right about that. I already asked Mr Hayakawa here about it."

"So then, how is it there are no footprints?"

"If the wind had been strong last night, the powdery snow would have blown over the footprints," said Sasaki. "But there wasn't that much wind."

"I don't believe it was blowing at all around midnight," said Eiko.

"And what about the other mysterious aspects of this crime?" continued Sasaki.

"Right, right. The string attached to the knife. And that weird dancing pose that Mr Ueda was in," said Togai.

"The position of the body was hardly something unusual as far as we are concerned," said Ushikoshi. "It's obviously agony to have a knife stuck into you. Kazuya Ueda was in terrible pain. I've heard of cases where the victims died in all kinds of convoluted poses. As for the string, I've heard of cases where someone was lightly dressed for summer and had no pockets to hide a knife in, so tied it to his body instead."

Everyone had the same immediate thought: *But it's winter!*

"What about the cord tying his right hand to the bed?"

"Yes, that is one of the unique aspects of this case."

"So you don't have a precedent for that one, then?"

"Hey, hey, calm down, everybody!"

Okuma, the local cop, looking as if he rather regretted the frank exchange between the laymen and the professionals, placed himself between the two camps.

"That's our job to investigate. You can trust us to get it done properly. We'd appreciate your total cooperation."

Cooperation? As suspects in a murder investigation? thought Sasaki privately. But of course all he could do was nod.

"So here's a simple diagram of the murder scene," said Ushikoshi, unfolding what looked like a sheet of writing paper. "Is this the state of the room when you found it?"

All the guests and staff stood up and leant forward to study the paper.

"Right here there should be a circular dot that looked like it was drawn in blood," said Togai.

"Yes, yes, the blood mark," replied Ushikoshi, as if it were a childish prank that he didn't particularly care about.

"Looks about right to me," said Kikuoka in his gravelly voice.

"Is this chair usually in this position, Mr Hamamoto?"

"Yes, it is. The top shelf is just too high to reach, so it's there to stand on."

"I see. And then there are the windows. The one on the west side has bars on the outside, but the south side doesn't. It's made of clear glass, and unlike in all the other rooms, it isn't a double window."

"That's right. That's because the south-side window is on the middle floor. I believed it was far enough from the ground that it was too difficult for an intruder to enter. On the west side he could climb the stairs and break open the window. But there's nothing much of value in there, really."

"There are some shot-puts on the floor here. Are they always there?"

"Hmm. I hadn't noticed them."

"Are they usually kept on the shelf?"

"No, they could be anywhere in the room."

"These shot-puts seem to have string wound around them several times with a wooden tag on the end. What's that for?"

"Yes, I own two types of shot-put—four-kilogram and seven-kilogram. When I purchased them I attached wooden tags to write their weight on them, so I could tell them apart easily. I'm afraid after I bought them they met the same fate as the discuses I purchased too—I never used them and they just got left sitting around."

"That's how it seems, except that the string attached to the tag on the seven-kilo shot-put seems to be rather long…"

"Really? I wonder if it came loose? I never noticed."

"Actually, it looks to us as if more string was added to make it longer. The length of the string from the shot-put to the tag was a total of 1 metre 48 centimetres."

"What? Do you think the killer did that?"

"Probably. This wooden tag that reads '7kg' is 3 centimetres by 5 centimetres, and about 1 centimetre thick. Here it has a piece of Sellotape attached that extends about 3 centimetres beyond the tag. It looks like a fresh piece of tape."

"Wow."

"Do you have any knowledge of this?"

"No, none at all."

"Is it some kind of trick?" Sasaki asked. "Do you think the killer stuck it there on purpose?"

"I wonder… And then, over here, there's an approximately twenty-centimetre-square ventilation hole. It faces the open space by this indoor staircase. Is that right?"

"That's correct. But it's not at a height that would allow anybody in the main building to stand in the corridor and be able to see into Room 10. If you stand in front of Room 12, you'll be able to tell—Room 10's air vent is way up high in the wall on the inside. The other rooms, Room 12 for example, if you stood on a step stool or something, I suppose you might be able to see inside, but not Room 10…" (See Fig. 1.)

"Yes, I'm aware of that. I already checked it for myself."

"So this isn't a perfect locked room after all," said Togai. "As there are no footprints outside, the killer must have performed some sort of trick using this air vent."

Sasaki was quick to respond.

"A twenty-centimetre-square hole isn't even big enough for someone to get their head through. And what about the cord tied around the victim's wrist? And the trick with the shot-put? He had to have been inside the room."

"So what happened to his footprints?"

"Beats me. But it wouldn't have been all that difficult to lock the room from the inside."

"I see," said Ushikoshi, with interest. "I'd love to hear how."

"May I?" asked Sasaki. The Detective Chief Inspector nodded.

"This whole thing is very simple. Room 10 is normally used as a storeroom, and has a padlock on the door. Whenever a guest stays there, the padlock is removed and the door then has only a simple latch that can be raised to open and clicked down to lock, like the door of a toilet stall. (See Fig. 4.) It was added so people could stay in that room, and it's very rudimentary. All the killer needed to do to this simple lever was to prop it up with a snowball as he left the room. After a while, the heat of the room would melt the snow and the lever would drop into place, locking the door from the inside."

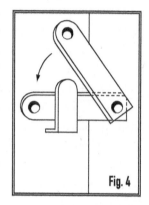

Fig. 4

There were cries of "Amazing! Incredible!" from the Kikuoka Bearings contingent. But Ushikoshi was not so easily impressed.

"We already thought of that," he said. "But that metal bracket was attached to a wooden support, and it's completely dry. Not even slightly damp. It's highly unlikely that they tried that method."

Sasaki was taken aback.

"That's not how they did it?"

"I'm afraid not."

There was a short silence.

"And yet, I feel the locked-room mystery won't be too much of a challenge to solve. It's not all that mystifying. No, it's another matter altogether that has us stumped."

"What's that?"

"Yes, well, it looks like this one's going to take some serious thought. I'd like to ask for everyone's help to puzzle it out. Well, it can't be helped—better to just be up front about it, I suppose. The murderer doesn't seem to be among you."

There was a slight ripple of laughter.

"I know it contradicts everything I've said up to now, but I can't see any of you as the murderer. And that's my problem. I'm talking about motive, of course. There are very few of you who were even acquainted with Kazuya Ueda before yesterday. With the exception of the people from Kikuoka Bearings, this was only the second time for most of you to meet him, following his visit here last summer. That would be Mr Kozaburo Hamamoto, Ms Eiko Hamamoto, Mr and Mrs Hayakawa, Mr Kajiwara, Mr Togai, Mr Sasaki and finally, Yoshihiko Hamamoto, is that right? And I'm sure you hardly spent any time with him, given what a taciturn type Mr Ueda was. I can't imagine any of you having known him well enough to even think about murdering him."

There was another outbreak of nervous laughter.

"Murder isn't a profitable business. Someone with a good name and status in society, who lives in such a good house, if they commit murder they lose all that and are thrown in jail just like anyone else. I can't imagine there being anyone so reckless among you. And Mr Kikuoka, Ms Aikura, Mr and Mrs Kanai are in practically the same situation. To put it bluntly, I don't see anyone having any reason to kill Kazuya Ueda, a simple chauffeur. That's my conundrum."

That makes sense, thought Togai, Sasaki and also Eiko. Ueda had been the kind of man that nobody had given a second thought to. If he'd been a little more handsome, he might have had women troubles, or perhaps if he'd been outspoken or arrogant, he'd have been a more likely candidate for murder.

But he was without money or status, or anything in his personality to cause someone to hold a grudge.

Detective Chief Inspector Saburo Ushikoshi watched the expressions on the faces of the assembled guests and wondered for a moment if there'd been a mix-up. Perhaps the murderer had mistaken Ueda for someone else, for someone he meant to kill? Perhaps Ueda was just an accidental victim?

But then again, Ueda had been given Room 10 from the outset, and everyone staying in the house that night knew it. There had been no switching of rooms at the last minute. Room 10 was a unique room because it could only be accessed from the outside of the building. It would be a mistake to think that someone had intended to enter Room 9, for example, but had accidentally ended up in Room 10.

He couldn't figure it out. Still, this man, Kazuya Ueda, was the most unlikely victim ever. There was nothing for it but to assume that someone else had been the intended victim.

"If the murderer is indeed one of the people here in this room, then I fully expect you to try to do a runner tonight. So I'm going to speak more quickly."

Ushikoshi didn't sound entirely as if he were joking. Then, almost as if talking to himself,

"There is always a reason for everything, especially for murder. No one kills another human being for no reason. It seems that this investigation is going to hinge on discovering the motive. Before I begin to ask each of you uncomfortable questions, there is one more thing I want to put to everybody. Last night, around the time of the murder, did any of you see or hear anything unusual or odd? A cry or scream that might have come from the victim, or… well, anything at all, however small or insignificant? Did you notice something that was a little different from usual? Anything you glimpsed, even for a moment? Often this kind of thing can be vital to an investigation."

There were a few moments of silence, and then Kumi Aikura spoke up.

"I did."

She had hesitated because what she had to say did not exactly fit into the parameters suggested by the detective. Her previous night's experience couldn't possibly be classified as something she'd "glimpsed just for a moment", or "small and insignificant".

"Ms... er... Aikura, isn't it? What is it?"

"Well, lots of things, actually."

Kumi was excited to find someone who was ready to take her story seriously.

"Well I'll be, love, what did you see?"

The local detective, Okuma, seemed mesmerized by Kumi's adorable face.

"Well, saw *and* heard."

"Could we have the details, please?"

Kumi needed no more encouragement. She wasn't sure where to start though, and went with the less shocking part of her story.

"I heard a scream. In the middle of the night. It was... it could have been the dead man, Mr Ueda. I mean, it sounded like a man's voice, it was like he was in pain, a kind of strangled roar."

"I see."

Ushikoshi nodded, apparently satisfied with Kumi's story.

"And do you know what time that was?"

"Yes, I looked at my watch. So I know exactly what time it was. It was just after five past one."

Suddenly everyone felt a little sorry for the detective.

"What do you mean, just after 1.05? Are you sure? You must be mistaken, surely?"

"I'm absolutely certain. Like I just told you, I checked my watch."

"But…"

The detective turned around and his whole chair tilted sideways, looking as if it were going to fall over backwards. It was one of the optical illusions created by this mansion.

"But that's absolutely ridiculous! Are you sure your watch isn't broken?"

Kumi took off her watch. She was left-handed, so wore it on her right wrist.

"Here. I haven't touched it since."

Almost reverentially, Ushikoshi took the expensive ladies' wristwatch from Kumi's outstretched hand and compared it to his own cheap watch. They showed the exact same time.

"It's supposed to lose less than a second a month."

This was Kikuoka's addition to the conversation. Of course, he was the one who had purchased the watch. Ushikoshi nodded his thanks and returned the expensive timepiece to Kumi.

"That's fine. However… this creates a fresh problem. I think everyone is aware, so I really don't need to repeat it, that Kazuya Ueda's estimated time of death, or in other words, the hour that the crime was committed, is, as I told you earlier, between 12 and 12.30. If the scream that you heard was indeed the victim's, then it was made more than thirty minutes after that time frame. This new information is about to cause us no end of trouble.

"So how about the rest of you? Did you hear this noise like a man screaming? Would anyone else who heard it mind raising your hand?"

Mr and Mrs Kanai, then Eiko, then Kozaburo, all raised their hands. Kumi glanced at Eiko and felt rather put out. What the hell? Now she was saying she'd heard it?

"Four of you. Hmm. Five, including Ms Aikura. Mr Togai? Didn't you hear it too? You were sleeping in the room directly beneath Room 10."

"I didn't hear anything."

"Mr Sasaki?"

"Me neither."

"Mr Kanai, you were staying in Room 9 on the top floor, weren't you? Not necessarily that close to Room 10… Did any of you happen to check the time?"

"I didn't look at my watch," said Kozaburo. I heard Ms Aikura screaming and rushed over right away to see what was wrong."

"Mr Kanai, how about you?"

"Let me think, it was…"

"It was just after five past one," Hatsue Kanai interjected. "Six minutes past, to be precise."

"I see." Ushikoshi sounded perplexed. "This is a very worrying problem. Anyway, is there anyone else who saw or heard anything else strange last night?"

"Just a minute. I haven't finished yet," said Kumi.

"There's more?" asked Ushikoshi warily.

Kumi felt a bit sorry for the policeman. If he'd got so upset over the scream, how was he going to react to the next part of her story? However, she decided not to pull any punches and recounted the whole story exactly as it had happened. As she'd expected, Ushikoshi listened open-mouthed.

"Did you think I'd have screamed just because I heard a man's voice?" asked Kumi.

"Is this for real? But, but, it can't possibly…"

"Wasn't it just a nightmare?"

The two detectives spoke at once.

"Everyone kept saying the same thing to me. But I am absolutely sure. Being here now feels more like a dream than what happened in the night."

"Is there anyone living around here who looks like that? I mean with dark skin and burn scars on his cheeks?"

"And something of a sleepwalker to boot."

It was Okuma who'd decided to throw this in.

"A monster who decides to go for a walk in the snow by the light of the moon," he elaborated.

"There are definitely no such people around here!"

Eiko spoke as if it were her own honour that was being impugned.

"And of course, there's nobody fitting that description within the mansion?"

Ushikoshi's question managed to offend Eiko even more. She laughed scornfully.

"Obviously not!"

From then on, she sat there in annoyed silence.

"And the residents of this mansion are: Mr Kozaburo and Ms Eiko Hamamoto, Mr and Mrs Hayakawa and Haruo Kajiwara. There's no one else?"

Kozaburo shook his head.

"Well, this is very depressing news. Ms Aikura, I believe you were sleeping on the top floor? Specifically… let's see… Room 1. Now, there are no footholds beneath the window of Room 1, nor were there any footprints in the snow below. So this monster somehow came floating through the air and peered in through your window?"

"I'm sorry, I don't know how he did it. And I never said it was a monster!"

"Tell you what, it'd be a lot more bloody helpful if you could make up your mind whether you heard a scream or saw some creepy bloke."

It was Okuma again, unable to resist commenting.

Kumi flashed him a look that said she wasn't prepared to say any more if he insisted on making disparaging remarks.

"Right, then... Is there anyone else who would like to throw a spanner into our investigation?"

Everyone looked as if they were trying to think of something. At that moment, one of the uniformed police officers standing guard outside hurried into the salon and began to whisper something into the ear of Chief Inspector Ushikoshi. The lead detective got up and approached Kozaburo.

"Mr Hamamoto, it seems we've found what appears to be the missing head from your doll. It's out in the snow, quite a distance from Room 10."

Kozaburo jumped to his feet.

"Oh, that's wonderful news!"

"Please go with this officer. For now we may be keeping it for forensics, but what will you do with it when you get it back?"

"Well, obviously I'm going to reattach it to its body, and return it to Room 3—my display room."

"Understood. You're free to go."

Kozaburo and the police officer left the room.

"So, is there no one else who observed anything odd? Mr Togai, you were right below Mr Ueda's room?"

"No, nothing. I went to bed around 10.30."

"Nothing unusual happening outside your window?"

"My curtains were shut. And the window's double glazed."

"And yet, the killer took that massive doll from Room 3—for what purpose I have no idea—and carried it into the back garden. And after that, he carefully took it apart, tossing only the head farther away from the other parts. The head section that we found was buried in the snow, at such a distance from the rest of the body that it suggests someone flung it with all their might. It's quite deep, and there are no footprints around it.

"The snow stopped falling around 11.30 last night. From the state of the doll's body, we can guess that the killer arrived shortly before then. Right outside Mr Togai's window. Are you sure you didn't hear anything at all?"

"I'm sorry. I was already asleep soon after 10.30. I didn't even hear Mr Ueda scream."

"Everyone seems to have gone to bed surprisingly early."

"Yes. We tend to get up early here."

"Ah!"

Sasaki suddenly cried out.

"What is it?" asked Ushikoshi, who looked as if nothing could shock him any more.

"The stakes! The stakes sticking out of the snow. Two of them. It must have been a few hours before the murder!"

"What do you mean? Could you explain more clearly?"

Sasaki explained how, looking out of the salon window the evening before, he'd spotted two wooden stakes sticking out of the snow.

"And what time was that?"

"It was after we'd eaten, right after we finished drinking tea. So I reckon about 8 o'clock, or maybe half past."

"Um, Mr Kajiwara, 8 o'clock-ish, would that be about the time people finished drinking their tea?"

"Yes, I think that would be about right."

85

"Did anyone else besides Mr Sasaki notice these two stakes?"

Everyone shook their head. Sasaki remembered the moment he'd spotted them. He really should have called somebody else over to take a look.

"Was it snowing at the time?"

"Yes, it was."

"And then in the morning, when you went out to wake Mr Ueda, how was it then?"

"You mean the stakes? Now that you mention it, this morning they were gone."

"How about a trace or mark where they'd been?"

"Ah, I'm not sure. I wasn't really paying attention, but I don't think there was anything. One was near the area we found the doll's parts, so I guess I was even standing around that spot this morning… Oh, do you think the killer put those stakes there?"

"No idea, but I have to say it's yet another mysterious story. Mr Hayakawa, did you not notice these stakes?"

"We hardly went out into the garden yesterday. I'm afraid I didn't notice anything."

"These stakes, were they standing completely upright?"

"Yes."

"So, perpendicular to the ground?"

"Yes, pretty much."

"Do you think they were stuck all the way into the ground?"

"No, that would be impossible. There's stone underneath the snow in both spots."

"Meaning?"

"I mean that part of the back garden is covered with a kind of paving stone."

"Hmm. Do you think you could show me whereabouts these stakes were?"

Ushikoshi handed Sasaki a pen and paper, and the younger man drew him a sketch of the back garden. As soon as he'd finished, Okuma came over to look. (See Fig. 5.)

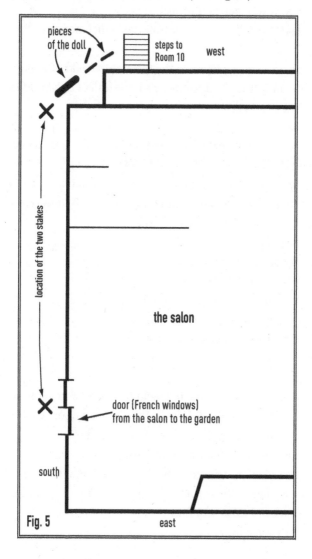

Fig. 5

"Aha! Now it's getting interesting!"

"How far away from the building were the stakes?" asked Ushikoshi.

"About two metres, I think."

"And the doll, was it about the same distance away?"

"Probably."

"So a line drawn between the two stakes would be about two metres away from, and parallel with the wall of this building?"

"Yes, it would."

"Hmm."

"But say they were connected to the crime, what on earth would they be used for?" asked Sasaki.

"Never mind that for now. We'll think about it later. It could very well be a completely unrelated matter. By the way, last night, who was the last person to go to bed?"

"That would be me," said Kohei Hayakawa. "Every night I lock up before going to bed."

"What time last night?"

"After half 10… I don't think it was as late as 11."

"And did you notice anything unusual?"

"Everything seemed the same way it always is."

"So you noticed nothing in particular."

"No."

"When you say *lock up*, that includes the door from the salon to the garden, the front door and the kitchen door? Can all of these be opened again easily from the inside?"

"Yes, they can. If it's from the inside…"

"The room that normally houses the doll that was in pieces at the corner of the main building, is that door kept locked?"

Ushikoshi turned to Eiko.

"Ms Hamamoto?"

"Yes, it is. But there's a large window facing the corridor and that isn't kept locked. If you wanted, you could get something out that way. And the doll was kept in the corner by the window."

"A window facing the corridor?"

"Yes."

"Ha! I see, I see. Well, that will be all for now. Next I'd like to ask each of you a few questions privately. And then we police need to have a meeting. It doesn't need to be a very big room, but do you happen to have a place we could use?"

"You're welcome to use our library," said Eiko. "I'll show you the way."

"Much obliged. It looks as if we still have enough time today. So shortly we'll begin calling people one by one. When you hear your name, please make your way to the library."

SCENE 6

The Library

As soon as the butler, Kohei Hayakawa, had shown them to the library, Sergeant Ozaki lost it.

"I can't believe what kind of shit people are into! Just for the hell of it, building a mansion with crazy sloping floors. I don't even own a decent house of my own. This guy's a total whack-job, if you ask me. The hobbies of the filthy rich. It really pisses me off."

Outside, the wind had begun to howl. The sun was already going down.

"Forget it," said Chief Inspector Ushikoshi, trying to calm down his colleague. "The rich have their hobbies, while we regular people struggle to get by. It's the way of the world. Just ignore him."

Ushikoshi pushed one of the chairs with its filed-off legs towards Ozaki.

"If everyone in the world was exactly alike, then it would be a very boring place. There's the rich lot like him, and poor coppers like us, and I think that's all right. Money doesn't necessarily make you happy, you know."

"Talking of coppers, what do you want me to do with my lot?" asked Inspector Okuma.

"I think you can let them go now," said Ushikoshi, and Okuma left the room to go and tell his local officers they could leave.

"But like I was saying, the layout of this house is completely insane, it's a total nuthouse. I was checking it out earlier."

Ozaki clearly wasn't ready to drop the subject.

"I tried to make a drawing of the place as I went around. Take a look." (See Fig. 1) "It's like a real mansion you'd find in a European country, and they've even given it a fancy name: the Ice Floe Mansion. It's made up of the main building here which has one underground floor and three above ground, and that Leaning Tower of Pisa-thing next to it. The thing that makes this tower different from the Pisa one is that, except for Kozaburo Hamamoto's own room at the top, there are no rooms whatsoever in the whole tower. There's not even a staircase. Which means there are no doors or other entrances anywhere. You can't even enter the bloody thing at ground level and climb up.

"So how, you ask, does Hamamoto get to his own bedroom? He lowers a drawbridge complete with chains and everything from this main building and climbs across to go to sleep. When he gets to the tower he pulls the chains and raises the bridge again. Like I said before, he's a complete whack-job.

"And then this main building's got fifteen rooms, and they're all numbered, starting from the top on the east side, the side next to the tower, and working down. Okay, now look at this drawing. This is Room 3, the one that had the doll in it, a kind of display room. And next to it, Room 4, is the library—where we are now. Underneath us is Room 5, the salon we were in before, and the kitchen. And then over to the west side, there's Room 10 where the murder took place, which is normally a storeroom for sports equipment. They don't usually put guests up in that room. Room 11 next door is set up for table tennis only.

"The reason I'm telling you all this is that apart from the six rooms I've just mentioned, every room has its own en suite bath and toilet. The place is like a five-star hotel. Ten

91

guest bedrooms, all sorts of leisure activity rooms—it's a fully equipped non-paying hotel."

"Hmm. Hmm. I see."

At this point Inspector Okuma returned and joined in the conversation.

"So that means that Ueda didn't get put in one of those rooms with its own bathroom. He got stuck in a storeroom, right?"

"That's right. When they have a large number of guests they sometimes run out of rooms, they said. So they move a folding bed into Room 10."

"Which means that there weren't enough guest rooms last night?"

"No, in fact there were enough. Room 15 was empty. In other words—"

"In other words, someone thought the humble chauffeur deserved to sleep in a storeroom. Who was in charge of allocating the rooms?"

"That would be the daughter, Eiko."

"Of course."

"There are four storeys, including the basement. The building is divided up into an east and a west wing, so there are eight mini-floors in total. Each of these floors is divided again into north and south, so sixteen rooms. Except that the salon is extra-large, two rooms in one, with an adjoining kitchen. I've labelled the kitchen Room 16 on the plan.

"Then, I noticed that all the rooms on the north side are larger than the ones on the south. The staircases are all on the south, and that takes a little space from the rooms on that side."

"I see."

"That's why both of the couples were given rooms on the north side. Mr and Mrs Kanai and the house staff, Mr and Mrs Hayakawa. The Kanais were on the top floor in Room 9, and the Hayakawas in the basement room number 7. Of course the Hayakawas have been living in that room since the mansion was built.

"Now about the staircases—this is totally bizarre. There are two, one in each of the east and west wings. The east staircase leads up from the ground-floor salon. You'd take this one if you were going to Rooms 1 and 2 or to Kozaburo Hamamoto's room in the tower. But for some reason those are the only places you can get to that way. It completely skips Rooms 3 and 4 on the middle floor. You can't get to the middle floor at all by those stairs."

"Really?"

"I couldn't work out why anybody would have created something so weird. Why would you want to go upstairs from the salon directly to the top floor, skipping the middle? And on top of that, the east wing doesn't have any stairs down to the basement at all. It's like a bloody maze—the more you walk around the more irritated you get."

"So what you're saying is if you want to go up to the middle floor or down to the basement, you have to use the stairs in the west wing that we used to get here? But I thought that staircase went beyond the middle floor. It looked like there were steps leading farther up."

"That's right. To get to the middle floor and the basement you have to use these west wing stairs. As the east wing stairs go up to the top floor, you'd think there was no need for the west stairs to go any farther than the middle floor, but they do go all the way up to the top."

"So anyone staying on the top floor can choose either of the staircases?"

"As a matter of fact, no, they can't. The west stairs only go up to Room 8 and 9 in the west wing. The occupants of Room 1 and 2 have to use the east stairs. On the top floor, there's no corridor at all joining the east and west wings. And so the occupants of Rooms 8 and 9 have no way of going and visiting the occupants of Rooms 1 and 2. They'd have to go all the way down to the ground floor, walk through the salon and climb up again."

"What a pain!"

"That's what I mean when I say this place is a nuthouse. It's a proper maze. I tried to go and check out Room 1, where Kumi Aikura says she saw the freaky man, but I took the west stairs. I got completely confused and had to come back down to the salon to ask the way."

"I suppose you would have."

"This bloke, Kozaburo Hamamoto, seems to love watching people being shocked or confused. I reckon that's why he had all the floors made on a slope like this. I'm sure people keep falling over until they've got used to it. Once you're used to it, you can use the windows on the east and west sides for reference, but you end up guessing wrongly which way is uphill and which is down."

"Yes, the windows look like they're leaning at an angle. They have me defeated. Somehow the side of the window frame that's farthest from the floor is the uphill side."

"But the floorboards are lying in the direction of the slope."

"I don't get it at all—it's like one of those house-of-mirror things you get at funfairs. Anyway, can you get from the north side rooms to the south? For example, if you're in Room 8 can you get to Room 9 next door to it?"

"That's possible. They're at the top of the same staircase. And then another thing about these stairs. The way they're arranged, they bypass the two rooms at the west end on the middle floor completely. The west staircase is just like the east one in that way. Room 10 where the murder was committed and the table tennis room, Room 11, next to it can't be accessed at all from inside the mansion."

"Hmm… Yes… That's right."

Ushikoshi was checking the diagram as he answered. It wasn't easy to make out.

"But as these two rooms are just a games room and a sports storeroom, I suppose it doesn't really matter if you can only access them from the outside."

"I get it now. It's pretty well thought out."

"To get into these two rooms you have to use the steps on the exterior west wall of the house. So whoever got assigned this room to sleep in must have found it tough in this season having to go around the outside of the house to get to his room. Well, I suppose they thought he's just the chauffeur, so he'd have to put up with it."

"It's a hard life when you're a lowly employee."

"Since they began to use Room 10 for guests, they had to store all the dirtiest stuff elsewhere, like gardening equipment, brooms, an axe and a scythe, and all the other odds and ends; so they built a shed at the bottom of the garden. The Hayakawas look after all that.

"And so Eiko allocated the guests their rooms, taking into consideration the unique layout of the house. First of all, there's Kumi Aikura, the woman with the face that all the men fall for. This morning, Tokyo HQ got right on the case. They've dug up plenty of information for us. It's an open secret at Kikuoka Bearings headquarters in Otemachi in Chiyoda Ward that Kumi Aikura is Kikuoka's mistress. And so to avoid anything going on at night, Eiko placed them at the very opposite ends of the house: Aikura in Room 1 on the east wing's top floor, and Kikuoka in Room 14 in the basement of the west wing.

"It seems that it was planned well in advance that Kikuoka would be in Room 14. That's normally Kozaburo Hamamoto's study. He keeps personal items—important books and stuff like that in there. The wall decorations and light fixtures are imported from England, and there's a priceless Persian rug on the floor. A lot of money has been spent on that room. Normally, people don't sleep in there—the bed is very narrow. Well, it's more of a couch really, but the cushions are supposed to be very comfortable.

"Kikuoka is the guest of honour in the party, so it follows that he was put in the most expensive room. And why did Hamamoto choose that room to use as a study? It seems that out of all the rooms in the main building, it's the warmest due to being in the basement. All the other rooms, despite being double paned, are rather cold through the windows' contact with the outside air. But Hamamoto seems to go backwards and forwards on his feelings about there being no windows. When he feels like it, he heads back up to his bedroom in the tower and enjoys a perfectly unobstructed 360-degree view.

"And it also looks like Eiko put Kumi Aikura in Room 1, next door to her own bedroom, Room 2, so that she could keep an eye on her. And for the very same reason, she put Yoshihiko Hamamoto in Room 8 on the top floor. As I mentioned before, there was no way to come and go between Room 1 and Room 8, even though they're physically so close.

I reckon Eiko was worried that Aikura might use her charms to tempt the young lad.

"Next we come to Rooms 3, 4 and 5—as I've already said, they can't be used as guest rooms. Room 6 in the basement belongs to the chef, Kajiwara. Room 7 is also occupied by staff—the Hayakawas. I'd say, no matter how warm the rooms, might be, I can't see how staying in a room with no windows would be appealing to short-term guests. Ever since the house was built, those two east-wing basement rooms have been reserved for the staff.

"Now, moving over to the west wing and starting from the top, Room 8 was Yoshihiko Hamamoto, Room 9, Mr and Mrs Kanai. The middle floor had Ueda in Room 10, of course. On the ground floor in Room 12 was Togai, and next to him in Room 13, Sasaki. Room 14 in the basement was occupied by Kikuoka, and Room 15 next to him was empty. And that's everybody."

"Way too complicated to take in in one go. For a start you're saying that Kumi Aikura in Room 1 and Hamamoto's daughter in Room 2 wouldn't be able to slip downstairs and remove that doll from the Room 3 display room? There are no stairs between the top and middle floors in the east wing at all?"

"That's right. While you could come down one flight of stairs from Room 8 or 9 in the west wing and be right in front of that display room, from 1 and 2 you'd have to take a long detour down to the salon and back up the west stairs. Even though the room is right underneath you."

"Just like the way you can't get down from Room 8 or 9 to the scene of the murder in Room 10. This place really is a damn maze. No exaggeration. Anything else we need to know?"

"Room 3, right there next door to us, seems to be known by the other occupants of the mansion as the 'Tengu Room'.

If you look inside it you'll understand why. It's full of all this junk that Kozaburo Hamamoto spent a fortune on when he was travelling around Europe, and the walls are decorated with masks of Tengu, the red-faced, long-nosed goblin."

"Whoa!"

"The south side wall is completely red from floor to ceiling with Tengu faces. And the east wall is pretty much covered too. That room doesn't have any windows facing the exterior of the building, so the surfaces of those two walls have completely uninterrupted surfaces. Plenty of room to hang all his masks.

"The wall on the west side has a large window facing the interior corridor. The north wall slants inwards and overhangs the room, so no masks can be hung on the north and west walls."

"Why does he have so many?"

"Tokyo police visited the headquarters of Hama Diesel in Chuo Ward to ask about that. The story goes that when he was a kid, the thing he was most afraid of were Tengu masks. Apparently, he wrote about it somewhere. For his fortieth birthday, as some kind of joke, his older brother gave him a mask, and so Hamamoto made up his mind to collect them. Went all out and hunted down some of the most unusual Tengus in Japan.

"Hamamoto was already quite the celebrity, so when people heard about it they fell over themselves to be the first one to send him an interesting mask, and before he knew it he ended up with all those. The story has been published several times in trade magazines. Anyone who knows Hamamoto has heard about it."

"Hmm... And what's happened to that doll that got taken to pieces?"

"Forensics have taken it for the time being, but it looks as if they'll be able to return it soon."

"And when they do give it back, can it be restored to its original condition? The head and the limbs?"

"Yep."

"So it was made to be taken apart easily?"

"Looks like it."

"So it wasn't damaged... What sort of doll was it?"

"Something that Hamamoto bought at a specialist shop in Europe. Apparently, it was made in the eighteenth century. I don't know any more than that. Should I ask Hamamoto directly about it?"

"Why would the suspect want to remove that doll from the display room? Was it one of Hamamoto's most expensive antiques?"

"Not particularly. There were plenty of items in that room that were worth a lot more."

"Hmm... I don't get it... There are too many strange things about this case. For a start, if someone held a grudge against Hamamoto, then why do away with Kikuoka's chauffeur?..."

"I have a theory about how it might have been done. Although Room 10 was a locked room, on the corner of the east wall there's that small ventilation hole, twenty centimetres square. It faces the west wing staircase, right?"

"That's right."

"I wonder if it could have been used in some way?"

"It doesn't look possible. If you look you see that the staircase on the middle floor goes to the opposite side from Room 10. If you look up from the corridor in front of Room 12, directly below it on the ground floor, you'll see that the ventilation hole in Room 10's wall is really high up in the wall and far away from anything. So if you tried to reach up there, you'd have to scale the full height of Room 12's wall and then the whole of

Room 10's. It's about the height of a prison fence. I can't see anyone being able to do it."

"That vent is in all the rooms of the house?"

"Almost every one. It looks as if they planned to put a fan in every room, but didn't get around to it yet. Every room has the same kind of hole facing onto the nearest stairwell.

"There's one more thing I should mention about these vents. The way the house is constructed, the west wing rooms 8, 10, 12 and 14 are identical, piled on top of one another like building blocks, so that the vent is in the identical spot—in the far south-east corner of the east wall. However, Rooms 9, 11, 13 and 15 are also identical and built directly on top of one another, but in their case, in order for the vent to face out into the space of the stairwell, their ventilation hole is up near the ceiling in the middle of the south wall, slightly towards the east side.

"Then if you go over to the east wing, Rooms 1, 2, 3 and 4 on the top and middle floors match up with their counterparts in the west wing. So 1 and 3 have the vents in the south corner of the east wall like 8, 10, 12 and 14. Rooms 2 and 4 in the middle of the south wall like 9, 11, 13 and 15.

"Rooms 6 and 7 in the basement are different though. Room 7's vent is the same as Rooms 2 and 4 above on the south wall, but over to the west side. Room 6 is the one that's different from the rest. It's the only room in the entire building that has its ventilation hole in the southern corner of its west-facing wall. Room 5 is, of course, the salon, and I imagine if it were to have a ventilation hole facing the stairwell, it would have been in the same west wall as Room 6 below, but in fact the salon doesn't have a vent. And that's all the rooms. I don't suppose any of it is really relevant to our investigation though.

"But while I'm on the subject, I'll go on to the windows. None of the walls that contain a ventilation hole has a window. Besides Room 3, all the rooms have exterior-facing windows. In other words, windows you can open to let in fresh air. The vent holes and the doors face the interior of the building, the windows face the exterior. Anyway, that appears to be the basic concept of the mansion's layout.

"If you imagine the rule as being that all the exterior walls have a window in them, and all the interior walls facing a stairwell have a ventilation hole and a door, you've got the idea. Then we move onto the floors, ceilings and walls shared with the next room. Obviously, nobody would think about making holes in any of those.

"Take this library, for example, there's something slightly strange about the position of the door in relation to the corridor. There's something slightly off about it, but it still follows the general rule. Right where the east wing stairwell should be, in the south-facing wall, in the corner towards the east—look, there's the ventilation hole. But there's no window, because this wall is facing an interior space. And as you can see, the windows are on the north and east sides, which both are exterior-facing walls. The position of the door, as I just mentioned, is not quite the same as Room 2 above us or 7 below us; or even 9, 11, 13 and 15 in the west wing. You can see it's at the westerly edge of the south wall. It's because of the construction of the corridor outside, but you can see that the rule that there is always a door in the wall with the ventilation hole has not changed."

"Huh? This is getting too complicated. I don't follow."

"But there is an exception—Room 3. That's the only room in the building without a window in the south-facing exterior wall.

Instead, it has a large window in the interior-facing west wall. In addition, in that same wall, there's a door. The ventilation hole is in the opposite wall, on the east. Hamamoto probably set it up that way to protect his valuable antiques from direct sunlight. And so he needed to put in an extra-large window for ventilation."

"All right, all right. That's quite enough. You've definitely done your homework. You could become an architect after all this is over. I'm really not getting half of it, but do you think it's relevant to this case?"

"Probably not."

"I hope you're wrong, because otherwise this is getting too complicated for no reason. We're brand-new students of this house of mirrors, and right now we don't understand a thing. The guests are mostly way ahead of us. This winter isn't their first visit, is it?"

"No, but in fact there are some first-timers amongst them— Kumi Aikura and Kanai's wife, Hatsue. Kikuoka and Mr Kanai were here in the summer."

"Hmm. But still, the majority of the folks here are used to this cursed jack-in-a-box of a place. They might have even worked out a clever way of using this cockeyed construction to do away with someone. Personally, I'm still suspicious of that air vent in Room 10."

Ushikoshi fell silent, and spent a few moments gathering his thoughts.

"Just now, you said that the hole is far away from everything else, high up in the wall. You said you were looking up from the corridor on the ground floor in front of... let's see... er, Room 12?"

"Yes, I did."

"Incidentally, the staircase we took to get here was made of metal, wasn't it?"

"Yes."

"The section that leads up from the salon to the middle-floor landing is made of wood. It's covered with a red carpet—a good quality one. But all the rest of the stairs are made of metal. Now why would that be? Even the stairs back at Sapporo police HQ are better than that. These ones—they're new but made of the kind of cheap stuff you find in a public building. If you're not careful and walk too heavily, they make a terrible clanging noise. Rather out of place in a medieval European-style mansion, don't you think?"

"You're right. But the angle is pretty steep, so I guess they needed to make it from something durable and safe."

"I suppose… they certainly are steep. Maybe that's it. And the landings—I guess I should say corridors—the corridors on every floor seem to be metallic too."

"Yes."

"This floor's different, but with the ground floor of the west wing and the top floor too, all the corridors seem to be L-shaped."

"They are. The top floor in the east wing here is the same. This floor is the only one constructed differently."

"The tips of the L—in other words the ends of the corridors, look as if there was some kind of design flaw or something. I don't know why, but they're not joined completely up to the walls. There's about a twenty-centimetre gap there at each end."

"Whoa! That's a bit creepy if you ask me. I suppose someone could lean over and press their head against the wall and see all the way down to the bottom of the house. For example if you stood by the gap at the end of the corridor in front of

Room 8 on the top floor, with a gap on every floor you could see all the way down to the corridor in the basement. Even though there's a handrail, it'd give me the creeps."

"So what I'm thinking is that you could use that gap, push a rope or a wire through the ventilation hole and manage to pull off some sort of clever trick. At any rate, the ventilation hole in Room 10 is directly under the gap on the top floor, right?"

"Yes, I thought of that too. I tried getting right up against the wall at the very end of the corridor by Room 8, but the ventilation hole to Room 10 is far below, way out of reach. It's at least a metre down. I guess you could possibly work out some kind of plan with two people working together, but it would be very difficult."

"You can't see into Room 10 through the hole, then?"

"No, definitely not."

"Pity. Anyway, I suppose that a twenty-centimetre-square hole is too small for anything like that."

"Yes, too difficult to pull anything off through that kind of space."

And with that, Detective Sergeant Ozaki's lecture on the nuthouse mansion was complete.

Ushikoshi turned to the local detective, who had sat there throughout the discussion in a kind of stunned silence.

"Inspector Okuma, is there anything you'd like to add?"

"Nah, nothing special," he replied automatically. His expression suggested he was relieved not to be responsible for such a complicated case.

"Reckon there'll be a blizzard tonight," he added.

"You may be right. The wind's really getting up," said Ushikoshi. "But then again this is a pretty desolate location.

There's no other human habitation for miles around. You know, I can't imagine wanting to live out here. It's just the kind of place you'd expect murders to happen."

"No kidding."

"I don't understand how anyone can live in a place like this," said Sergeant Ozaki.

"I guess if you're filthy rich, you're always surrounded by hangers-on, people sucking up to you, after your money. Anyone would be about ready to escape a life like that."

For someone from such meagre circumstances, Ushikoshi seemed to have a pretty good handle on the way the rich thought.

"So, who shall we call first?"

"Well, I'm most interested in the three staff members. I'd like to have a go at getting them to talk," said Ozaki. "I bet you with that kind of employer they've got a whole bunch of grievances to get out of their system. In a big group they'd keep a lid on it, but get them alone and it'll all come pouring out. They're probably total wimps when it comes down to it, just shake them up a bit and they'll spill."

"Do Kohei and Chikako Hayakawa have children?"

"It seems they had a child who died. We haven't found out the details yet."

"So they don't have any kids at all?"

"Seems not."

"And Kajiwara?"

"He's single. Still young—only twenty-seven. Who do you want me to call first?"

"You know, I don't think we ought to call the staff first. Let's call that medical student, Sasaki. Would you mind?..."

*

105

The police officers arranged themselves in a row like the three judges of the underworld, forcing each witness to sit across the table from them. As Sasaki took his seat he joked that it felt like a job interview.

"Please don't include any unnecessary chat. Just answer the questions as we ask them," said Ozaki sternly.

Ushikoshi opened the questioning.

"You're staying here to check Kozaburo Hamamoto's health. Is that correct?"

"Yes, it is."

"We have three main questions for you. First, what relationship did you have to the murdered man, Kazuya Ueda? How close were you to him? I promise you that we can easily discover whether you are lying or not, so to save time all around, please don't try to hide anything. Just tell the truth.

"The second question concerns your alibi. I know it's probably difficult, but as long as you weren't in Room 10 between the hours of 12 and half past, in other words, if you have proof you were elsewhere, we'd like to hear it.

"Our third question is the most important one: just like the information you gave us earlier about the stakes in the garden, we'd like to hear of anything strange you noticed last night. And also, of any strange behaviour on the part of anyone. We know that in matters like this, it can be hard to speak up in front of everyone. Of course, we won't reveal from whom we got any of the information, so please let us know if there is something you think we ought to know. That's all, thank you."

"I understand. First, question number one: I think I can answer that with perfect accuracy. I only ever had two interactions with Mr Ueda in my life. That was 'Where is Mr Kikuoka?' And one more that I've forgotten the details of. But that kind

106

of thing. Apart from that, I've never met the man, not back in Tokyo—I've never had the occasion to. In other words, he was a complete stranger to me. I think I could even say I have a closer relationship with you three detectives than I had with him.

"As for an alibi, that's a bit difficult. I went up to my room around 9.00 p.m. I'm due to take the National Medical Examination to get my licence very soon, so I was reading some reference books. I never left my room again after that, so I don't have anything to say in response to your third question either."

"So you're saying that after you went up to your room you never even went out into the corridor again?"

"That's right. There are bathrooms attached to every room. There's no need to go outside."

"You were staying in Room 13? You didn't pay a visit to Togai next door in Room 12?"

"I have done in the past, but last night he was wrapped up in something else, and I was studying for my exams, so at least last night we didn't see each other."

"What do you mean by he was wrapped up in something else?"

Sasaki related the story of Kozaburo and the flower bed puzzle.

"I see," said Ushikoshi. Ozaki snorted scornfully.

"And from your room you didn't hear any strange noises?"

"No… The window is double-paned."

"How about sounds from the corridor or the stairs? The killer managed to remove that huge doll from Room 3. He must have passed very close to Room 13."

"I didn't hear anything. I never had any idea that there had been a murder. Of course I'll be paying more attention tonight."

"About what time did you go to sleep?"

"Around 10.30, I think."

They hadn't got much out of Sasaki, and Togai wasn't any more helpful. The only difference was that he was able to be even clearer about his relationship with Ueda—he'd never spoken to him in his life.

"That was the son of Shunsaku Togai, the politician," said Ozaki, when Togai had left.

"Whoa! *That* Togai!"

"A Tokyo University student? Must have brains, that one," said Okuma.

"Those two, Sasaki and Togai, are both after Eiko Hamamoto."

"As I see it, Togai's only advantage is that he's from a famous family."

"Sad to say, but I agree."

"Call the Kikuoka Bearings group next. Now is there anything I should be aware of before we begin?"

"Well, we already know that Kikuoka is having an affair with his secretary, Kumi Aikura. Apart from that, Kanai has been Kikuoka's personal doormat and brown-noser for the past decade and more, and has only recently been promoted to a managerial position."

"What's the relationship between Kikuoka Bearings and Hama Diesel?"

"Back in 1958 when Kikuoka Bearings was just a fledgling company, Kikuoka managed to get into bed with Hama Diesel. His company owes everything to Hamamoto. Around half of all the ball bearings used in Hama Diesel's tractor-trailers are made by Kikuoka Bearings."

"So the two companies are affiliated?"

"Right. Anyway, that's why they were invited."

"Have they had any kind of dispute or falling-out recently?"

"Nothing at all like that. Both companies are doing extremely well, particularly their export business."

"Got it. And there was nothing going on between Kumi Aikura and Ueda, the chauffeur?"

"Nothing at all that we can find. Ueda seems to have been the most quiet, unassuming man. Kikuoka's the nosy type, and jealous to boot. A gold-digger mistress like that one is hardly going to risk it all for someone like Ueda."

But there turned out to be little difference between the Kikuoka Bearings contingent and Sasaki or Togai. Kumi Aikura had encountered Ueda through work, but they'd had next to no direct contact and almost no conversation. The detectives were able to check this information in a casual way with the others and decided it was most likely the truth.

Mr and Mrs Kanai had had the same experience as Kumi. The biggest surprise for the officers was that Eikichi Kikuoka himself made the same claim. The only things he seemed to know about Ueda were that he was unmarried, rarely spoke, had no brothers or sisters, and his father was deceased. In other words, he was the only child of a single mother from Moriguchi near Osaka. And that was about it. Kikuoka had invited Ueda to have a drink with him a couple of times, but they had no kind of relationship to speak of.

Besides the three questions they'd asked Sasaki and Togai, the police had added an extra one—*Who do you think might have wanted to kill Ueda?*—but it was hopeless. They all said the same thing: they had no idea.

"Mr Kanai, what time was it when you went running to Room 1?"

"I heard Ms Aikura screaming just after 1.05 a.m. and stayed in bed for about ten minutes I think, not sure what to do."

"Did you hear a man's voice scream too?"

"Yes, well…"

"Did you look out of the window at all?"

"No."

"When did you finally get back to your room?"

"Just before 2 a.m."

"And you had to make a round trip through the salon to do that?"

"Yes, of course."

"On your way there or back did you meet anyone, or see anything strange?"

"No, nothing."

And so they only got one single piece of useful information—namely that if Kanai was telling the truth, around 1.15 a.m., and again around 1.50 a.m., there were no suspicious characters along the route connecting Room 9 with Room 1.

At any rate, none of the people interviewed had anything that constituted a solid alibi. All of them had retired to their respective rooms around 9.30, changed into pyjamas, and then never once after that ventured out into the corridor (with the exception of Michio Kanai, of course). After dinner, all of the guests seemed to have shut themselves away in their rooms like bears preparing to hibernate for the winter.

With each room in the mansion having its own en suite bathroom, this behaviour was no different from that of guests at a hotel, but to the three police officers who hadn't been brought up in a life of luxury, it was a little hard to imagine. At night, back at the hall of residence at the police academy, there were more people hanging out in the corridors than in their own rooms. They decided to ask the next person, Yoshihiko Hamamoto, the reason for this.

"You said the same things as everyone else: no one seems to have ever exchanged words with Mr Ueda; no one set foot outside their rooms after dinner; no one heard anything; no one saw anything. Therefore, nobody has an alibi. Why did everyone shut themselves away and never come out again?"

"I think... maybe it was because everyone brought pyjamas with them but..."

"Yes? Go on."

"There weren't any robes or dressing gowns."

The detectives all nodded knowingly, but in fact they didn't get anything from Yoshihiko's reply other than to wonder what kind of a house they had found themselves in.

And what on earth were they going to do that night without so much as a pair of pyjamas?

The next person they called was Eiko Hamamoto. Ushikoshi repeated their three questions.

"I'm sorry but I don't have an alibi. If you want to know where I was between just after 1 and just before 2 in the morning, then I was in Room 1 with my father, Kumi Aikura and Mr Kanai. I'm afraid I can't answer for the half-hour after midnight."

"Hmm. But finally we've found someone besides Mr Kanai who actually left their room. It looks like you had a dressing gown."

"I beg your pardon?"

"I'm sorry, private joke. Were you close to Kazuya Ueda?"

"I hardly spoke to him."

"Of course not. You wouldn't have."

"Remind me of your other question."

"Did you see anyone behaving suspiciously or hear anything strange?"

"No, I didn't see anything."

"Hmm. So once you went to bed you never left your room until you heard Kumi Aikura's screams and went to the next room?"

"No... Actually, yes, to be accurate I did leave my room one other time."

"Oh, yes?"

"It was so cold I woke up. I opened my door to check if the drawbridge was completely up or not."

"And was it?"

"No. As I'd guessed, it wasn't properly shut."

"Does that happen often?"

"Yes, occasionally. Sometimes it's difficult to close from the tower side."

"And so you closed it?"

"Yes."

"What time was that?"

"I'm not sure... Maybe about twenty or thirty minutes before I heard Ms Aikura scream... I didn't check my watch."

"So it was around 12.30?"

"Yes, I suppose it was. But it might have been later."

"Could you tell us exactly what happened when you heard Ms Aikura screaming?"

"I was in bed but awake for the reason I just explained. Then I heard screaming. Really loud screaming. So, wondering what was going on, I tried to listen, and then I heard what sounded like a man's yell. Then I got out of bed, opened my window and looked outside."

"Did you see anyone, or anything?"

"No. The moon was out and reflecting off the snow, so I could see quite well, but I couldn't see anything out of the ordinary. And then I heard her screaming again, so I went and knocked on the door of Room 1."

"Hmm. And then your father appeared?"

"That's right. And finally, Mr Kanai."

"And what do you believe it was that Ms Aikura had seen?"

"I'm sure she had a nightmare."

Her tone was emphatic.

Next was Kozaburo Hamamoto. He listened to Ushikoshi's three questions, then surprised them all with his first response.

"I've had several conversations with Ueda."

"Oh?… And why was that?"

Both Ushikoshi and Okuma looked suspicious.

"Why? Now that's a difficult question to answer. Was it wrong to want to get to know Ueda?"

Ushikoshi forced a laugh.

"No, no, of course not. But when I hear that the celebrated Mr Kozaburo Hamamoto, a person so famous that there could well be a statue made of him one day, made the effort to get to know a humble chauffeur, it just seems very odd to me."

"Ha! Well, it seems just as odd to me to hear an opinion like that from a member of the police force, who are supposed to be the keepers of peace and public order. If I desire intellectual stimulation, I'll happily strike up a conversation with whomever I like. I don't discriminate. I liked to talk to Ueda because he had been in the military. I wanted to hear first-hand all about the current state of the Japanese Self-Defence Forces."

"I see. But your relationship with Mr Ueda was only at this mansion, right?"

"Yes, naturally. There was no other place I could have met him, seeing as I never leave this house. But I only finished construction a year ago. Before that, I used to live in Kokura City. I noticed Ueda was Mr Kikuoka's chauffeur back then when he used to visit my home, but we never exchanged any words at that time."

"Would I be right in thinking Mr Kikuoka and Mr Ueda have only visited you here at this house twice—once in the summer, and this current visit?"

"Right."

"How long did they stay in the summer?"

"A week."

"I see."

"And then, as for your second question, I went up to my room around 10.30. I'm sorry but I can't provide an alibi."

"10.30? That was rather late, wasn't it?"

"I was chatting with Eiko. However, I don't know if this information is enough to be my alibi, but as you know, my room is at the top of the tower, and the only way for me to get back to the main building is by a staircase in the form of a drawbridge. Whenever I lower or raise that bridge, it makes a noise that echoes throughout the whole of the main building. It's winter now so I don't leave it down for any period of time, because while it's in the down position it means that the door to the main building is left open, and it's much too cold for that. Therefore, if you hear the drawbridge being lowered and then raised at night, and you don't hear that sound again until the next morning you can be sure that I haven't left my room in the tower."

"Aha, I understand. But of course, Mr Hamamoto, you aren't under suspicion. It's hard to imagine any reason that a man of your social standing and prestige would destroy everything he had by murdering a simple chauffeur. What time did you lower the drawbridge this morning?"

"Around 8.30, I believe. If I get up any earlier my daughter complains that the noise of the bridge wakes her up. By the way, you do realize that the murderer isn't in this house?"

"Well, if the murderer isn't in this house, then Mr Ueda must have killed himself. But in our experience we've never seen anything like that manner of suicide. If it does indeed turn out to be murder, then I regret to say the murderer must be here in your house."

"But it doesn't appear that he or she is."

"You are quite right. But we have our colleagues in Tokyo working on this case too, and I'm confident they will discover the hidden motive for this crime. By the way, regarding this noise that the drawbridge makes, can it be heard by anybody anywhere in the main building?"

"I'm pretty sure you can hear it anywhere. It's very loud. But I couldn't swear that you can hear it down in the basement. In that sense, it makes Room 14 where Mr Kikuoka is staying such a special room. The people in Room 1 or 2 would definitely be able to hear it."

"And how about question number three?"

"You mean whether I noticed anything suspicious? Well, my room is up in the tower, far away from everyone else, so I have no idea whatsoever. That said, I did hear that man's voice and Ms Aikura screaming. Apart from that I didn't see or hear anything out of the ordinary."

"Hmm. And what do you think it was that Ms Aikura saw, Mr Hamamoto?"

"Well, that's quite a mystery. I can't imagine it being anything besides a nightmare."

"But you definitely heard a man's scream?"

"Yes, I heard it. But it was very faint. At the time I thought it came from somewhere far beyond this house—a drunk yelling or something."

"I see. And then I'd like to ask you why someone took—what's its name again?—from Room 3?"

"You mean Golem?"

"That's it. Do you think someone deliberately carried it out?"

"I really don't know. It was right by the window, and therefore quite easy to remove from the room."

"If someone wanted to make you suffer, would taking that doll and dumping it in the snow be a good way to do it?"

"Not at all, really. There are other smaller, lighter and more valuable items that I truly care about. And if they really wanted to upset me, rather than taking it apart, they could have smashed it to pieces. And they could have done that inside Room 3. There was no need to take it outside."

"So it isn't something you really care about?"

"Not at all. It was something I just picked up on a whim."

"Why do you call it—er… Golem?

"It was a doll shop in Prague. That's what they called him. There's a bit of an odd story behind the name. Surely you don't need me to tell that story to the police?"

"What kind of story?"

"There's a belief that he can walk by himself and always heads towards water."

"What the...!"

Hamamoto laughed.

"You don't believe me! But in medieval Europe there was a great folklore tradition, and they believed in all sorts of myths."

"It's a grotesque-looking doll. Why did you want to buy something like that?"

"Why did I buy it...? Hmm... I suppose it's because I just don't feel the appeal of those cute French dolls."

"That reminds me, this is quite an unusual residence, isn't it? I'd like to ask you about it. The stairs and the corridors—or perhaps the right word is landings—on every floor are made of metal. Even the handrails are metal.

"And then, at the far end of every L-shaped corridor, the floor doesn't quite reach as far as the wall. There's an open gap, and that has a handrail too. What was your reason for making it like that?"

"That gap was a mistake. A young architect placed an order for metal floorboards and the wrong size was delivered. He said he'd redo it but I told them it would be all right. Actually, I preferred it that way. It makes them look like a kind of aerial walkaway. But I asked them to put in the guard rail. My staircases and passageways are all metallic, and I've gone overboard and put in metal handrails too. And then my stairs are steep, and look as if they're getting rusty. I kind of like that grim, gloomy effect.

"Ever since I was a university student, I've loved the copper-plate prints of the Italian artist, Giovanni Battista Piranesi. Piranesi left many sombre prints of prisons. He was a portrayer of imaginary prisons. Floor upon floor of high ceilings and dark metal staircases, and also towers and aerial walkways. And of course metal drawbridges. His prints were full of those kinds of things. I wanted to build this house in that image. I even thought about calling it 'Piranesi Mansion'."

"I see. That's fine," said Ushikoshi, but Kozaburo didn't notice. He was passionately caught up in his story.

Next Hamamoto's members of staff were called. Haruo Kajiwara turned out to have no other interests besides cooking and watching TV in his own room. He'd never spoken to Ueda, nor seen anything unusual the night before.

Chikako Hayakawa was the same, but her husband, Kohei, left a different impression. He was around fifty but came across as a rather timid character who looked much older than he was. Kohei Hayakawa's replies were exactly like those of a politician denying a scandal. It sounded as if everything he said was a lie. The detectives had a hunch he was hiding something.

Sergeant Ozaki raised his voice. Up to now, everyone's answers had been so pedestrian and conventional, his irritation had been building.

"So you didn't even exchange a single word with the victim, Ueda; you went to your room around 10.30 and never came out again, and therefore you have no alibi; and finally you saw nothing suspicious. Is that what you're claiming?"

Hayakawa looked startled, then stared down at his feet. The veteran detectives recognized that this was a person who, given one more push, would spill the beans. Outside, the wind was getting louder, the prelude to a heavy blizzard.

Chief Inspector Ushikoshi and Sergeant Ozaki began to wonder which of the three questions Kohei Hayakawa had answered untruthfully. If they could discover that, the extra push would be much more effective. If they guessed wrong, then the suspect might clam up for good. Ushikoshi took a gamble.

"We won't repeat anything you tell us in this room," said Ushikoshi, making his choice. "Are you sure you didn't see anything at all suspicious?"

And just as Hayakawa seemed about to crumble, he lifted his head and said, "Absolutely nothing."

From that point on, no matter what the detectives asked him, he gave no concrete response. Ushikoshi realized he'd gambled and lost, and quickly changed the line of questioning.

"So tell us, Mr Hayakawa, do you believe that somehow last night a stranger managed to break into this mansion?"

"Reckon that'd be impossible. Kaji's always right by the service entrance to the kitchen, and everyone else was near the glass doors in the salon. I go around and lock all the doors in the house before everyone goes to bed."

"The ground-floor toilet window too?"

"That toilet window's always locked. Got iron bars on it too."

"Hmm. And you're in charge of the windows in all the guest rooms?"

"If there's a guest staying, I've been told not to go into their room unless they ask me. But of course Ms Hamamoto is always telling the guests to call me if they need anything."

"Hmm, I see," said Ushikoshi but the question itself was a little off-point. Asking whether a stranger could have broken into the Ice Floe Mansion with the intention of murdering Kazuya Ueda was irrelevant really. Room 10 was in the perfect location for someone to enter directly from the outside. There was no need whatsoever to sneak into the main building.

So what was the business with the Golem doll all about? Ushikoshi decided that he had better confirm one more time with Kozaburo Hamamoto that it had really been in Room 3 in the daytime yesterday.

"Thank you."

And with that, Ushikoshi set Kohei Hayakawa free.

"What a pain in the arse," said Ozaki, staring out at the whirling snow. "It's going to be a real storm. I don't think we can get back tonight."

"The Snow Queen says she's not letting you go home."

Another unfunny joke from Inspector Okuma.

"Yes, that's what I'm hearing," said Ushikoshi. He was distracted, thinking back over the completely fruitless investigation.

What they had learnt was this: Ueda was not the kind of man who someone would want to kill; when Eiko Hamamoto had gone to close the door to the bridge around 12.30 or 12.40, she hadn't seen anyone or anything—in other words, there was nobody hanging around Room 1 or 2 at that time of night; at 1.15 a.m. and again at 1.50 a.m. when Michio Kanai had been taking the circuitous route between Room 9 and Room 1, he hadn't noticed anything suspicious. So probably by that time the killer had completed his task and had already returned to his room. Or had the killer heard the sound of footsteps and hidden himself away somewhere? Well, that was if the murderer was even one of the guests staying at the mansion.

"Chief Inspector, you never know what might happen. I reckon I'd better call up at least one of our young toughs. If we stay the night we may end up making an arrest."

No objections to that, thought Ushikoshi to himself.

"We've got one real bruiser I can think of. I'll put him on night duty, okay?"

"Yes, please, Inspector Okuma. If you've got someone right for the job, let's do it."

"Yes, better safe than sorry."

ACT TWO

Why no! It's but a mask, a lying ornament

CHARLES BAUDELAIRE,
The Mask

SCENE 1

The Salon

The detectives left the library and came down to the salon. Eiko was the first to spot them. She addressed the room in her distinctive, perfectly enunciated tones.

"Attention, everyone! Here they are! Our guests from the police have joined us, dinner's ready so let's sit down. Tonight we're going to be treated to the wonderful flavours of the north."

The meal was as delicious as Eiko had promised. Snow crab, scallops au gratin, salmon sautéed in butter, something called *kenchin*-style steamed squid—all specialities of the Hokkaido region. Inspector Okuma and Chief Inspector Ushikoshi were both Hokkaido born and raised, but were seeing most of these dishes for the first time. They had a sense that this was traditional Hokkaido fare, but hadn't the faintest idea where in Hokkaido people might eat food like this every day.

When dinner was over, Eiko got briskly to her feet and strode over to the grand piano in the corner of the salon. The next moment, Chopin's "Revolutionary Étude" reverberated through the room, almost like a challenge to the blizzard outside. The guests exchanged looks as if to say, *What's going on?* And then as one they turned to look in the direction of the piano.

Out of all of Chopin's works, this intense piece was Eiko's favourite. If she were to choose something to listen to, there were other pieces that she liked just as well (except for "Chanson de l'adieu", which for some reason she couldn't stand), but when she wanted to play, it was his "Revolutionary Étude" or his "Héroïque" that she preferred.

Her fingers struck the keys fiercely, and when this tour de force was over, the enthusiasm of the applause that followed must have rivalled that for Chopin's own performance of his piece. An encore was begged for. Caught up in the moment, having enjoyed such a delicious meal, the detectives felt they ought to add their polite applause to the crowd.

Eiko turned to her audience and smiled, then began softly to play one of the nocturnes. As she played, she lifted her head and looked outside. The blizzard had grown stronger, the wind had begun to howl and was rattling the large window with the flakes of snow brushing the glass as they fell.

Eiko felt as if everything were a prop especially prepared for her. This snowstorm, these gracious and cultivated guests, even the murder—she felt as if the gods had furnished her with all of these as a tribute to her own beauty. Beautiful people should enjoy the privilege of seeing others grovel in their presence. She felt that even the chairs and the doors should yield to her.

At the end of her second piece, she stood without closing the lid, and after waiting for the applause to die down, she addressed the room.

"It's a little early to be closing the lid on this keyboard. Who'd like to be next?"

Kumi Aikura felt as if someone had just stabbed her in the stomach. Eiko's intentions had just become clear to her.

"It shouldn't be difficult to follow such an amateur performance," Eiko continued.

Of course, the truth was that Eiko had purposely chosen her best piece, and her performance had been flawless. She pretended to be trying to persuade Sasaki, Togai and others to volunteer to play, but in fact she was steadily stalking a different prey.

It was a terrifying scene. The wolf was casually circling the flock of sheep, waiting to pounce on the petrified lamb. This performance was as impressive as the one that had just finished,

"Oh, here's someone who surely must be an accomplished pianist!" she cried, as if the thought had just occurred to her. "I've always wanted to chance to sit in this salon and listen to someone else play my piano. How about it, Ms Aikura?"

With the howling blizzard as a backdrop, the audience was on tenterhooks to see how this scene would play out.

From the way Kumi Aikura had turned pale and was looking back and forth between Eiko and her sugar daddy, it was clear to everyone that she wasn't a pianist. When she finally spoke, her voice was barely audible.

"I'm sorry, I don't play."

No one had ever heard Kumi sound like this before. Eiko, however, didn't seem satisfied yet with her victory. She remained standing in front of Kumi.

"This lass is not the type for all that. Always so busy studying she never had time to learn the piano. Forgive her, Ms Hamamoto."

At last, Kikuoka had come to Kumi's rescue. She sat looking at the floor in misery.

"Let's hear some more of your playing, Ms Hamamoto," called Kikuoka in his raspy walrus voice, and Michio Kanai quickly saw his opportunity to earn himself a few points.

"Ms Hamamoto, your skill on the piano is superb. I would love to hear some more."

Eiko eventually relented, and returned to the piano to play another piece. Again, with the exception of Kumi Aikura, the audience's reaction was ecstatic.

When everyone had drunk their tea, the robust-looking policeman that Inspector Okuma had called from the Wakkanai Police Station turned up at the Ice Floe Mansion, a layer of snow adorning his peaked cap. He was introduced to everyone as Constable Anan.

Eiko suggested that Constable Anan and Inspector Okuma spend the night in Room 12. Togai, the current occupant, looked up in surprise.

"Togai, you can move to Room 8 and share with Yoshihiko," said Eiko.

Togai and Sasaki both wondered why Eiko didn't put them together in Room 13, which was larger than Room 8. They each privately decided it was because she knew that they were rivals for her affections, and thought it best to keep them apart. She was always so thoughtful! But if that were the case, then surely she should have moved Sasaki to Room 8? Room 13, where he'd spent the previous night, was so much more spacious than Room 12, and would therefore have been much better suited to lodging the two policemen. It must be because Sasaki's exams were coming up soon. Letting him keep his own room would give him time to study.

Eiko's decision was in fact somewhat self-serving. She believed in ensuring her suitors were as successful in their careers as possible. In that way she could have the choice of men who in the future would be a doctor or a lawyer or a Tokyo University professor, or at the very least, some kind of famous person.

"Chief Inspector Ushikoshi, Sergeant Ozaki, the room next to Mr Kikuoka's in the basement is currently unoccupied. Please take that tonight. I'll have it prepared for you right away."

"Much obliged."

Chief Inspector Ushikoshi expressed thanks on behalf of all four officers.

"I don't suppose you've brought any sleepwear?"

"No, we haven't. But please don't go to any trouble."

"We do have several spare sets of pyjamas, but I don't think we have enough for all four of you."

"Oh, please don't worry about anything like that. Compared to the pancake-thin futons we get at the police station, it'll be heaven."

"Anyway, we have toothbrushes for everyone."

Okuma privately thought that this was about the same as a night in prison. Even criminals got a toothbrush.

"So sorry to trouble you."

"No, not at all. You are keeping us safe, after all."

"We'll do our best."

As he brought his second cup of black coffee to his lips, Kozaburo Hamamoto struck up conversation with Eikichi Kikuoka. Kikuoka's personal terror of developing diabetes meant that he also took his coffee black and sugar free.

Kikuoka had been staring out of the window as if dumbfounded. The glass was covered in drops of condensation; beyond it snowflakes were whirling like deadly splinters.

Up here in northern Hokkaido, there was at least one night of extreme weather each winter. It was a blessed relief to be inside with the double windows keeping you warm on such a night as this.

"How do you like our blizzards up here in the north?" asked Kozaburo.

"What?... Oh, it's amazing. I've never seen anything like this before, such a powerful storm. It feels as if the whole house is shaking."

"Does it remind you of anything?"

"What do you mean?"

"Never mind. We're just a single house in the middle of a huge, empty plain. Someone once said that the constructions of man are just molehills to Mother Nature, powerless against her."

"Very true, very true."

"Doesn't it remind you of the war?"

"Where did that come from?"

"Ah, it just brought back some memories for me, that's all."

"The war... there are no good memories... But this is the first time we've had a night like this while I've been visiting. There was nothing like this back in the summer. It's like a typhoon."

"Maybe it's Ueda's revenge."

"What the...? Lay off the jokes, please. Tonight's going to be hard enough to get to sleep as it is. That noise and all that's happened... I ought to be tired but all this is stopping me from sleeping."

At this point, Kanai opened his mouth and said something that was sure to get him a pay cut.

"I wouldn't be surprised if Ueda's ghost turned up by your bedside, saying 'Sir, should I fetch the car?'"

Kikuoka's face turned red with rage.

"Don't... Don't talk such utter crap! You idiot! What are you thinking?"

"Mr Kikuoka?" interrupted Kozaburo.

"What?"

"I'd just like to ask you, do you still have any of those sleeping pills I gave you?"

"Huh? Yes, I've got a couple left."

"All right, then. That's fine. You'll take some tonight, then?"

"Yes, I suppose so. You know, I was just thinking it might be a good idea."

"Right. I can always go and get some more from Sasaki. And I really think you ought to take two. I don't think a single pill is going to do it on a night like this."

"Yes, you're right. Anyway, I think I'd better get to bed as soon as possible. This storm is getting heavy."

"I think that's a good idea. For a couple of old men like us. And I think you ought to be very careful to lock up your room—don't forget your door. After all, they do say there's a murderer on the loose in the house."

"You don't say!"

Kikuoka laughed heartily as if he found it amusing, but it was clear that he was actually quite nervous.

"Hey, you never know. If I were a bloodthirsty killer, I'd be after you, Mr Kikuoka!"

This time Kikuoka positively roared. He was trying to seem amused, but there was sweat visible on his forehead.

At that moment, Chief Inspector Ushikoshi came over to Kozaburo and asked to speak to him for a moment.

"Yes, of course!" replied Kozaburo, still in high spirits.

He glanced over to see the other three police officers huddled together at a corner of the dining table, discussing something in hushed tones.

Seeing Kozaburo turn away to talk to Ushikoshi, Kikuoka decided to talk to Kumi instead.

"Hey, Kumi, does your bed have an electric blanket?"

But his secretary appeared to be in an unusually foul mood.

"Yes."

She still had the same wide-eyed expression as always, but tonight her catlike eyes were not turned on her sugar daddy. She was sulking about something.

"Didn't you find... Well... that it wasn't all it's cracked up to be?"

"No," she said curtly. The implication was, *And neither are you.*

"You know, it's the first time in my life I've slept under an electric blanket. But it wasn't quite enough. I can't criticize the heat it gives off but... Was there a duvet in your room too?"

"Yes."

"Where? I mean, where did you find it?"

"In the wardrobe."

"What kind of duvet?"

"A down one."

"In my room there didn't seem to be anything like that. Guess it's because it's not really supposed to be a bedroom. The bed's so narrow that if you turn over you end up on the floor. The cushions are nothing to complain about though. Have you seen it? Hey? It's like this chair but with the sitting part pulled way out like this... Well, it's a sort of couch, I guess, but there's like a backrest on the end. Odd sort of a thing, really."

"Oh?"

Kumi's responses were so brief that even Kikuoka noticed the change in his lover.

"What's the matter with you?"

"Nothing."

"Obviously, it's not nothing. You're in a really crabby mood."

"Am I?"

"Yes, you are."

Anyone observing this exchange would realize that Kikuoka was capable of speaking in a low voice after all.

"Let's go and talk in my room. I was just about to go to bed anyway. Look, I'll say goodnight and head downstairs. You wait a bit and then casually follow. We'd better *look over my schedule*."

Kikuoka got up. From the far corner of the table, Okuma spotted his move and came over to speak to him.

"Ah, excuse me, Mr Kikuoka, if you're off to bed, please make sure you lock up your room properly. Don't forget the door. After all that's happened, you can't be too careful."

SCENE 2

Room 14, Eikichi Kikuoka's Bedroom

"I can't take it any more! I want to go home. I told you I didn't want to come. I can't put up with it a moment longer."

Kumi Aikura was sitting on Kikuoka's lap, pouting.

"What are you talking about? You know that nobody can leave right now. After what happened we're under house arrest. What on earth is wrong?"

Right now Kikuoka was displaying an expression of utter Zen Buddhist calm, one that none of his employees had ever even glimpsed (except once in 1975 when the company's gross income had suddenly doubled).

"You know how I feel, don't you? You're so mean!"

This scene had repeated itself over the decades and not once had the women's lines changed. Why did this never go out of fashion?

Kumi lightly punched Kikuoka right where he sported what he believed to be a fine crop of chest hair. This required some level of skill. The punch shouldn't be too hard or too gentle. Kumi didn't realize there were genuine tears in her eyes. Tonight had been so incredibly mortifying. Heaven had happened to send her the most effective tool to get what she wanted.

"You are awful!"

She buried her face in her hands.

"I can't understand what you're saying if you cry like that. Come on, love, what's made you so unhappy? Huh? Was it Eiko?"

Kumi nodded, her face dripping tears.

"Poor thing. You're such a sensitive soul, Kumi. I'm afraid if you're going to survive in this world, you just have to get used to stuff like that."

Believe it or not, his words came from the heart.

Kumi nodded again charmingly.

"But you know I really love that about you—you're so sensitive, it's cute how naïve you are."

Kikuoka put his arms around Kumi and hugged her tight—a gesture that he hoped made him seem like her dashing protector—and brought his lips to hers. But if anyone had happened to be watching, the view would have seemed more like a massive bear devouring its prey from the head down.

"Stop it!" said Kumi, pushing his chin away. "I am so not in the mood for that!"

There was an uncomfortable silence.

"I told you I didn't want to come, and now Ueda's been killed! And I never imagined there could be such a bitch as that woman. That's why I wanted you to go alone, Daddy—"

"I told you not to call me Daddy!"

Daddy was angry. If he didn't put a stop to it right away, one day she might say it in front of an employee.

"I'm sorry."

Kumi looked crestfallen.

"It's not that I don't want to take a lovely trip with you to a snowy place. I was looking forward to going away together so much. But I never imagined I'd meet such a horrible woman. It was such a shock."

"Ah, that one—she's not like a woman at all."

"Right? I've never met anyone like her before."

"But what do you expect? She's the daughter of the kind of nutty old man who would build a weird place like this just for fun. You know she's got to be a bit touched in the head. The crazy daughter. If you take everything she says seriously, then you're going to end up driving yourself mad."

"But I—"

"Society has rules. They say we're all equal but there's still social status. You can fight against it all you like, there's nothing you can do to change it. And so when somebody bullies you, you can always turn and look over your shoulder, and there'll be someone standing right behind you, ready to be bullied too, so you just start beating on them. This world is the domain of the powerful. Just keep on bullying those weaker than yourself. That's why I have my minions, so I can treat them however I want. In this life there's no pleasure without pain. You can't let yourself be the loser."

From Kikuoka's mouth these words were very convincing.

"It's common sense."

"Yes, but—"

"What is it with young people these days? Always questioning everything. It's all 'But... But... But...' They're all wishy-washy, can't make a decision. I just don't get what they're thinking, all these airhead types. Just be a man! Go for it! God put sheep on this earth to feed the wolves. Unwind, relax, enjoy life by bullying your minions; it builds up your strength. That's what we pay them for!"

"Be a man? But what about me? Who am I supposed to bully?"

"Well, you could start with that brown-noser, Kanai."

"He's got that wife. I'd be too afraid."

"Afraid? Of Kanai's wife? What are you on about? If she says anything to you, I'll get her husband to start drafting his letter of resignation."

"But when I think that I'll have to come face to face with Eiko again tomorrow…"

"You can ignore her. Just nod your head and pretend she's a turnip or something. You've seen me. I bow and scrape to Hamamoto, but while I'm doing it I'm thinking 'What a moron'. He's valuable to me in my business, so I kowtow to him. That's the way of the world."

"I understand. So then, when we leave this place, how about taking a little trip to Sapporo City? If you buy me something nice, I'm sure it'll put me in a better mood."

This was rather a leap of logic, but President Kikuoka nodded effusively.

"Let's do it. Visit Sapporo and get something for my Kumi. Anything you like!"

"Really? Wonderful!"

Kumi put one arm around Kikuoka's thick neck and gently pressed her lips to his. It seemed she was in the mood after all.

"Well now, Kumi, you are adorable. You and that crazy Eiko are like chalk and cheese."

"Hey! Don't compare me to her."

"You're right," he chuckled. "Probably best not to."

Right then there was a knock at the door. Kumi leapt from Kikuoka's lap with lightning speed, and Kikuoka grabbed for a patently dull-looking business magazine. Both displayed impressive speed and agility. Right on the third knock, the door burst open with such force that the visitor must have put all their weight behind it.

The door of Room 14 had been fitted with a much more elaborate lock than most of the other rooms in the main building, but despite his being there with his secretary, it wasn't

135

Kikuoka's company office, and accordingly he hadn't locked the door behind him.

Eiko had realized quite a while earlier that Kumi wasn't in the salon or up in Room 1, and had a very good idea where she might find her. Ms Hamamoto had the strict idea in her head that no one should behave in a morally corrupt manner in her house (she never stopped to consider that technically this was her father's house).

Therefore as she opened the door, her eyes went straight to the bed. However, its sole occupant was Kikuoka, sitting upright, deeply absorbed in a business magazine. Kumi was standing by the wall, apparently fascinated by a painting of a yacht.

The magazine wasn't upside-down as such, but Kikuoka couldn't be finding it easy to read. He'd previously let slip that he couldn't see any letters close up without his reading glasses, and he didn't appear to be wearing them right now.

Kikuoka looked up from his magazine as if he had just now noticed Eiko (although it made no sense that he wouldn't have looked up the moment the door opened).

"Oh, Ms Hamamoto!" he said cordially, giving himself away by being anxious to speak before she did. "We've just been sorting out my schedule. Lots of things to do."

There wasn't a single document or appointment diary on the table, the company president was busy reading a magazine and his secretary was staring at a painting on the wall. There was no indication that anyone was doing any scheduling.

"I was just stopping by to see if you needed anything," said Eiko.

"Need anything? Oh, no. How could anyone be dissatisfied with a wonderful room like this? And it's my second time here."

"Yes, but some of our guests are here for the first time."

"What? Oh, I see! This young lady. Oh, don't worry. I've explained everything she needs to know."

"Have you plenty of hot water?" Eiko asked.

"Hot water? Yes, I believe so."

"And how was it in Room 1?" she said, turning to Kumi.

"What? Oh, me?"

"There's no one else here from Room 1."

"There was hot water."

"Good. So is your meeting done?"

"It's over."

"Then please don't let me stop you from getting to bed. You can go to sleep anytime—in Room 1."

Kumi was speechless.

"Kumi, I was just saying, wasn't I, that you ought to go to bed early... I'm sorry, Ms Hamamoto, she's afraid of sleeping alone now after that incident. You know how she saw a strange man at her window last night, you can imagine how scared she must be. She's still so young, so very childlike."

Kikuoka laughed.

Eiko didn't appreciate this explanation at all. However young Kumi might be, she was only about the same age as Eiko herself—maybe there was a year between them at most.

"So you needed your father to read you a bedtime story?"

Kumi turned and glared at Eiko. But she was only able to hold it for a few moments before suddenly dashing for the doorway, slipping past the mistress of the house and scurrying off down the corridor, footsteps echoing behind her. Eiko smiled sweetly.

"If she's got that much energy, then she'll be fine sleeping alone."

She left the room, closing the door behind her.

SCENE 3

Room 9, Mr and Mrs Kanai's Bedroom

"Hey, Hatsue, come and see! The blizzard's getting heavier, and I think I can just about make out something that looks like an ice floe."

They'd left behind the busy salon and come up to their quiet room on the north side of the house, but now the sound of the wind and the rattling of the window frame seemed much louder than before. It was a full-on blizzard. And all of a sudden, Michio Kanai's usual demeanour had changed. He seemed to have developed a backbone.

"Now this is what you call a snowstorm! It's really desolate. We've come all the way to the farthest north point—the Okhotsk Sea. How about that? Face to face with the wildest that Mother Nature can bring. This is awesome. Makes you feel like a real man."

He continued to peer out of the window.

"The view from this room is great. Doesn't matter if it's clear or snowing. I think it'll be even better tomorrow morning. Can't wait… Hey, aren't you going to look?"

His wife had flopped down on the bed and just answered in a tone that said she couldn't be bothered,

"I don't want to see."

"Are you sleepy already?"

Hatsue didn't reply. It wasn't that she was especially sleepy.

"I don't know—that Ueda," he went on. "Somehow now that he's been killed I can't help feeling that he was a decent bloke—you know. When he was alive, I always found him kind of awkward—a bit slow on the uptake…"

Kanai had completely misunderstood the reason for his wife's depressed mood.

"I'm going to make sure the room's tightly closed, because there could be a stone-cold killer in this house right now, hiding there in the midst of everyone. This has turned into a right dangerous mess. We wouldn't have come if we'd known all this was going to happen. But I do think we need to take care. Those detectives kept repeating 'lock up' and 'secure your room'. We should be careful too. Did you lock the door?"

"I just can't stand that woman. She gets worse every time I see her."

Hatsue's comment took her husband completely by surprise. He was struck dumb for a moment, but his expression quickly became irritated. If Eiko had been there in the room, in one evening alone she would have seen a whole variety of faces of Michio Kanai she'd never seen before.

"What now? You're not starting that again, are you?… Oh! You mean the director's new squeeze? No one can ever stand his secretaries."

Hatsue looked amazed.

"I'm not talking about his little piece of arm candy. I'm talking about that bitch, Eiko!"

"Huh?"

"Who does she think she is, calling me fat? She doesn't have all that great a figure herself. What the hell is her problem?"

"Are you talking about what she said yesterday? Don't be stupid, that wasn't what she said at all."

"That's exactly what she meant! Didn't you get it? That's why everyone calls you a fool. Stand up for yourself. Can't you see everyone's laughing at you? They call you the limp celery."

"What are you talking about?"

"How can you not see it? Acting all moonstruck, going around simpering, *Ms Hamamoto, your skill on the piano is superb! I would love to hear some more!* Why are you trying to worm your way into the affections of such a child? You're an executive. Top management. Behave like it! You're making me ashamed."

"I am behaving like it."

"You're not! The only time you're not smiling like a fool is when you're with me. And then you do nothing but find fault. At home you're always in a foul mood but when you're out in public, you're always sucking up to people. Try putting yourself in my shoes. She sees me as the wife of a man like that and that's why she treats me that way. That's what's really happening, isn't it?"

"That's just the salaryman's lot. Sometimes that stuff is unavoidable."

"It's not just sometimes. That's why I'm bringing it up!"

"And who do you think you owe it all to—that you even have the opportunity to complain like this? There are wives all over Japan stuck in public housing, never able to go out anywhere, go travelling. But you can call yourself an executive's wife now, you've got your own house, and a car to drive yourself wherever you want. Who do you owe all that to?"

"Am I supposed to say that I owe it all to your bowing and scraping and fawning over everybody?"

"Exactly!"

"Really, now?"

"Well, how else do you expect me to have got where I am?"

"Have you heard what that old lech, Kikuoka, and his slut secretary call you? It'll open your eyes."

"What does the wilting old chrysanthemum call me?"

"He calls you 'that brown-noser, Kanai'."

"Everybody says that kind of thing behind people's backs. It's not a bad price to pay for a generous annual bonus."

"But people are bothered by the way you suck up to the old walrus. There's no way I'd be caught doing that."

"You think it's fun for me? The only way I've ever been able to stand it is by thinking of my wife and children. I'm doing it with clenched teeth. You should be thanking me. You've no right to complain at all. Or perhaps I shouldn't have brought you? Eh?"

"Oh, no, I wanted to come. I think that I've earned the right to visit nice places with you from time to time, to eat good food. Usually you're the only one who gets to do this fun stuff."

"Now you think I'm having fun? Don't contradict yourself! You just said that I'm humouring the old pervert. You can't just turn it around and say whatever you like. You've got a nerve, woman!"

"It's that Eiko and Kumi who are ruining the whole thing for us. Why did I come? I don't understand it. Kumi's a complete airhead. And she treats you like her own employee."

"Are you kidding? You're really imagining things now."

"I'm not imagining anything!"

"She actually has her good points. She has quite a good heart."

Hatsue's mouth fell open.

"What did you say?"

"What now?"

"You are absolutely beyond hope. You have no idea how she sees you, do you?"

"And you really do overthink things."

"Are you saying that I think too much?"

"Yes. You're too suspicious. You can't go through life being that way. You've got to toughen up."

"You call sucking up to Kikuoka, and being bossed around by his mistress being tough?"

"I sure do. A weaker man would never be able to kowtow to someone all day long. I'm tough enough to do it."

"Ugh. I've heard enough."

"I don't have any respect for the Chrysanthemum. He's just got a good head on him for making money, and so I've plenty to gain by sticking by him. Most of the time I feel like killing him; in fact last night I had a dream where I split his bald head open and a bunch of petals came showering down. It felt really good."

"What about Kumi?"

"Kumi? She wasn't in the dream. Only Kikuoka. I told him to get down on his knees and beg for mercy. I laughed as I picked up an axe and cracked his—"

The story was interrupted by a knock at the door.

"Yes?" called Hatsue automatically. Her husband was still lost in the pleasant memories of his dream. But when he pulled himself together and went to open the door, there stood the object of his tale, the man whose head he had cracked open with an axe just the previous night.

Michio Kanai was so thrown off balance that he couldn't bring himself to speak. Hatsue came to the rescue by immediately adopting a very convincing meek demeanour.

"Oh, good evening, Mr Kikuoka, sir. Please come in. You'll find that this room has quite a wonderful view."

"Sounds like the two of you are having a very lively conversation," said Kikuoka as he came in.

"Er... yes, well... the view from here is really splendid. And it is all thanks to you, sir. I feel incredibly lucky to have the chance to take this break in such a relaxing place. We both do."

"Yes, yes. Well, there's no outdoor view from my room—it's a bit boring to tell the truth. No complaints about the decor though. Is it really coming down out there?"

"Yes, still the same, isn't it, dear? A major snowstorm."

"Yes, really. The same as ever. Still a blizzard out there, Mr Kikuoka."

Kikuoka looked around the room.

"Wow, this is a deluxe room, isn't it? Such a dramatic view! It's a little dark now to be able to see it properly, but I imagine the view tomorrow morning'll be amazing. Makes me wish I could change rooms with you."

"Oh, would you like us to switch with you?"

"Eh? What? Oh, no, seems old Hamamoto personally chose that other room for me. Think I'll just pop up here tomorrow morning and take a look."

"Please do," said Hatsue. "You're welcome anytime. It's kind of dull here with just the two of us. My husband really is the most unsociable type. Not a thing to say for himself."

"Ho, ho! That's a bit harsh, isn't it? Ha! But I suppose it's true," said Michio.

"Hang on! Is that drift ice? That white thing in the distance?"

"Where? Ah, yes, sir. You're quite right. They say that on a fine day you can see as far as Sakhalin from here."

"I'm just asking about drift ice."

"Ah, yes, of course. Yes, it's an ice floe."

"There are ice floes visible out there. Ms Hamamoto was kind enough to tell us earlier," added Hatsue.

"I see. Well, I think it's about time I was getting to bed. It's not good for the body to stay up late. If I end up with diabetes from partying into the night, then half the fun of life will be over."

Kikuoka laughed.

"Diabetes?... Oh, you're joking? Diabetes? But, sir, you're so young..." Michio Kanai forced himself to laugh. "You think you might get diabetes! Oh, that's a good one!"

"I'm not joking at all. You ought to be careful too. You get diabetes and you'll never be able to satisfy your wife again."

And with another roar of laughter, he punched Michio playfully in the shoulder a few times, and left the room. The executive husband and wife waited to hear his footsteps going down the stairs, and then exchanged a sour look. The reason was that just two weeks earlier sugar had been found in Michio Kanai's urine. Since then he'd been using a special sweetener for diabetics which was an extremely unpleasant substitute for the real thing. Only someone who had been forced to try it could understand just how unpleasant it was.

"It just makes me want to cry. How come a fat old lecher like him doesn't get diabetes and a skinny, clean-living man like you ends up a diabetic? He deserves to get it! Then he wouldn't be able to sleep around so much! Life really isn't fair."

"Shut up! Let's just go to sleep."

"You can sleep by yourself. I'll go and sleep in the bath or somewhere."

"Do what you like!"

"When I think how tomorrow we're going to have to sit through that irritating cow's piano recital again, I get too angry to sleep. I don't know why she can't just shut the hell up."

Right then, there was another knock at the door. Hatsue was panting like a wild beast from the effort of spitting out so much invective, but when she saw who was at the door, her voice instantly took on the sweetness of a teenage girl's.

"Oh, hello, Ms Hamamoto! What can we do for you?"

"I was just doing the rounds of all the rooms to check that there's nothing you need. I wondered if you had any questions about anything."

"No, there's nothing at all we could possibly want," said Michio. "This is such a wonderful room. And as it's my second visit, I don't think there's anything we need to ask you."

"Is there enough hot water?"

"Yes, plenty, thank you."

"I'm glad to hear it. I just wanted to make sure."

"Thank you so much for inviting us to such a lovely party," said Hatsue. "And your piano recital was such a treat!"

"Yes, Ms Hamamoto, you're a truly gifted player. Have you been studying long?"

Michio Kanai's face wore its usual plastered smile.

"Yes, I suppose it has been a rather long time. I started taking lessons when I was four. But I'm really not a very good player. I'm rather embarrassed that my performance was so poor."

"Not at all. It was absolutely delightful," simpered Hatsue. "This husband of mine has nothing interesting about him at all. He's like a limp stick of celery. Unless we come for a little holiday like this, we never get to do anything fun at all."

"Hey, Hatsue, that's not true! But I really hope you'll play for us again tomorrow, Ms Hamamoto."

"Yes, please!"

"Ah, I'm so sorry. Tomorrow my father plans to play everybody something from his record collection."

"You're so talented, Ms Hamamoto! I wish I'd taken the piano when I was a girl. I was just saying the same thing to my husband."

145

"Oh, don't. You're embarrassing me. Anyway, if there's anything I can do for you, anything you need, don't hesitate to ask Hayakawa and he'll come and let me know."

"Thank you. We will."

"Well, then, be sure to lock up properly. Goodnight."

"Yes, we will. Thank you for everything. Goodnight!"

Back in the Salon

Kumi Aikura wasn't in the mood to be all by herself in Room 1, so instead she made her way back to the salon and hung around there.

Apart from Kikuoka, the Kanais and, of course, Eiko, everyone was still there. And it wasn't long before the west-side door opened and Eiko returned from her visit to Room 9.

Mr and Mrs Kanai and Kikuoka seemed to be the only ones concerned about getting an early night for their health. Like Kumi, the others seemed more worried about being alone on this stormy night.

The police detectives, on the other hand, didn't seem too bothered.

"Ahh! I'm getting sleepy," said Okuma, stretching. "Didn't get much sleep last night. Work and all."

And with that excuse, he got to his feet. Eiko noticed and called Chikako Hayakawa to show him to his room.

The Inspector left for Room 12 and Chikako soon returned to the salon. But that was the only change. No one else from the crowd made any move to head off to bed. Mr and Mrs Hayakawa and Kajiwara could hardly leave before the guests, so they took three of the chairs and seated themselves inconspicuously in the doorway between the salon and the kitchen.

The clock turned 10. The salon had no television, so that normally by this time of night it would be deserted. Eiko went over to the stereo and put on Colin Davis conducting *The Rite of Spring*.

Togai and Yoshihiko were sitting together at the dinner table. Sasaki was opposite, reading one of his medical textbooks.

"Hey, Yoshihiko," said Togai. "You know the flower bed, was that a design from a catalogue or something that could be ordered?"

"Nah, I don't think so. Uncle Kozaburo drew the sketch himself, and called in a landscape gardener to do it."

"So he designed it himself?"

"That's what I heard. And when they started landscaping it, he was there for the whole thing, giving directions and stuff."

"Wow."

"But that's only what I heard from my cousin, Eiko."

"What are you two talking about?"

Eiko came over and took the chair next to Yoshihiko.

"That flower bed."

"Oh, that."

She didn't seem very interested in the topic.

"It's always a big thing when Daddy has the idea for a design. It's all, 'fetch me this, get me that'. You know that he's an artist at heart. He never really wanted to be the president of Hama Diesel. What he really enjoys doing is listening to Wagner while he paints."

"Does he really demand that people bring him all kinds of things?" asked Togai.

"He's quite the autocrat, Uncle Kozaburo," said Yoshihiko.

"It's because he's such an artist. Back then he insisted on drawing all his sketches on aluminium foil. He sent me off to Kajiwara to borrow rolls of it."

"Aluminium foil? That's what he drew on?"

"So it seems. And after borrowing it, he never gave it back. Kajiwara told me that he needed it for his cooking, so I told Daddy to take what he needed and to give the rest back, that he was wasting it. But he just told me to go and buy more. So I had to go down to the village to stock up."

"Wow."

This time Sasaki was the one to react.

Constable Anan carefully placed his cap on the dining table, adjusted his expression and seated himself at the very far corner. He was immediately accosted by Kumi.

"Constable?"

"Yes?"

Anan kept his face rigidly facing forward.

"Constable Anan, isn't it? That's rather unusual. Is it a local Hokkaido name?"

Kumi waited for a reply, but none came. She had just given up and decided to go and try the billiard table, when Anan suddenly spoke up.

"My father's from Hiroshima. My grandmother was from Okinawa."

"Do you have a girlfriend?"

Kumi seemed determined to make the constable uncomfortable.

"I'm sorry, but I'm unable to answer that kind of question."

Ignoring his obvious reluctance, Kumi grabbed Anan by the arm and began to pull him from his chair.

"How about a game of billiards?"

"I'm, er… I'm sorry but that's not possible. I'm afraid I didn't come here to play billiards."

But Kumi was not that easily discouraged.

"It'll be fine. You'll still be doing your job while you're play-ing. You're supposed to be protecting us, right? Come on, if you haven't played before I can teach you."

Chief Inspector Ushikoshi was deep in conversation with Kozaburo Hamamoto, but that didn't stop him from throwing glances in the direction of the billiard table, where he saw the junior officer start up a game with a young woman.

Eventually Togai and Yoshihiko got up and looked ready to head off to bed. They went over to Kozaburo as if to say goodnight, but for some reason he signalled to them to stay. Then Kozaburo and Ushikoshi both got up, Kozaburo called Eiko over and the five of them headed to the billiard table.

Anan, who by now was enthusiastically potting balls, noticed his boss coming in his direction and quickly stood to attention. Kozaburo smiled and urged him to continue.

Back at the dining table, Sergeant Ozaki was getting bored. He got up, threw a scornful glance towards Constable Anan at the billiard table and whispered in Chief Inspector Ushikoshi's ear that he was going to retire for the night.

Eiko spotted the interaction and sent Chikako Hayakawa to show the Sergeant to his room. When Chikako returned, she went straight back to her seat next to her husband and the chef.

Kozaburo Hamamoto was in a cheerful mood, enthusias-tically demonstrating different shots to the beginner, Anan. Chief Inspector Ushikoshi found himself surprised and impressed by the older man's skills, but when asked if he'd like to play, he quickly demurred. Like Anan, he had never played before either.

Kozaburo turned next to Eiko and Yoshihiko.

"Constable Anan here seems to have some talent. I'm count-ing on you two to give him some proper coaching. "Mr Anan,

I don't mind if you'd like to keep playing all night. There are no other houses nearby, and knowing you are here all night staying awake makes me feel safer. I'll look forward tomorrow to seeing how much improvement you've made. And if you're up to it, I'll challenge you to a game. But if you come face to face with the killer, please take a break from practising.

"Yoshihiko, Eiko, teach him well. I have a feeling this man has it in him to become quite a player after only one night of practice. And it might be a good idea for you to stay close to a policeman on a night like this one."

For his part, Ushikoshi hadn't seen anything in Anan that suggested he might be a billiard genius, so he found Kozaburo's suggestion rather surprising.

"Now then, Chief Inspector, would you care to visit my room? I think it would be a great chance to get to know each other. I have a rather good bottle of cognac in there. I'm not keeping it to share with some celebrity visitor; I'd much prefer to drink it with someone I can get along with. But more than anything I'm feeling a bit vulnerable tonight, one night after someone was murdered in my house. I think that cognac will taste even better tonight if I'm drinking it with a police officer."

"I don't mind if I do."

Togai, left alone at his side of the table, moved over to sit next to Sasaki. Perhaps he didn't feel like heading back to his room alone, or maybe he just wanted the companionship.

Kozaburo was about to climb the stairs from the salon, when he suddenly stopped at the first step. He seemed to have changed his mind.

"Chief Inspector, I'd forgotten. There's something I need to say to Mr Kikuoka. I wonder if he's already asleep. I'm sorry to bother you, but would you mind coming with me for a moment?"

151

"No problem."

The two men crossed back through the salon, and this time headed down the stairs to the basement. They stopped at the door of Room 14.

"If he's already sleeping I feel bad about waking him..." murmured Kozaburo, knocking gently on Room 14's door. There was no reply.

"Mr Kikuoka? It's me, Hamamoto. Are you asleep?" he called softly. The noise of the blizzard echoed faintly in the basement corridor.

"No answer. He must already be asleep."

Kozaburo tried turning the doorknob, but the door was locked from the inside.

"Let's go. He's asleep."

"Are you sure it's okay?" asked Ushikoshi.

"It doesn't matter. It can wait till tomorrow."

The two men went back upstairs. Kozaburo went to speak to the Hayakawas.

"It's going to get very cold tonight. Please turn the heat up."

Then Kozaburo and Ushikoshi climbed the east wing staircase. After a while, the sound of feet crossing the drawbridge mingled with the noise of the blizzard.

Kumi Aikura was not at all happy that Eiko had joined the game of billiards. As soon as Kozaburo left the game, she decided it was time to head up to her own room.

Now the occupants of the salon were down to eight: at the dinner table were Togai, looking at the sketch he had made of the flower bed, and Sasaki, reading a medical textbook. At the billiard table were Eiko, Yoshihiko and Constable Anan; and near the door to the kitchen, Mr and Mrs Hayakawa and Haruo Kajiwara.

Kozaburo's Room in the Tower

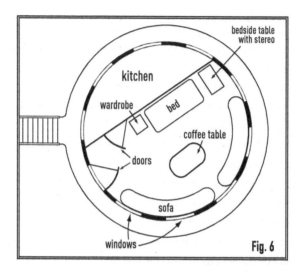

bedside table
with stereo

kitchen

wardrobe

bed

coffee table

doors

sofa

windows

Fig. 6

"This house is so strange and magnificent at the same time. This is another great room." (See Fig. 6.)

"It's just right for an old man like me to kill time. I can dabble in my sinful pleasures. I sit here asking myself why I built such a whimsical thing, and suddenly a whole day goes by… But you're fed up with this place, aren't you?"

"It's one surprise after another. They're never-ending. Hold on, is the floor of this circular room crooked too?"

"Yes, this tower is built to resemble the Leaning Tower of Pisa. My plan started out to build this tower on a slant. The Leaning Tower of Pisa leans at an angle of about 5.5 degrees. This tower was built to lean at the exact same angle."

"Wow."

"I'm going to prepare some snacks for us. Could you excuse me a minute?"

"Sure, sure. No problem. Is there a kitchen or something through there?"

"Well, it's not quite what you'd call a kitchen. There's a sink and a refrigerator and a stove. Take a look if you'd like."

"Yes, I would. This is the first time I've visited such an unusual building. I'm sure it'll be useful for reference purposes…"

Kozaburo opened the door to the kitchen area and turned on the light. Ushikoshi peered in.

"Wow. There are so many windows in here too! Do they go all the way around?"

"Yes, this room has nine windows and one door, covering its whole circumference. Four of them are in the kitchen."

"I see. The view must be excellent."

"It is a very good view. It's dark so you can't see anything right now, but in the morning you can see the sea on one side. You know, you'd be welcome to stay the night here. The early morning view is the best. You won't miss it if you spend the night. How about it? I was going to admit it to you eventually after a few glasses of brandy but I'm a little scared. I've come all the way up here to Hokkaido but I've still managed to make an enemy. If there's a killer hiding away here somewhere, it'd be safe to say he's likely to have me in his sights next. It'd be reassuring to think that there was a police officer in the same room all night."

"Fine with me. But is there anywhere for me to sleep? I can only see one bed."

"Yes, right here, under this…"

Kozaburo reached down under his own bed and pulled something out.

"See, it's a mini version of my bed. You pull it out like a drawer."

He took the cushions off one of the sofas and arranged them on the bed.

"Because it needs to slide under the other bed, this one doesn't have a mattress on it."

"Ha, another surprise. It's all very well thought out."

The two men sat on the sofa and drank Louis XIII cognac. The wind seemed to grow louder, drowning out the sound of the ice clinking in their glasses.

"Couldn't a strong wind like tonight's blow over a tower that leans as far as this one?"

Kozaburo chuckled.

"It'll be fine."

"And the main building too?"

Kozaburo laughed a little harder.

"Fine, fine!"

"Okay, then, but if this mansion does collapse, at least the hidden killer'll be trapped underneath it."

This time Ushikoshi laughed at his own joke.

"And if the killer is out there in the snow, he's probably frozen solid by now," added Kozaburo.

"Yes, he would be. He'd probably need a drop of this brandy to warm him up. Is this Louis XIII? I've heard people talk about it, but I've never even seen it in real life, let alone drunk it. It's really quite fine."

"It doesn't give you a hangover. Anyway, Chief Inspector, can you tell me whether you've got a possible suspect in mind for the murder?"

"Ah, so that's what you want to know, is it? In mind... Someone in mind... Well, I guess I'll have to confess to you that we don't. We're really quite stumped. It's a bizarre case. I've never heard of another murder where a scream was heard a full thirty minutes *after* the victim was killed."

"And the corpse appeared to be dancing."

"That's right. And the suspect seems to be a non-existent, bearded, swarthy sleepwalker with burn scars on his cheeks. It's like something out of a horror movie. There's nothing the police can do here."

"After murdering a man, he flew through the air and peeped in through a young woman's bedroom window… May I ask you some questions about that?"

"Yes. I'll answer to the best of my ability."

"Why did the murderer take my doll outside, break it into pieces and scatter it in the snow?"

"Um, well, I think that was a kind of smokescreen. At first sight, it seems to have some important meaning, but it was really done just to mislead us. I don't believe it had any more significance than that."

"And why was Ueda in that strange position?"

"That wasn't at all significant. The dead bodies of murder victims often end up like that—in weird contortions from the agony of death."

"What was that round mark on the floor by the small of Ueda's back?"

"It got there by chance. While he was writhing in agony, his fingers just happened to touch the floor."

"The stakes that Sasaki says he saw in the garden, stuck in the snow?"

"Ah, yes, about that… If those stakes had something to do with Mr Ueda's death, then I'm sure that the killer suffers from some sort of psychosis. When it comes to criminals, especially murderers – and this is something difficult for lay people to understand – they often need to perform some kind of ritual before committing their crime. There are too many examples of this to count. There was once a burglar for whom wearing women's stockings was some kind of good luck ritual for him. He said that if he left the house with women's stockings on, then his next break-in would always go well. So that's what we believe the stakes were about. Some kind of good luck ritual."

"Hmm. Then who was the man who looked into Ms Aikura's bedroom—the one with the burn scars on his face?"

"There's no one fitting that description here in the house or in the neighbourhood, right? Nobody in the village has seen anyone like that either. So obviously—"

"Ms Aikura must have been dreaming. But do you really think so? The scream, the lack of footprints… it's not a straightforward case at all, is it? And you can't find any motive at all?"

"That's really the problem. Trying to narrow down the occupants of this mansion to one suspect, well, no matter how difficult it may be, we will get there eventually. But whoever we pick, it always comes back to motive. Not one of the people in this house had a motive for murder. This is the toughest part of the whole thing for us police. But we have Tokyo Headquarters on the job and I'm confident they're eventually going to come up with something we couldn't possibly have found by ourselves."

"I hope so. If you don't mind my asking, Mr Ushikoshi, if I may call you that, have you been a detective long?"

"About twenty years."

"I've heard that veteran detectives like yourself tend to have very strong intuition when it comes to spotting a criminal. Is there somebody in this case who you've got a hunch about?"

"Unfortunately not. But I think it's going to turn out to be someone quite unexpected… By the way, do you definitely want me to spend the night here?"

"If you could, that would be great."

"In that case, I need to inform Ozaki. I'm sure he'll have left the door to our room unlocked for me. I'd better go and check in with him."

"No need. I'll just call someone. If I press this button, a bell rings in the salon and the Hayakawas' room. Chikako will come and we'll ask her to let Sergeant Ozaki know. She'll be here right away."

Minutes later, Chikako Hayakawa appeared, brushing the snow from her head. Kozaburo asked her to let Sergeant Ozaki in Room 15 know that Ushikoshi would stay the night in the tower, and asked her who was still up. Chikako responded that everyone was still awake.

"Wait about thirty more minutes, then feel free to go to bed," said Kozaburo.

Ushikoshi glanced at the wall clock and saw it was 10.44 p.m.

A couple of minutes after Chikako had left, Eiko appeared at the door.

"Oh, Eiko! What brings you up here?"

"I'm thinking of going to bed soon. I'm really tired."

"Ah, I see."

"I was hoping you'd put the bridge up if Chief Inspector Ushikoshi plans to sleep here. The people in the salon are getting cold."

"Ah, yes, of course. Who's still there now?"

"Sasaki and Togai. Yoshihiko's playing billiards with the policeman. And then there's the Hayakawas and Kajiwara."

"Do any of them look ready to go to bed?"

"No, not yet. Sasaki and Togai are watching the billiard game."

"Has Ms Aikura gone up to her room already, then?"

"Her? A long time ago."

"Got it. Well, you'd better get some sleep."

Kozaburo saw his daughter out, closed the door and returned to the sofa. He took a sip of his cognac.

"Ah, the ice has all gone."

His voice was strangely subdued.

"It's a brutal night, isn't it? Let's put on some music. I only have a cassette tape player up here though."

On the bedside table there was a desktop-sized stereo.

"My daughter always says she hates this one."

The piano piece that began to play was a tune that Ushikoshi recognized, but he couldn't put a name to it. He knew that if it was something familiar even to him, then it must be famous, which of course made him hesitate to ask the title. He really didn't want to show himself up too much. It wouldn't be good for the future of the investigation.

"I enjoy operas and symphonies and other more grandiose stuff too, but piano compositions are my favourite type of classical music. How about you, Chief Inspector? Do you like to listen to music? What kind do you like?"

"Ah... I, er..."

Ushikoshi shook his head apologetically.

"I'm not musical at all. Can't sing, I'm tone-deaf. All Beethoven sounds the same to me."

"I see..."

Kozaburo sounded a little sad to find that this wasn't a topic the two men could discuss.

"I'll go and get some more ice."

He picked up the ice bucket and went into the kitchen.

Ushikoshi heard the sound of the refrigerator door being opened. Kozaburo hadn't quite shut the kitchen door behind him and Ushikoshi could see Kozaburo through the opening as he moved backwards and forwards in the kitchen.

"This a real blizzard!" said Kozaburo, raising his voice.

"Sure is!" called Ushikoshi in response. The piano music continued, but the blizzard outside was about the same volume. The door from the kitchen opened and Kozaburo reappeared with a full ice bucket. He sat on the bed and dropped some cubes into Ushikoshi's glass.

"Thank you," said Ushikoshi, studying Kozaburo's face. "Is something the matter? You don't seem very well."

Kozaburo smiled a little.

"I'm not very good on stormy nights... Anyway, let's keep drinking until we've used up all the ice. Are you up to keeping me company?"

As Kozaburo spoke, the antique wall clock struck eleven.

SCENE 6

The Salon

It was some while later that Kozaburo realized that he'd forgotten about the drawbridge. He and Ushikoshi hurried out into the snowstorm and pulled the chain that raised the bridge, becoming so chilled in the process that it took several more drinks to warm them up again. It was just after midnight by the time the two men got to sleep.

The next morning, in anticipation of the view from the tower, they woke up well before 8. The wind had completely dropped and the sky was no longer full of swirling snowflakes. However, there was no blue sky to be seen; the drift ice sat on a desolate sea under a gloomy sky. There was just one brighter, white cloud over to the east, concealing the morning sun.

But for those used to living in a northern climate, this view was as impressive as any other. It looked as if someone had taken a vast white sheet and placed it on top of the sea, hiding the water completely. How much labour would that have taken to achieve? To Mother Nature it was a breeze.

They lowered the drawbridge. As they were crossing, Ushikoshi noticed a vertical line of metal rungs embedded in the main building wall ahead of them. He guessed it was a kind of ladder for use by someone needing to climb up to the roof of the building.

They arrived in the salon just after 9.00 a.m. Perhaps because most people had stayed up so late the previous night, the only person already awake was Michio Kanai. He was sitting alone at the dining table. The three house-staff members seemed to be in the kitchen, but the rest of the guests must still have been asleep.

The three men greeted each other, and Kanai went back to the newspaper he'd been reading, while Kozaburo went over to the fireplace and took a seat in his favourite rocking chair. Ushikoshi also sat down in a nearby chair.

The firewood burned and the smoke was sucked up by the massive funnel of a chimney. The glass of the windows was all fogged up. It was a perfectly normal morning in the Ice Floe Mansion.

Nevertheless, Chief Inspector Ushikoshi had an uncomfortable feeling. And he soon realized why. Because Sergeant Ozaki and Inspector Okuma had not got up yet. He'd just begun to wonder about this when the salon door burst open and Ozaki and Okuma themselves hurried in.

"I'm sorry, I was a bit tired." said Ozaki. "Is there anything to report?" he continued, pulling up a chair to the dining table. Ushikoshi got up from his chair by the fire and went over to the table.

"So far so good. But it's still early yet. Nothing to report."

"S'pose not." Okuma sounded half asleep still.

"I'm sorry, sir, I couldn't get to sleep with the noise of the wind," said Ozaki.

"What happened to Anan?"

"He was playing all night, so I don't expect he'll be getting up any time soon," said Okuma.

The next to come down was Hatsue Kanai, then Eiko, followed closely by Kumi Aikura. But more than an hour later the rest of the party still hadn't shown up.

Everyone was drinking hot tea as they waited.

"What shall we do? Should I go and wake them?" Eiko asked Kozaburo.

"No, let them sleep."

Just then there was the sound of a car coming up the hill, followed by a young man's voice calling from the front entrance hall.

"Excuse me? Hello?"

"Just a minute!"

Eiko went out to see who was there. A moment later she let out a shriek that had the three police officers start after her, but she immediately reappeared with an enormous bunch of irises.

"Did you order these, Dad?"

"I did. Winter is so dreary without any flowers. I had them flown in."

"Dad, you're the best!"

Behind her was the sound of the car going back down the hill. Eiko laid the irises gently on the table.

"You and Chikako divide them up and put some in here and everyone's rooms. There should be a vase in every room. If there isn't, I know we've got a few extra around somewhere. I know we have enough."

"Thank you, Daddy. Let's do it right away. Auntie! Auntie!"

The guests volunteered to go and fetch the vases from each of their rooms. Right about the time the flowers had been divided up, Sasaki and Togai finally appeared, but went right back out again to fetch the vases from their rooms.

At that point it was almost 11.00 a.m. Eiko took some of the flowers and went to wake Yoshihiko. That was when Constable Anan finally turned up.

At 11.50 a.m. everyone was assembled in the salon except Eikichi Kikuoka. No one had considered disturbing a company president from his sleep. But now that they thought about it, it was strange that he wasn't already up. He'd gone to bed early the night before. It had been around 9 o'clock when he'd left the salon. He'd stopped by the Kanais' room after that, but he must have been back in his own room by 9.30. For him to still be asleep past 11 the next morning…

"Strange…" mumbled Kanai. "Perhaps he's not feeling well?"

"Should we go and check on him?" said Kumi. "But then again he might be in a bad mood if we wake him up."

"I hope he hasn't been—" said Okuma, stopping himself. "I reckon it's safer if we do wake him up."

"All right, then, let's take him some flowers," said Kozaburo. "Eiko, pass me that vase."

"But this one belongs in the salon."

"It doesn't matter. This room'll be just fine without flowers… Thanks. Shall we all go and check on him?"

Everyone made their way down to Room 14 in the basement. Kozaburo knocked on the door.

"Mr Kikuoka? It's Hamamoto."

Chief Inspector Ushikoshi had an attack of déjà vu. Last night he had participated in the exact same scene, except that at that time Kozaburo had called his name with less urgency.

"He's not waking up." Kozaburo turned to Kumi. "You try, dear. He might respond better to a woman's voice."

But the result was the same. Everyone exchanged looks, but Ushikoshi's face turned completely white.

"Mr Kikuoka! Mr Kikuoka!"

He began to bang violently on the door.

"What the hell? Come on!"

The detective's panicked tone made everyone's stomach drop.

"Can I break it down?"

"Yes, but…"

Kozaburo hesitated a moment. This was his beloved study after all.

"From up there, can't you see inside a little bit?"

Sasaki was pointing to the ventilation hole high up in the wall. But there weren't any tables or chairs or anything that could be used to stand on.

"Ozaki, wasn't there something in your room?" said Ushikoshi, but Ozaki was ahead of him. He ran into Room 15 and came back with the bedside table, then placed it directly under the vent and clambered up.

"It's no good. I'm too low to see anything."

"The stepladder!" shouted Kozaburo. "Kajiwara, isn't there a ladder in the outside shed? Run and get it!"

Time crawled by as they waited for Kajiwara to get back with the ladder. When he did, he set it up and climbed to the top.

"What the…"

"Is he dead?"

"Has he been killed?"

The police officers were anxious for news.

"No. Mr Kikuoka isn't in his bed. But there's something on the bed that looks like blood."

"What? Where is he?"

"I can't see. Not from here. I can only see the area around the bed."

"Let's break it down."

Ushikoshi was not going to wait for permission this time. He and Okuma threw themselves against the door.

"I don't mind, but this door is particularly sturdy. And the lock is custom-made. It's not going to break that easily. And I'm afraid there isn't a duplicate key."

What Kozaburo said seemed to be true. Even with Constable Anan joining the other two, the weight of three men slamming against it, the door didn't budge.

"The axe!" shouted Kozaburo. "Kajiwara, go back to the shed. There's an axe in there, right?"

Kajiwara shot off.

When he returned with the axe, Anan told everyone to get out of the way, and held them back with outstretched arms. Okuma lifted the axe. It was clear to everyone that this was not the first time this man had chopped wood. Soon woodchips and splinters were flying, and a crack opened in the door.

"No, not that spot. It won't work."

Kozaburo stepped forward from the group of onlookers.

"Here, here and here. Hit it in those three spots."

Kozaburo indicated spots at the top, bottom and the very middle of the door. Okuma looked dubious.

"You'll see when you break it."

Okuma managed to make three holes, then tried to stick his hand inside. Ushikoshi pulled out a white handkerchief and offered it to Okuma, who wrapped it around his hand.

"Near the top and the bottom of the door are two bolts that you have to turn to lock or release. Reach in and turn them. The upper bolt will swing downwards. The lower one will lift upwards."

Because it was so hard to picture, the instructions were difficult to follow, and it took Okuma a long time.

When the bolts were finally undone, the police officers all tried to rush in at once, but the door hit something and got stuck. Ozaki pushed on it with all his strength, and it opened far enough to reveal something that looked like a sofa stuck behind the door. Weirdly, it was the base of the sofa that was visible from the outside—in other words, it had been tipped over on its back. Ozaki stuck a leg through the gap and tried to kick it away.

"Don't be so rough!" said Ushikoshi. "You'll disturb the crime scene. Just get the door open."

When the door finally opened, the semicircle of onlookers gasped. It wasn't only the sofa; the coffee table was overturned too. Beyond that lay the bulky, pyjama-clad form of Eikichi Kikuoka. There were clear signs that he'd fought, but now he lay face down, a knife protruding from the right side of his back.

"Mr Kikuoka!" cried Kozaburo.

"Mr President!" This from Kanai.

"Daddy!" blurted Kumi.

The police officers all hurried in.

"Damn it!"

The voice came from directly behind them. As Ozaki turned to look there was a smashing noise, and the flower vase was suddenly in pieces on the floor.

"Damn, damn! I'm sorry."

Kozaburo had attempted to follow the police into the room and had tripped on the upturned sofa.

The irises lay scattered over Kikuoka's ample body.

"I'm really terribly sorry. Shall I pick them up?"

"Never mind. It's fine. We'll do it. Please stay back. Ozaki, pick up the flowers."

Ushikoshi surveyed the crime scene. (See Fig. 7.) There was a lot of blood—a little on the bed sheets, some more on the electric blanket that had slipped off and was now on the floor, and much more on the Persian rug that decorated the parquet floor.

The bed was bolted to the floor so it hadn't moved from its original spot. The only furniture that had been moved was the sofa and the coffee table, and both of these had been tipped on their side. At first glance there didn't seem to be anything else out of place or broken. There was a gas fire in the fireplace, but it wasn't on, and the stopcock was closed.

Ushikoshi examined the knife in Kikuoka's back. Two things surprised him; first, that the knife was stuck very deeply in, right up to the handle. It must have been plunged in there with all the killer's might. But more surprising was that the knife was identical to the one that had killed Ueda—a hunting knife with a piece of white string tied to the handle. The victim's pyjamas were soaked in blood, but the string was completely clean.

The knife was in the right side of Kikuoka's back so it had missed his heart.

"He's dead," said Ozaki.

This meant that he must have died of blood loss. Ushikoshi looked back at the door.

"That's impossible!"

The words had slipped out. But how could it be?…

It was the most solid door he had ever seen. Looking at it now from the inside, he realized that it had been made as sturdy as anyone could wish. The door itself was made of thick oak, and its lock was completely different from the simple one on Ueda's door. There were three separate locking systems. It was as well constructed as a vault.

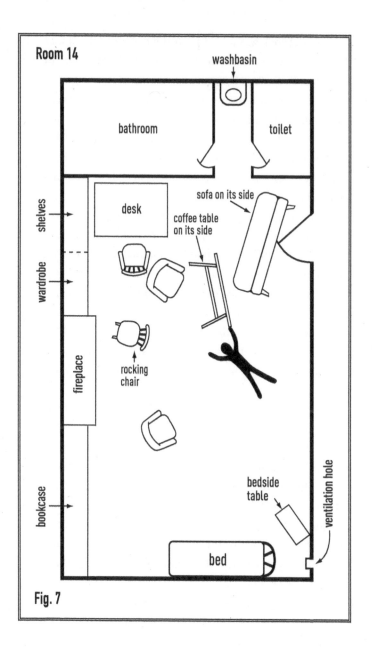

Room 14

washbasin

bathroom

toilet

shelves

desk

sofa on its side

coffee table on its side

wardrobe

fireplace

rocking chair

bookcase

bedside table

ventilation hole

bed

Fig. 7

The first lock was a button in the centre of the doorknob that you pushed in, the same type as on all the doors in the mansion. The other two were quite a tour de force. On the upper section and lower sections of the door, there were two bolts installed, with metal cylinders that were at least three centimetres in diameter. Each one required turning 180 degrees until they dropped into place. No matter how adept somebody might be, there was no way the locks could be manipulated from outside the room. And the door frame was just as sturdily constructed—there was not a millimetre of space on any side.

Ushikoshi couldn't comprehend how the room had got in such disorder and a knife had been plunged into the victim's back. However, he decided to feign complete calm.

"Ozaki, please escort everyone to the salon. Anan, call the station."

"What to do about these pieces of vase?" asked Okuma.

"Just pick them up and chuck 'em away."

Along with my own reputation, thought Ushikoshi morosely.

Another team of around a dozen police officers swarmed up the hill, and the mansion became a hive of activity again. Ushikoshi felt steadily more defeated by the moment. What kind of bloodthirsty monster was responsible for this? Four police officers had spent the night in the house. Could the killer not have shown some restraint? Why did he have to escalate to serial murder? And why the locked-room scenario? It wasn't as if either of the deaths could have been suicide. You'd have to be crazy to think it. In Kikuoka's case the knife was in his back, no less!

He'd been publicly humiliated. And this wasn't going to be easily forgiven. He'd completely miscalculated, made wrong assumptions. As a police officer he shouldn't have dismissed the possibility that it would turn into a serial murder. He was going to have to start over from the beginning.

That evening he got the time of death from forensics—11 p.m. or within thirty minutes either side.

"Let's get on with the questioning."

Ushikoshi addressed the surviving guests, hosts and house staff in the salon.

"Last night between 10.30 and 11.30, what was each of you doing, and where?"

Instantly, Sasaki spoke up.

"We were still in the salon. That police officer was with us."

"Who is 'we'?"

"Togai and me. And Yoshihiko. And then Mr and Mrs Hayakawa and Mr Kajiwara. Six of us."

"I see. Until what time?"

"Past 2 in the morning. I looked at the clock and saw it was already 2 a.m., so we all hurried off to bed."

"All six of you?"

"No."

It was Chikako Hayakawa who spoke.

"Actually, we went to bed around 11.30."

"'We' being you and your husband?"

"And me too," said Kajiwara.

"So you are saying that all three of you passed by the door of Room 14 around 11.30 last night?"

"No. We don't go that way. After you go down the stairs, you turn the opposite way to get to our rooms."

"Hmm. And you didn't notice any strange noises or figures in the vicinity of Room 14?"

"Well, the wind was so loud."

"True…"

Ushikoshi decided that it was a close call, but timewise, he could probably exclude the three staff members from the list of suspects. However, it was very significant that three people had passed close by the door of Room 14 around 11.30. The killer must have already done the deed and left by then.

"So the other three of you were in the salon until 2 a.m.?"

"That's correct. With Constable Anan."

"Anan, is that right?"

"Yes, it is."

So Sasaki, Togai and Yoshihiko could safely be excluded too. Kozaburo Hamamoto had spent the evening with Ushikoshi himself, so he could be counted out completely.

"Mr Hayakawa, did you lock up completely last night?"

"I did it around 5 yesterday evening. After the first murder, figured we couldn't be too careful."

"Hmm."

That confirmed that somewhere in this house was a homicidal maniac. In other words, the killer was sitting there right before his eyes, one of these eleven people. He'd already ruled out seven of them. That left Eiko Hamamoto, Kumi Aikura, and Michio and Hatsue Kanai. Four suspects, and most of them women!

"Ms Eiko Hamamoto and Ms Kumi Aikura, where were you?"

"I was in my room."

"Me too."

"In other words, neither of you has an alibi?"

The two women turned a little pale.

"But…"

Kumi seemed to be working something out in her head.

"To get from Room 1 to Room 14, you'd have to go through the salon. The police constable and the others were all in there."

"That's right. That goes for me too. There's absolutely no way to get to Room 14. That room is in the basement, and has no windows. Even if we'd taken an outdoor route, there's no way in."

"I see."

"Just a… Hang on there!"

Michio Kanai was in a state of panic.

"Does that mean that we're suspects? I was in Room 9 the whole time. My wife can attest to it!"

"Well, in the case of a husband and wife—"

"No, no… Listen! I'm the one most affected by this murder. And therefore my wife too. Mr Kikuoka's death is the severest blow to us both. I hate to put it this way, but I'm going to have to say it. At the company, I've always been a Kikuoka supporter, among all the company factions. I've been his follower, if you like, for fifteen years or so. It's been thanks to Mr Kikuoka that I've got where I am. You can investigate me all you like. Go ahead! But my future without the president is bleak. I can't even imagine what it'll be like for me tomorrow now. There was no reason for me to kill him. I have no motive whatsoever. In fact if anyone had tried to kill Mr Kikuoka, I would have had to do everything I could to protect him. For my own sake. There's no way I could have killed him. Apart from anything, look at me! I'm a wimp. Do you see this feeble body winning a face-off against that man? It wasn't me. No way. And for all the exact same reasons, it wasn't my wife either."

Ushikoshi sighed. This man was quite a talker when cornered. That said, what Kanai claimed was most probably true. And

173

therefore, yet again, there were no suspects. It was incredibly frustrating.

"Mr Hamamoto, would you mind letting us use your library again? We need to have another meeting."

"Oh, of course. You're most welcome to use it."

"Thank you. Come on!"

Ushikoshi hurried his men out of the salon.

SCENE 7

The Library

"Never known anything like this damned case!" said Inspector Okuma. "What the heck is going on? Has the cause of death been confirmed yet?"

"Yes, it has," said Sergeant Ozaki. "Forensics says it was the knife in his back. They detected some sleep medication in his system too, but nothing like a lethal dose."

"What is going on in this cursed house?"

"They've gone over Room 14 but they haven't been able to find anything. No hidden doors, secret cabinets, nothing like that. Same as Room 10."

"What about the ceiling?" asked Ushikoshi.

"Same goes for that too. Just an ordinary ceiling. If we looked inside the walls and above the ceiling, we might find something, but we don't need to go that far just yet. There's plenty else they need to do first."

Okuma decided to throw in his two pence worth.

"I reckon they need to check that ceiling out more carefully. It's that string. Why was it attached to the knife? Everyone in this house besides the Kanai couple has an alibi for around 11 p.m. But the Kanais have no motive. If the killer is one of the people who slept in this house last night, it's starting to get a bit like a murder mystery novel. Someone planned this trick ahead of time, so that right around 11 o'clock a knife would plunge itself into Kikuoka's back. That's the only explanation. Don't you agree?"

"Hmm. I suppose we have to agree that that is a possibility," said Ushikoshi.

"Right, eh? And so if you think that, the ceiling's gotta be fishy. Because of that string. What if they hung the knife from the ceiling so that it fell onto the bed at 11 o'clock?"

"But we've checked the ceiling," said Ozaki. "It's made of perfectly normal boards. We've knocked all over every inch of it, and there are no gaps, no places where it's been disturbed. No sign of any kind of trick. And besides, as for that theory... Well, I can I think of at least two reasons why it would be impossible. The first is the height of the ceiling. That knife was buried in Kikuoka's back right up to the hilt. If it had been hanging from the ceiling and then dropped, there is no way it would have gone in so deeply. In fact it's not even clear that it would have inflicted a wound at all. A knife dropping from ceiling height might have been painful, but probably no more than a bee sting. It would have just barely touched him and then fallen sideways.

"Then could the killer have dropped it from a higher place? Well, you were sleeping in the room above, Inspector Okuma. To have a knife pierce so deeply, it would have to be dropped from at least one more storey up. But then we still don't know whether it would have gone in so far. But at the very least the fact remains that the killer couldn't have dropped it from inside Room 14. He would at least have to have dropped it from above the floor of Room 12."

"Huh? Yes, I guess you're right."

"The other reason it wouldn't work is the blanket," Ozaki continued. "The knife would have had to pierce him through an electric blanket. And then it wouldn't have been in his back. It would have been in his chest."

176

"But what if he slept on his stomach?"

"Yes, he might."

"I know that this is too simple, but it's all I can come up with… Somewhere in this house there is one more person, someone that none of us has seen. That's all it could be. No matter how you look at it, not one of those eleven people could be considered a suspect."

"But is that possible?" asked Ushikoshi. "We've already searched that spare room where no one's staying. Surely no one's harbouring a killer in their room?"

"Well, we can't really say."

"Hmm. For now, while we have them all gathered here, we should perform a thorough search of all the rooms in the house. But I don't—"

"No, I reckon you're right," said Okuma. "Likely a house like this has some secret space that a person could hide in. I say we should focus on that. That could be how it's being done. In a weird messed-up place like this, I'll wager you there's some trick built in."

"So what you're saying," Ozaki interjected, "is that we have to consider that the owners of this place—in other words, Kozaburo Hamamoto and his daughter, Eiko—must have been in on the plan. But when we consider motive, the Hamamotos, together with Sasaki and Togai, have to be excluded off the bat. They had no connection at all with Kazuya Ueda. And obviously Eikichi Kikuoka is counted out now.

"According to the data when we were researching Ueda, Kozaburo Hamamoto and Eikichi Kikuoka don't go back all that far. They weren't childhood buddies or anything like that. They met when they each became presidents of their respective companies. It was through work that their relationship began, specifically when Kikuoka Bearings had dealings with Hama Diesel.

"That all began fourteen or fifteen years ago, but it doesn't seem that the two men were ever particularly close. Their companies didn't seem to have any friction in their dealings either. Hamamoto and Kikuoka have met fewer than ten times in their lives. Kikuoka had only become Hamamoto's house guest very recently—only since Hamamoto built this holiday home. It certainly doesn't seem that they had the kind of relationship that might lead to murder."

"And they're not from the same part of Japan?"

"No, completely different. Hamamoto's from Tokyo, Kikuoka from the Kansai region. All of their employees told the Tokyo police that until their companies became successful, the two men had never met."

"Eiko had never met Kikuoka either, I assume?"

"Definitely not. Before this visit, Eiko had only ever met Kikuoka last summer when he came to stay."

"Hmm."

"Others have confirmed that Kikuoka only visited this house on those two occasions. Sasaki, Togai, Yoshihiko Hamamoto and Haruo Kajiwara – they all say the same thing, that this was the second time they had met Kikuoka. However you look at it, there really wasn't enough time for any kind of feud to have developed between them and Eikichi Kikuoka."

"Yes, common sense would suggest that all the people you've named should be excluded as suspects."

"Yes, as far as motive is concerned."

"And yet, in all the cases we've ever handled, there has never been such thing as a motiveless crime, except for those committed by some sort of pervert or psychopath," Ushikoshi pointed out.

"That's right."

"Grudges, theft, jealousy, sudden rage, sexual urges, money… all kinds of petty reasons like these."

"And of the names you didn't mention, there's the secretary and the protégé and his wife. But there's also the housekeeper couple, the Hayakawas. How about them?" asked Ushikoshi hopefully.

"Until yesterday we knew nothing about them, but now we've found something. We received new information today. Tokyo HQ told us that Mr and Mrs Hayakawa had a daughter around twenty. That daughter met Kikuoka here when he was visiting last summer."

"Aha!"

Immediately, Ushikoshi and Okuma's eyes lit up.

"On the curvy side, fair-skinned and rather attractive according to reports. I don't have access to a photo of her though. If you'd like one I think we can ask the Hayakawas."

"Got it. And then?"

"The daughter used to work at a bar called Himiko in Asakusabashi in Taito Ward, Tokyo. In August of this year, she came up here for a visit. Kikuoka probably showed an interest in her—apparently, he was an infamous womanizer. Everyone says that about him."

"Was Kikuoka still single?"

"Far from it. He has a wife and two children—a high school-aged son and a daughter in middle school."

"Really? He had plenty of energy, then, that one."

"Kikuoka, although he seemed an open-minded, generous type, also had a rather underhand side to him. It seems that if anyone ever showed him ingratitude at work, he would seem to laugh it off, but later he'd always be sure to get his revenge."

"Again, the hard life of the lowly employee."

"With Yoshie, the Hayakawas' daughter, the same kind of thing happened. Here in front of her parents he didn't show even a hint of interest, but when he got back to Tokyo, seems he kept showing up at her bar.

"Himiko is one of those places that young people like to hang out. Kind of modern but not too expensive. There are just two people working there—the *mama-san* and Yoshie. So it was this kind of place that the president of Kikuoka Bearings began to turn up at daily. Was a bit awkward, really."

"Old lechers with money and status are the worst."

"That one believed deeply in spending money on women, they say."

"Quite a philosophy."

"So it seems. He was kind of a reckless spender. That relationship with Yoshie went on for quite some time, until Kikuoka suddenly stopped coming to the bar."

"Hmm."

"By the way, according to the *mama-san* of Himiko, he'd promised to buy Yoshie an apartment and a sports car but he never did. She was pretty pissed off with him."

"Very interesting."

"The *mama-san* says that Yoshie used to get excited about all the presents he was going to buy her, and so after he disappeared she got very depressed. Anyway, Yoshie got dumped, and her phone calls to Kikuoka were never answered. If she ever did manage to get a hold of him, he claimed that he had never made her any promises."

"So what did she do?"

"She attempted suicide."

"What? She died?"

"No. She didn't succeed. She took sleeping pills, but she was found and had her stomach pumped. I think there was a strong element of revenge against Kikuoka in it. And, according to the *mama-san*, she probably felt ashamed of having talked about everything so openly too."

"Well, you could say they're both at fault in their own way, I suppose. And how are things now?"

"She had recovered quite well, and was getting out and about again, but then at the beginning of last month she was killed in a traffic accident."

"So she did die!"

"It really was just a traffic accident and had absolutely nothing to do with Eikichi Kikuoka, but the Hayakawas blame Kikuoka for it. They say he killed her."

"Well, they would… She was their only child… And does Mr Hamamoto know about all this?"

"I'm pretty sure he does. Well, he must know that the Hayakawas' only daughter died in a traffic accident, surely."

"So, Kikuoka just nonchalantly decides to turn up at the house where Kohei and Chikako Hayakawa live?"

"He was personally invited by the esteemed president of Hama Diesel. He couldn't refuse."

"How terribly unfortunate for him!" said Ushikoshi with heavy sarcasm. "I get it. Kohei and Chikako Hayakawa had a motive for murdering Eikichi Kikuoka. Yesterday they kept it quiet, didn't they? But what about Ueda?"

"Now that's still as strange as ever. The Hayakawas had absolutely no reason to kill Kazuya Ueda. The only contact they ever had with him was the couple of times he came to the house."

"Hmm. So they had a motive to kill Kikuoka, but none to kill Ueda. That *is* strange… And to make matters worse, the only two people with a motive to kill Kikuoka have an iron-clad alibi.

"Well, never mind that for now. How about the next married couple? Is there any news about a possible motive for Michio and Hatsue Kanai to kill Kikuoka?"

"Actually there is. And it's straight out of a gossip magazine."

"Oh?"

"It seems to be true that Michio Kanai was a huge supporter and member of Kikuoka's faction at work. He's been sucking up to Kikuoka for just shy of the past twenty years. And it worked. He's really come up in the world. It's all exactly as Kanai said himself in his big speech just now. Everything's pretty much confirmed to be true. The problem is his wife."

"The wife?..."

Ozaki was enjoying leaving the others hanging on his words. He paused to take a cigarette and light it.

"It was Kikuoka who set Kanai up with Hatsue around twenty years ago. But before that, Hatsue Kanai used to be Kikuoka's lover."

"Again!"

"The playboy!"said Okuma, with a hint of grudging admiration.

"He's just that type, I guess."

"I take my hat off to him," added Ushikoshi, rather sarcastically. "Well, did Kanai have any idea about this?"

"That's still unclear. On the surface it seems that he knew nothing, but he might have had his suspicions."

"But even if he did suspect something, would that be a strong enough reason to murder someone?"

"Difficult to say for sure, but probably not. As far as Kanai is concerned, losing his employer means he's nothing any more.

Company Executive Kanai only existed because of President Kikuoka. So I'm saying that even if Kanai had realized about his wife's past with Kikuoka, it was something that happened a long time ago. If he'd ever attacked Kikuoka, it'd be fair to say he'd lose everything.

"If for some reason, he had been desperate to kill him, if there had been something festering in him that was forcing him to do it, how would he have gone about it? Well, it would be more sensible for him to have got in first with members of the opposing faction or factions at the company. He'd need to protect his position after the death of his patron. But there's no evidence at all that he did anything like that."

"So he was Kikuoka's bootlicker right to the end?"

"Seems so."

"I see."

"To me it makes no sense to think of Kanai having a motive to kill Kikuoka."

"How about his wife?"

"Ah, the wife... I don't think she could have done something like that."

"How about Kanai's relationship with Ueda?"

"Just as we discovered from the earlier investigation, there was no particular relationship between the two. As for motive, I think it's impossible to find one."

"Then let's take a look at Kumi Aikura."

"It's no secret at the company that she was Kikuoka's lover. But as far as Kumi's concerned, she relied on his being there... It really wouldn't be a great idea to kill him. Even if she had some kind of motive that we don't know about, it would make sense to squeeze as much out of him as she possibly could for now, then pick the moment right when he was about to leave

183

her. But at the time he was murdered, Kikuoka was still totally infatuated with her."

"So this thing with Yoshie Hayakawa, he was two-timing her with Kumi?"

"Yeah. It looks like it."

"Nice behaviour."

"What a charmer!"

"And yet, let's imagine there were some particular circumstances that we don't know about, and Kumi managed to get herself hired as Kikuoka's secretary with the sole purpose of murdering him?"

"I don't think it's possible. She's from Akita Prefecture. Growing up, neither she nor her parents ever left the area. Kikuoka never visited Akita in his life."

"Huh. Got it. To sum up, the only people with a motive to kill Kikuoka seem to be Mr and Mrs Hayakawa. And there is absolutely no one with a motive to kill Kazuya Ueda. That's it? And on top of that, we have another one of those cursed locked-room mysteries. Inspector Okuma, what's your opinion of all this?"

"I've never seen anything like it. This case is downright bonkers. Some dirty old man gets murdered in a locked room with no way of it being done from the outside, and there's no goddamn suspects with any motive. And the only ones who might have done it were in the salon with one of our officers at the very time!

"I reckon there's only one thing for it—we'll have to rip out all the wall and ceiling boards in Room 14. May be some sort of secret passageway behind them. That fireplace is fishy if you ask me. I'll bet you'll find a secret passage back there. Follow the passageway and there'll be a secret room, and that'll be where you'll find the twelfth person in this case—a little person or a dwarf or something—someone who's been hiding very quietly this whole time... I'm not kidding. This has to be it. If he was a little person he could hide in narrow spaces—you know—and move around through secret passageways."

"That fireplace is just decorative. You can't light a real fire in there. There's just a gas heater in it. So there's no chimney or flue, no open hole above it. We've knocked on all the boards around it, we've tried all the seams and joints – there doesn't seem to be anything suspicious at all about it."

"So tell me what you're thinking, Chief Inspector," said Okuma.

Ushikoshi just gave his customary "Hmm..." He turned to his junior officer.

"Ozaki? What about you?"

"I think we have to look at everything logically."

"I totally agree."

"There have been two murders, in two separate locked rooms. Or to put it another way, the suspect set up the two rooms for the murders. In the case of Room 10, for reasons unknown, he tied a cord around the murdered Ueda's wrist, and added string to the shot-put on the floor. In Room 14, he fought with Kikuoka, knocking over the sofa and the coffee table, so in both crime scenes there was clear evidence that the murderer had been inside the room. I think we have to take it that both crime scenes were constructed after the murder had been committed."

"Fine, but is that really possible?"

"But both of the scenes had the doors properly locked. Room 14 in particular, had those bolts and a knob with a locking button—a very complicated and difficult locking system.

There was no crack or gap anyway in the door—Room 14's was very well constructed. There wasn't the hint of an opening in the top, bottom or either side. There was that heavy door frame on all sides.

"Which leaves us with that twenty-centimetre-square ventilation hole, high up in the wall. I think the murderer must have somehow manipulated the scene via a piece of string or something run through that hole. But it's pure conjecture. There were no signs that anything had been secured to the wall anywhere around the hole. No pins had been stuck in the wall or around the door and there was nothing that looked like a pin that had come loose and fallen on the floor. I searched pretty thoroughly. In other words, there's no forensic evidence left behind that proves they used that method."

"Huh."

"I think it may be possible that the sofa and coffee table being knocked over had something to do with a locked-room trick."

"I wonder. And then there's the question: why use this locked room at all in the first place? There's no one dumb enough to wonder whether a knife in the back might be suicide."

"You're right. But let's imagine for now that the sofa and table were somehow instrumental in the locked-room trick. By knocking over both pieces of furniture, somehow a cord was pulled and the bolts on the door were unlocked. You'd need to use a really strong piece of cord to do that, and then the cord would have to be retrieved from the ventilation hole. You told us, didn't you, Chief Inspector, that you knocked on the door of Room 14 last night?"

"Well, technically it was Mr Hamamoto who knocked."

"What time was that?"

"Around 10.30."

"At that time was there any string or anything hanging from the ventilation hole?"

"No. In fact, when there was no reply, I glanced up at the vent. There was nothing there."

"No, probably not. At that point, Kikuoka was still alive and sleeping. And yet about thirty minutes later he was dead. And at 11.30 the three members of staff passed quite close by on their way to their rooms. None of them looked towards the air vent specifically, but it makes sense that by that time the cord had already been removed.

"We already found out that the ventilation hole is so high up in the wall that you can barely see into the room, even standing on a bedside table, so unless the killer used a step stool or a ladder, there must have been a long piece of cord hanging from the vent. And with people passing so close by, even if they didn't go right by the door, it would have been impossible to leave it like that without it being noticed."

"So what you're saying is that the murder was committed very quickly and done by about 11.10 p.m."

"Yes, that's right, but it just happens that the household staff went down to the basement at 11.30. It doesn't always happen that way—it was pure coincidence. Because normally they'd be going to bed much earlier than that. If the killer hadn't been careful, he could easily have been seen pulling the string. That's the flaw in that plan.

"If I were the killer I'd have done the deed much, much earlier. The later it became, the more likely the staff would have been coming down to the basement."

"Right. It would make sense to have committed the murder and removed all traces by the time I was at the door of Room 14."

"Yes, but the time of death can't be moved from around 11 o'clock. So with that in mind, we can narrow it down to who could physically have been there. Who among our suspects could have visited Room 14 at that time, unseen by anyone? Only the occupants of Room 9."

"That may be true… But I'm not convinced about the 11 o'clock time frame. It makes the whole plan much too risky. Don't you think?"

"Well, I wouldn't think of attempting it, but then again I've never thought about murdering anybody either."

"There is an alternative possibility that we could consider. A clever trick that gets the knife in Kikuoka's back by 11 o'clock. If the suspect can pull off a stunt like that, he's free to play a leisurely game of billiards with a police constable, or relax over a drink with the head detective on the case."

"Yes, I've been thinking about that too," said Okuma. "But it would be really difficult to set up a murder in a locked room with a piece of string. I mean if Room 14 was already set up ahead of time, well, you couldn't even have walked into the room."

Ozaki resumed his commentary.

"Room 14 itself had nothing particularly special about it. There's nothing there that lends itself to setting up a murder from outside the room. On the writing desk in the corner there was nothing but a pot of ink, a pen and a paperweight; the bookcase didn't seem to have been touched at all. Mr Hamamoto says that the books all seem to be in place. To the right of the fireplace there's a built-in wardrobe, but there's nothing strange inside it. The door was closed.

"If anything's unusual about the room, it's the number of chairs. There's the desk chair, which was in its usual place, pushed under the desk. Then a rocking chair in front of the fire which was also more or less in its normal position. Then the set of sofa and two armchairs. Without even counting the bed, which is a kind of converted chair too, that makes a total of five different seats. I suppose some sort of trick could be set up by using all of them. But the two armchairs hadn't been moved much either.

"Anyway, the important thing is that no one could get in there besides Kikuoka himself. There was no spare key for Room 14. I don't know whether they'd lost it, never had one made in the first place, or that Hamamoto was too neurotic to allow there to be more than one key for his personal study, but it has been confirmed that there was definitely only the one. And last night, Kikuoka had it. This morning our men retrieved it from the pocket of his jacket which he'd thrown off."

"So he left the key lying around in his room. What if he'd accidentally pushed the locking button on the inside of the doorknob and gone out, closing the door? That would've caused a bit of a problem, wouldn't it?"

"No, that would have been okay. If you push the button in first and then close the door, it doesn't work. The button pops back out and the door doesn't lock."

"I see."

"Anyway, we were told that while Kikuoka was staying here, he always made sure to lock the door from the outside every time he left his room. It seems he left his money in there. The Hayakawas and several others have attested to that."

"All right. So there's no way that anyone could have got into the room before the murder?"

"No, no way. All the other rooms had two keys. The Hayakawas would show the guests to their room and hand them one of the keys. The duplicates are with Eiko Hamamoto. Room 14 was the exception, so I guess they decided to put the richest bloke in there."

"Huh," said Okuma, sounding deflated.

"It's not something I'm going to admit to in front of all those folks in the salon, but I'm on the point of throwing in the towel on this whole thing. Just like you said yourself, Inspector Okuma, there is no killer. There is no murderer among those eleven people out there."

"Hmm…"

"It's the same as the last case," said Ozaki. "There's plenty about the Ueda killing that we've put on the back burner. We still haven't worked out why there were no footprints in the snow. That locked room had the simplest of locks on it, it could have been manipulated somehow, but the snow outside the door was completely undisturbed. By any of the entrances or exits to and from the main building, or anywhere around the house, even on the steps up to Room 10, there was nothing. As long as everyone is telling the truth, and Sasaki isn't lying either, the ground that they crossed to get to the scene of the crime was all covered in pure virgin snow. That's the first problem.

"And then the two stakes in the ground that Sasaki had seen the night before. Not to mention that disgusting-looking Golem doll… And then…oh, yes, that's right, Chief Inspector Ushikoshi, Ueda was murdered on the night of the 25th. How about the daytime of the 25th? We said we were going to check whether the doll was really in Room 3 earlier that day. Did we?"

"It was. Mr Hamamoto says he definitely saw it sitting there during the daytime."

"I see. So the suspect took it from the room shortly before committing the crime… Hang on! Just wait a minute while I go next door to check on the doll."

The doll had already been returned to its place in the Tengu Room. Ozaki leapt to his feet and ran out of the library. Okuma took the opportunity to offer a few words of his own.

"Me, I don't think anyone got into Room 10 by way of that door facing the outside. But the ventilation hole was facing inwards towards the rest of the house. Someone got up to no good with that open hole, I'll warrant."

"But it was way up high in the wall."

"Well, the only other explanation is that the bugger must have got in using some secret passageway, or some other trick like—"

"Chief!"

Ozaki was back.

"The doll's right hand—there's string wrapped around it."

"What?"

"Come and see!"

The three detectives rushed out of the library and over to the interior-facing window of the Tengu Room. The Golem doll was sitting just under the window, leaning back against the wall, and as Ozaki had said, wrapped around its right wrist was a piece of white string.

"This stinks," said Ushikoshi. "Let's go back. I'm not falling for this kind of bullshit."

"The suspect must have done this."

"They must have. Right after forensics returned it to the house. Someone's playing silly buggers with us."

They went back to their seats in the library.

"Getting back to the matter of the footprints, if they were made to disappear by some sort of clever ruse, I don't think it would mean very much. Since for Kikuoka's murder it's almost one hundred per cent certain that the killer is inside the house. If, back at the time of Ueda's murder, the killer had already planned to kill Kikuoka next, he might as well have left the footprints to cast suspicion on an outsider for the crime."

"Perhaps… Well, never mind. So in that case, where are we?"

"We're back to assuming that there were never any footprints in the first place, and that the killer used some kind of trick to commit the murder from inside the house—"

"That's what I've been saying all along!" said Okuma loudly.

"But how does that doll fit in with things? Did it fly through the air under its own power and land out there in the snow? It's not possible. And even though we're quite sure that someone in this house is responsible for these murders, there would still have been a surprising amount we could have learnt from footprints. For example, whether they were made by a man's or a woman's shoe. The stride can also tell us their height and their gender. If the length of the stride seems to indicate it's a woman, but the shoes are definitely a man's, then we could suspect a woman deliberately wearing a man's shoes. It would still have been safer to get rid of the footprints. As much as possible, anyway."

There was a knock at the door.

"Yes?"

Taken off guard, the three detectives all answered at once. The door opened very slowly to reveal a very nervous-looking Kohei Hayakawa.

"Um… Sorry to disturb you, but lunch is almost ready."

"Ah. Is it? Thanks."

Hayakawa started to close the door again.

"Mr Hayakawa? Did Kikuoka's death bring you some relief?"

Ushikoshi was as blunt in tone as he was in words. Hayakawa's eyes widened and his face turned ashen. His hand gripped the doorknob.

"Why are you asking me a question like that? You think I had any connection with—"

"Mr Hayakawa, please don't underestimate the police. We've looked into the business with your daughter, Yoshie. Tokyo police know that you attended your daughter's funeral in Tokyo."

Hayakawa's shoulders slumped.

"Please, take a seat."

"No, thank you. I'd rather stay standing… I don't have anything to tell you."

"He told you to sit!" yelled Ozaki.

Hayakawa shuffled towards the detectives and sat down.

"Last time we spoke, you sat in that very chair and deliberately hid the truth from us. Now we can forgive that just the once, but if you try lying to us again, I have to tell you we won't be able to let it go."

"Inspector, I don't mean to hide anything from you. I wasn't hiding anything back then either. I wanted to tell you. The words were right there on the tip of my tongue. But even though Mr Kikuoka is dead now, at that time it was Mr Ueda who had been killed. I thought bringing up that story would have seemed suspicious…"

"And how about today? Now it's Kikuoka who's dead!"

"And you suspect me? How on earth could I have done it? It's true that when my daughter died I hated Mr Kikuoka for it. My wife too—we lost our only child. I'm not denying it. But I couldn't kill him, no matter how much I might have thought about it. I was in the entranceway between the salon and the kitchen. And besides I'm not permitted to go into the rooms."

Ushikoshi stared Hayakawa straight in the eyes, as if he were trying to see through a keyhole into his mind. There was a long silence.

"So while Mr Kikuoka was still in the salon, you didn't go into his room at all?"

"Certainly not! Ms Hamamoto has specifically told us not to go into the rooms when we have guests staying, but anyway, with that room, there isn't even a key. There's no way to get in."

"Hmm. I have another question for you. This morning Mr Kajiwara went out to the storage shed to fetch an axe and a stepladder. Isn't that storage shed kept locked?"

"It is kept locked."

"But this morning I didn't see him taking a key."

"You have to put in the right numbers. It's one of those whatchama—"

"You mean a combination padlock?"

"Right."

"Does everyone know the combination?"

"Everyone who lives in this house does. Do you want to know it?"

"No, no. That's fine. We'll ask you if we need it. So you're saying that the guests didn't have the combination, but Mr and Ms Hamamoto, Mr Kajiwara, you and your wife did?"

"That's right."

"Nobody else at all would know it?"

"No. Nobody."

"I understand. Thank you, that's all for now. Please let our hosts know that we'll be down for lunch in about thirty minutes."

Hayakawa was out of the seat in an instant, a look of relief on his face. As the door closed behind him, Ozaki turned to his boss.

"That old man could have killed Ueda."

"Yeah. The fact that he doesn't have a motive is the fatal weakness in that theory."

Ushikoshi sounded as if he were only half joking.

"But it would be physically possible. If the husband and wife had colluded, it would have been easier. Anyway, someone working as a butler probably knows the ins and outs of the house far better than the master of the house."

"As for motive, how about this? They planned to kill Kikuoka, but Ueda was his bodyguard, so they had to get rid of him first."

"That's pretty feeble. If that was their motive, then the same night they did Ueda in was also the perfect opportunity to knock off Kikuoka too. If Ueda was a bodyguard, there was only one of him, and he was miles away from his employer, stuck in some sort of storeroom that could only be accessed from the outside. They had the perfect conditions to murder Kikuoka. The suspect wouldn't have hesitated to kill Kikuoka, and only Kikuoka.

"After all, Ueda was still young, he had the physical strength of an ex-Self-Defence Forces soldier. Kikuoka was much older, and quite overweight. Even Hayakawa might have stood a chance against him. There was absolutely no need to kill Ueda."

"But Ueda knew about the business with Yoshie Hayakawa. He could have caused trouble afterwards for the Hayakawas. Maybe they killed him to silence him."

"I suppose it's possible. But then wouldn't the Kanais and Kumi Aikura be even more of a problem? For sure Kikuoka wasn't particularly chatty with Ueda. He probably hadn't ever brought up the topic of Yoshie Hayakawa with him."

"Probably not."

"Even if the Hayakawas did it, I still don't understand the locked room situation in Room 14. And anyway, at the time of death the two of them were definitely still in the salon. There's nothing we can do about that. So for now we just have to throw the whole problem of motive to the winds, and narrow it down to whoever could physically have been the murderer."

"Yes, I suppose so... Which means..."

"Which means Mr and Mrs Kanai. And if we're going to stretch the point, Kumi and Eiko too."

"Eiko?"

"That's the problem we're faced with. We have to look at absolutely every possibility."

"But how was Kikuoka killed? Even if we try to narrow down the list of suspects, have you got even a rough idea of how it was done?"

"I think I might have."

"How?"

The two men turned to stare at Ushikoshi. Ozaki seemed eager to hear his boss's theory, but Okuma looked extremely dubious.

"I think we have to agree that the door was completely impenetrable. I don't believe that by using a piece of string, both of those bolts could be turned and the button in the doorknob pushed. I just don't think all that is possible."

"But you don't think the victim opened the door himself?"

"No, I don't. Which means that room – being in the basement and having no windows, and a door that doesn't open – leaves us with the ventilation hole."

"That twenty-centimetre-square hole?"

"The very same. I'm convinced that Kikuoka was stabbed through that hole."

"But how?"

"The vent is right above the bed. The killer must have attached the knife to the end of a long stick or pole to make a kind of spear and stuck it through the vent."

"Aha! But they would have needed something at least two metres long," Ozaki pointed out. "And the problem with something that length is that would be too long to fit across the corridor space—it'd hit the opposite wall. And then it would be a real pain to carry around. If they kept it in their room it would definitely be noticed, but even before that, how could they get it into the house?"

"I've already thought of that. It must have been one of those collapsible fishing rods."

"Aha! I see."

"A fishing rod could be extended to just the right length to reach into the room," explained Ushikoshi. He sounded rather proud of himself.

"Huh. But would a knife inserted that way really stay in the victim's body? The knife would have to be securely tied to the rod, wouldn't it?"

"It would. And that's the significance of the piece of string that was attached to the knife. But I still haven't quite figured out how it worked. It must have been a clever plan. That part I think we'll have to hear from the killer themselves—after we've arrested them."

"So you're saying that Room 10's murder was carried out the same way?"

"Ah, now that I'm not sure about."

"There was nothing in that basement corridor that could have been used to stand on. I mean that's why I brought a bedside table from the next room. But even when I stood on that I was still way too low to see into the room. A coffee table would be even lower. All the bedside tables in all the rooms in the house are the same height."

"Yes. That is a problem… Perhaps you could put one of them on top of the other?"

"On that slanting floor? In any other house you might be able to manage it… And anyway, there's only one table in each room. And then there's the skill it would take to climb up on two tables on top of each other. It'd be unstable."

"Maybe two people could manage together, one climbing on the other's shoulders. There must be many ways it could be done. But that's why I was asking Hayakawa just now about the key to the outdoor shed. I was thinking about that stepladder."

"This house has only three ways in and out, and all of them are connected to the salon. If anyone went out to the shed they'd have been seen by everyone in the salon. To get outside, you could possibly climb out through the window on the landing of the staircase from Room 1, but then there's nowhere to get back in. If you came back in through the same window, you'd have to go through the salon to get to Room 14 in the basement. So there's no point in climbing out in the first place."

"I'm beginning to believe that everyone in the salon was in on the plot."

"What, Anan too? You think my police constable was mixed up in this?" chuckled Okuma. "But seriously, ask anyone who was there, and they're going to say that they didn't happen to notice anyone resembling a house painter casually passing through the salon with a stepladder tucked under his arm."

Suddenly Ushikoshi had a thought.

Maybe there was one other way it could have been done. Only the occupants of the ground floor would be able to get in and out of their window. That meant either Sasaki or Togai. Those two had definitely been in the salon at the time of Kikuoka's murder, but Eiko and Kumi weren't. Either of those two could have climbed out of the window on the east staircase landing—

"How about a rifle or some other kind of modified gun?"

Ushikoshi's thought process was rudely interrupted by Okuma's own musings.

"Some kind of gun that could shoot the knife using a spring mechanism, or elastic. They'd have needed string for that kind of trick—"

"But we're still stuck on the problem of the stepladder," said Ozaki. "And how the sofa and coffee table in Room 14 got overturned. Plus, we can't ignore the signs of a struggle. The killer was definitely inside Room 10."

Ushikoshi glanced at his watch.

"Yes, we've been ignoring that aspect. I think we need to search everyone's room again. Let's focus on Mr and Mrs Kanai, Eiko and Kumi. Search for a fishing rod or some kind of pole longer than two metres, or some kind of modified gun or rifle. Also look out for something that could be used as a kind of collapsible stand or step stool. All of those kinds of things.

"Of course we don't have a warrant, so we'll need each person's consent. I'm sure the young students will be happy to let us take a look. And I think with so many people, everyone will probably give in and consent in the end. We've still got officers here, haven't we? Let's split the task up between them and Anan, preferably all working simultaneously. Let's not leave out the empty rooms either. And it's possible that someone's dumped it out of the window. I want the snow around the whole house thoroughly examined—a wide enough perimeter in case

199

the killer threw it. Oh, and the fireplace too. It's possible that the killer might have burnt the evidence in the hearth in the salon. Better check just in case.

"Right, let's get down to the salon. We'll announce the searches to everyone after lunch. We'll be careful to ask as politely as possible. Don't want to go offending the gentry."

When lunch was over, Ushikoshi and Okuma made their way back to the library in silence, sat down in the exact same chairs as before and watched the sun gradually sink in the sky. They had the feeling that they might be forced to watch the sun again tomorrow, and the day after that too. Neither man felt much like talking.

It wasn't that he didn't hear the door open, but Chief Inspector Ushikoshi didn't feel inclined to turn his head around until he heard his name spoken. His hopes were riding on this result. He could barely look Sergeant Ozaki in the eyes.

"What happened?"

"We searched every room in the house. And every person too. There were no women police officers available, so we'll probably be fielding complaints from the female contingent."

Ozaki's speech was a little more sluggish than usual.

"I see. And?"

"We found absolutely nothing. Nobody was hiding a fishing rod; there isn't one in the whole house. No long poles either. The billiard cues are about the longest thing here. And of course we didn't come across any modified firearms.

"There was no evidence that anything had been burnt in the fireplace besides regular firewood. We combed the ground around the house to a distance farther than an Olympic javelin champion could have thrown, but found nothing.

"There are no stools or stepladders. Just like Room 14, in Kajiwara's and the Hayakawas' rooms there are desks—well, not as fancy as that one—but they were both so large and solid that it would have been extremely difficult to move them anywhere. And their height wasn't that much more than the bedside tables—barely another twenty centimetres.

"Then I thought that perhaps the long object we were looking for might be a javelin, so we went to check the sports equipment in Room 10. But there was no javelin in there. There were pairs of skis and ski poles in there, and in the storage shed we found a long-handled shovel, a hoe, spade, broom—all those kinds of tools. But to bring those into the house would be just the same situation as with the stepladder. We give up."

"I'm so sorry. But I guess I kind of expected it," said Ushikoshi with a sigh. "Do you have any other ideas?"

"As a matter of fact," said Ozaki, "I did come up with something."

"All right, tell me more."

"I wondered about a frozen rope. Whether it could be used like a long pole."

"Clever! And what did you discover?"

"Nobody had any rope, but there was some in the storage shed."

Ushikoshi began to think furiously.

"You know that could be an important point. Some kind of long pole… Something inside this house that is long. Maybe something that is always there right in front of our eyes. Something that takes just a little bit of fixing up and suddenly you've got a long pole—something like that. Is there anything in that display room next door?"

"We searched it thoroughly, but a stick or a pole—"

"There has to be something somewhere. If there isn't, it means the suspect would have had to get in and out through the door, and then somehow lock it behind him… Something that you can disassemble and end up with a long pole… I don't think the bannister on the staircase is removable… the firewood… Did they tie several pieces together with string to make it longer?… No, not possible. Damn it! Are you sure there's nothing at all in the next room?"

"Nothing. But why don't you take a look for yourself?"

"I'll do that."

"There is one thing—the doll, Golem; its hands are constructed in a curved shape as if it were gripping something. I thought the knife could have fitted into one of its hands. I gave it a try."

"What? You're quite the detective, aren't you? Talk about an overdeveloped sense of curiosity! And, what did you find?"

"A perfect fit. Like putting a dummy into a baby's hand."

"Ha! Well, you certainly have an eye for the ghoulish. But no matter how you look at it, it has to be a coincidence, no?"

"Yeah, I guess so."

"But so much in this case has gone wrong or drawn a blank, the lack of alibi for the Kanais in Room 9 seems to be the only thing left that we can be sure of. At least that is not going to turn out to be a let-down, is it?"

Ushikoshi sounded as if he were trying to console himself. The three detectives lapsed into silence.

"Sorry? Ozaki, do you want to say something?"

Ushikoshi had noticed the junior detective fidgeting.

"Well, sir, the thing is, I've kept quiet about it up till now…"

"What is it?"

"It's a difficult thing to admit, but last night after I left the salon to go to bed, I just couldn't get it out of my head that the only people who had already gone to bed besides Okuma and myself were Kikuoka and the Kanais, and I began to wonder if they might be up to something while everyone else was still in the salon. So I went to each of their rooms and just under the doorknob, I used some hair oil to stick a hair across the space between the door and the wall. If the door was opened, the hair would get pulled off. I'm sorry that it wasn't a very mature thing to do. I'm a bit embarrassed—"

"What are you talking about? It was inspired! Did you do the same with any of the other rooms?"

"I didn't do any of the rooms where there was no way to come out except through the salon. I limited it to the rooms where you could get out without being seen. As for the other people staying in the west wing—Sasaki, Togai and the house staff—I planned to do the same with their doors, but they stayed up so late that I'm afraid I fell asleep before I could do it."

"What time did you stick the hair on those doors?"

"Right after I told you that I was going to bed. So around a quarter past or twenty past 10."

"Hm. And then?"

"I woke up once and went to check on those two rooms."

"And what did you find?"

"The hair on Kikuoka's door had come off. The door must have been opened at some point. But the one on the Kanais' door…"

"Was?…"

"…Still there."

"What?"

"The door hadn't been opened."

SCENE 8

The Salon

The morning of the 28th of December dawned without further incident. It was a very minor victory for the detectives. Nothing had happened in the night, but they could hardly claim it was because of their presence…

The increasingly bitter occupants of the Ice Floe Mansion had begun to notice that the expert detectives with their airs didn't seem to know any more about what was going on than they did. Of the three nights they had spent in the mansion since the evening of the Christmas party, there had been a murder committed on two, one of which the killer had impudently pulled off right under the noses of several police officers. And the bitter truth for these experts was that, beginning with the time of death, fingerprints and all the usual clues, all they'd managed to confirm was that there was absolutely nothing to go on.

Finally, the sun went down on what seemed to the guests a very long day, and to the detectives much too short. It was evening and both parties were called for dinner. They sat themselves without much enthusiasm around a table laden with the usual lavish food.

As the guests joined them, conversation began to dry up, which seemed to bother Kozaburo Hamamoto. He tried to keep up a jovial front, but everyone felt the absence of the gravelly voiced man with his exaggerated compliments.

"I'm so sorry that what was supposed to be a fun Christmas holiday has turned into something so dreadful," said Kozaburo, after dinner was over. "I feel truly responsible,"

"No, please don't feel that way, Mr President," said Kanai from the next seat. "You have absolutely nothing to feel responsible for."

"It's true, Daddy. You really shouldn't say things like that."

Eiko's normally shrill voice came out closer to a shriek. This was followed by a few moments of silence. It was Chief Inspector Ushikoshi who decided to pick up the conversation.

"We're the ones who should accept responsibility."

There was resignation in his voice. But Kozaburo continued speaking.

"There is one thing I am determined to avoid, and that is any kind of secret whispering among us about the identity of the killer. If amateurs like us get started on trying to solve these crimes, then the relationships between us will be destroyed.

"That said, the police do seem to be having a lot of trouble solving the crime, and we really do all hope for a swift conclusion to this awful matter. Is there no one here who has noticed something, or has some kind of wisdom that they can share with these detectives?"

Hearing this, the three detectives' expressions turned sour and their body language became defensive. Perhaps it was the detectives' behaviour, but nobody in the room took Kozaburo up on the idea. He decided a few more words might be appropriate.

"Sasaki, you're usually very talented at solving this sort of riddle."

"Well, I have come up with a few ideas."

He'd clearly been waiting for this moment.

"How about it, gentlemen?" said Kozaburo.

"We'd like to hear them," said Ushikoshi, without much enthusiasm.

"Well, first of all, the locked room in the murder of Kazuya Ueda, I think I can solve that mystery. It was the shot-put."

There was no reaction from the detectives.

"That shot-put had string wrapped around it, with a wooden tag attached. The string had been extended, probably by the killer, and clearly for the purpose of creating that locked room. The latch—the type that moved up and down like a railway crossing gate—was propped up with that tag, stuck to the latch with Sellotape. Then the shot-put at the other end of the string was placed on the floor by the door, and when the killer closed the door behind him, because of the sloping floors in this mansion, the shot-put rolled away until the string was pulled tight and the wooden tag peeled away. And then of course the latch dropped and the door was locked."

"Ah, of course!" said Kanai. Togai looked as if he had just swallowed something nasty. The detectives nodded wordlessly.

"Well, Sasaki, do you have anything else for us?" asked Kozaburo.

"I do have something, but I haven't thought it all the way through yet. It's the other locked room, Mr Kikuoka's room. I don't think it's completely impossible to achieve, because it wasn't really a completely locked room. There's a hole for ventilation—small, but still an open space. The killer could have stabbed him with the knife, then balanced the coffee table on top of the sofa, securing it with a cord, and then attached it somehow to the en suite bathroom knob, and out through the vent hole. Then he'd have let it go from the corridor, and the table would fall off the sofa so that one of its legs pushed the button on the inside of the door—"

"Obviously, we'd already thought of that," snapped Ozaki. "But there are no marks anywhere on the door frame or in the wall where a pin or staple or anything was used. And that method would require a huge amount of cord. There's no kind of rope or cord like that anywhere in this house, or in anyone's possession.

"What's more, the suspect had absolutely no idea when the Hayakawas might come down to the basement. To set up a trick like that would take more than five minutes; probably ten. And anyway, the way you just described it includes setting three different locks. It would take even longer than that for sure."

Sasaki didn't respond. And this time the silence was much more uncomfortable than before. Kozaburo decided to try to break the tension.

"Eiko, let's listen to some music. Put a record on."

Eiko got up and soon the gloomy air of the salon was filled with the sound of Wagner's *Lohengrin*.

SCENE 9

The Tengu Room

By the afternoon of the 29th of December, the residents of the Ice Floe Mansion were sprawled around the salon, listless. It felt like the waiting room for condemned prisoners. Today's sense of fatigue had been created by the previous days' excess of nervous tension and fear. But boredom too was setting in.

Seeing the atmosphere in the room, Kozaburo proposed showing the Kanais and Kumi his collection of mechanical dolls and automata that he'd brought back from Europe. He'd already shown them to Michio Kanai and Kikuoka back in the summer, but Hatsue and Kumi were yet to see them. He'd intended to invite them to view everything much earlier, but all the fuss had distracted him from his plan.

Kozaburo had a lot of Western dolls in his collection, and he imagined that they would interest Kumi. Eiko and Yoshihiko were tired of seeing everything, so they chose to stay behind in the salon. This meant that Togai also decided to stay. Sasaki was interested in antiques, so although he'd also seen everything several times already, he decided to tag along.

A few days previously when Kumi had been on her way to be interviewed in the library, she had glanced through the window of the Tengu Room. It had given her a bad vibe, but today she reluctantly agreed to go anyway, ignoring the vaguely bad premonition she had as they set out.

Kozaburo Hamamoto, along with Michio and Hatsue Kanai, Kumi Aikura and Sasaki took the west stairs up to the door of the Tengu Room. As she had done the previous time, Kumi looked in through the window, the only one in the house that overlooked an interior corridor rather than the exterior. It was a huge window, giving a view of the whole room.

The window stretched all the way from the south wall corner to about 1.5 metres shy of the doorway, a total width of about 2 metres. It could be slid open about 30 centimetres from either the left or right side, leaving either or both sides open. That's how all the glass doors of the cabinets in this room were usually slid open too.

Kozaburo got out a key and opened the door, revealing that no matter how much of an impression you could get of the room by viewing it through the window, it wasn't until you stood inside that you could really take in the spectacle. First of all, right by the doorway stood a life-sized clown. It had a cheerful smiling face, but a rather depressing, musty smell.

There were all kinds of other dolls in the room, both large and small, all a little threadbare. They had aged, and looked almost on the point of death, but their youthful expressions were still intact. Their grimy faces with their peeling paint seemed to Kumi to be concealing some kind of vague madness. Either standing or sprawling in a chair, each one smiled faintly with some kind of unfathomable emotion. They were suspiciously quiet, looking like something you'd see in the waiting room of a psychiatric hospital in your worst nightmare.

As if their flesh had gradually been stripped away over time, the paint of their faces had peeled and scabbed over, exposing a little of the craziness inside. The part that had decayed the most were the smiles on their red, peeling lips.

By now they didn't even seem to be smiling any longer—these dolls had the most enigmatic look of pure evil. Their smiles had the power to send an instant chill through anyone who looked at them. Decomposition—that was the perfect word for it. The smile that had been on the faces of these cherished dolls had transmuted, decomposed. There was no better way of putting it.

A deep-seated grudge. They'd been brought into the world by the whimsy of human beings, but then not permitted to die for a thousand years. If the same thing were inflicted on our bodies, the same look of madness would appear on our faces too. Ever in search of revenge, our madness would grow in intensity, fed by the grudge we harboured.

Kumi let out a small but genuine scream. However, it was nothing compared to the residents of this room whose mouths were permanently poised on the edge of a scream.

The south and east walls were completely red with Tengu masks, with their huge long noses and fiery eyes that glowered at the room's doll occupants. It seemed to the guests that the Tengus' job was to stifle the screams of the dolls.

Hearing Kumi scream seemed to put Kozaburo in a cheerful mood.

"Well, this place is as amazing as ever," said Michio Kanai, and Hatsue nodded with great enthusiasm. But this kind of small talk felt out of place in the heavy atmosphere of the room.

"I've always wanted to set up a museum, but I was always so busy with work. In the end, this display room is all I was ever able to put together."

"It's already a museum," said Kanai.

Kozaburo gave a little laugh.

"Well, this is, anyway."

He opened one of the glass cases and took out a small figurine, about fifty centimetres tall, of a boy sitting in a chair. The chair had a little desk attached to it, and the boy had a pen in his right hand; his left rested on the desk. He had a sweet expression on his face, and this figurine lacked the visible wear and tear of the other dolls.

"He's so cute!" said Kumi.

"It's a clockwork doll, or automaton, known as *The Writer*. It was made in the late eighteenth century. I heard about it and went to great pains to get hold of it."

The assembled guests made various admiring sounds.

"Did it get its name because it can actually write words?" asked Kumi, sounding a little scared.

"Of course. I think it can still manage to write its own name. Would you like to see?"

Before Kumi had a chance to respond, Kozaburo tore off a sheet from a memo pad and slipped it under the doll's left hand. Winding the spring in the doll's back, he gave its right hand a gentle nudge. The doll's right hand began to make awkward, jerky movements which started to leave marks on the memo paper. There was a small clacking sound that must have been the grinding of the cogs inside.

Kumi was relieved to find the movements delightful rather than menacing. Even the occasional change in pressure of the doll's left hand on the paper was charmingly realistic.

"That's adorable! But at the same time a little bit scary."

Truth be told, everyone present was feeling slightly relieved. No one had been sure what to expect.

The doll was only able to write a tiny bit. It came to an abrupt halt with both hands just above the desk. Kozaburo removed the paper and showed it to Kumi.

"Well, it's over two hundred years old, so it's not surprising it's not as good as it used to be. Can you make out the letters M, A, R, K? This boy's name is Marko so he almost got his full name down."

"Signing autographs, just like a celebrity!" said Kumi.

"Yeah, I'm sure there've been plenty of celebrities who couldn't write more than their own name," said Kozaburo with a grin. "Apparently he used to be able to write much more, but this is his whole repertoire now. I guess he must have forgotten his alphabet."

"His eyesight's probably failing with age, if he's really two hundred years old."

"That's a good one," said Kozaburo. "Maybe I'm the same way. But at least I've given him a ballpoint pen to use. The pen he used to have was much harder to write with."

"How wonderful! If you don't mind my asking, is it worth a lot of money?" said Hatsue.

"I don't think you can put a price on it. It's something that could easily belong in the British Museum. If you're asking me how much I paid for it, I'm afraid I can't answer that. I wouldn't like to shock you with my total lack of common sense."

"Ah!" said her husband.

"But if we're talking money, this piece here was even more expensive. This is *The Dulcimer Player*."

"Did it come with that desk?"

"It did. The mechanics are hidden inside."

The Dulcimer Player was a noblewoman in a dress with a long skirt, seated in front of what looked like a miniature grand piano. Both were attached to the top of a beautiful mahogany desk. The doll itself wasn't particularly large, probably no more than about thirty centimetres.

Kozaburo must have operated some sort of hidden device, because all of a sudden the noblewoman's hands began to move and music filled the room.

"She's not really playing, is she?" said Sasaki.

"No. That would be too complicated to design. I suppose you could think of this as a very elaborate music box. A music box with a doll attached. It's the same principle."

"But the music isn't that tinkling sound you get with a music box," Sasaki pointed out. "It's much more rounded and mellow than that—there're not only high notes but low ones too."

"Yes, it sounds more like bells to me," said Kumi.

"Probably because the box itself is so large. And unlike the little boy, Marko, she has quite a wide repertoire. About the number of tunes on one side of a long-playing record."

"Really?"

"Yes, it's a masterpiece from the French rococo period. And this one here is German-made from the fifteenth century. It's called *Clock with Nativity Scene.*"

Kozaburo showed them an elaborate metal clock in the shape of a castle. On the top was the Tower of Babel, and the T-shaped pendulum hung from a spherical rendition of the cosmos with the baby Jesus at its centre.

"And this one is *Goddess Hunting Deer.* The deer, the dogs and the horse all move.

"This one is *The Gardener.* Unfortunately, he doesn't sprinkle water from that watering can any more.

"And over here we have a tabletop water fountain made for a nobleman in the fourteenth century. This one doesn't spout water any more either.

"In medieval Europe these kinds of magical playthings were popping up all over the place. These new marvellous mechanisms came about and changed people's view of magic. It was fun to surprise people. For many long years that role was taken by witchcraft and sorcery. And then finally, these kind of automata were invented and took over the role. The worship of machinery, perhaps you could say. There was a trend for people to design machines that were copies of things found in nature. And so witchcraft and machinery for quite a while were synonymous. It was a transition period. Of course these were meant to be toys, something to play with, but that is only obvious when looked at from the standpoint of our modern-day science."

"You don't have any Japanese artefacts," Sasaki pointed out.

"That's right. Nothing besides the Tengu masks."

"What about Japanese *karakuri* dolls? Are they poorly made?"

"Not at all. There's the famous *Tea Server* and all the dolls that were made up in Hida Takayama. The inventor Hiraga Gennai and especially Giemon, the pseudonym of Tanaka Hisashige, were responsible for making the most sophisticated automata. It's just they're impossible to get hold of. The reason is that in Japan they have very few metal parts. Long ago the cogs were made from wood, and the springs from whalebone, and after a hundred years they'd be worn out. Even if you could get hold of one, it'd be a replica, a copy. But even those replicas are almost impossible to get your hands on."

"Are there any blueprints still in existence?"

"Yes, there are a few. Without the blueprints no one could have made those replicas. But they're only drawings, really.

"On the whole, Japanese craftsmen didn't tend to leave blueprints behind. They wanted to keep the art of making *karakuri* dolls their own secret. It wasn't a problem of poor technique at all. I really question this aspect of Japanese people's behaviour. For example, back in the Edo Era, there was apparently a rather splendid *karakuri* doll—a child playing the fife and drum. It could blow on a small flute and play the drum at the same time. Neither the original nor the blueprints have survived. So I've been complaining to the engineers of many countries: if you develop a new product or technology, please record the process in minute detail and leave it for future generations. It should be your legacy to the future."

"What a good story!" said Michio Kanai. "I also heard that *karakuri* craftsmen were looked down on in Japan. Is that true?"

"I think it is. Japanese automata were considered to be nothing more than toys, purely for amusement. Unlike in the West, where they were developed further into clocks and mechanical objects, and eventually computers."

For a while the guests wandered around the room, each taking in the collection at their own speed. Kumi was drawn back to the letter-writing boy and the noblewoman at her dulcimer; Michio Kanai and Kozaburo strolled together, while Hatsue Kanai headed off by herself at a much faster pace and soon found herself in the far corner of the room in front of a single doll. She was suddenly overcome with paralysing terror. The secret fear that she had felt as she entered the room was instantly revived. Or rather the unearthly feelings that had been slowly growing on her since she set foot in this room now all seemed to be embodied in this one antique figure.

Hatsue had always believed she had some kind of psychic powers. Even her husband admitted that she had some sort of special ability. And now, looking at this doll, she felt it giving off some sort of unusual presence.

It was Golem, the life-sized doll. She'd seen it before as a body lying in the snow, and again when it had been put back together in the salon, but this was the first time she had seen its face. It had huge eyes, a moustache and beard, and sat on the floor, just to the right of the Tengu-covered south wall, leaning against the west wall, under the window onto the corridor, both of its legs splayed out in front.

Its body was made of wood; also its hands and feet. Its head was probably wooden too, but although its face was carved in fine detail, and its hands and feet painted, the torso was made of rough, unfinished timber.

Hatsue guessed that the doll had once worn clothes. This seemed to be borne out by the way the arms from the wrists down were realistically depicted, and the feet were made to look as if they were wearing shoes; in other words, the parts of the doll that would not have been covered by clothing. On closer inspection, both hands were curled as if they had been holding a thin stick or pole at some point in the past. Right now, though, they were empty.

The whole of the doll gave off a ghostly aura, but the strongest sensation came from its head, that face. Its expression revealed a more extreme madness than that of the other Western dolls in the room, and the smile on its lips was closer to a sneer. Hatsue could understand a craftsman wanting to make cute dolls, but why would anyone think of making this giant of a man with its creepy smile?

She realized that her husband and Kozaburo were standing behind her. Bolstered by their presence, she leant towards Golem to examine his face more closely.

His skin was a little dark, like an Arab's maybe, she thought. But the tip of his nose gleamed whitish. The paint on his cheeks had started to peel away like the shell of a hard-boiled egg. He looked as if he had suffered severe burns or frostbite. But his smile seemed to say that he wasn't bothered at all by any of this. Apparently, the damage was painless.

"Ah, yes, this is the first time you've met this one," said Kozaburo.

"Yes, er... Go— something wasn't it?"

"Golem."

"Yes, that's it. Why does he have that name?"

"Everyone in the shop where I bought him used to call him that. So I just kept calling him by the same name."

"He has such a hideous face. I was just wondering what he was staring at with that sneer. It's kind of frightening."

"Do you think so?"

"There's nothing cute about him at all. Not like that doll that could sign its name. Why on earth did they make something with a grinning face like this?"

"Maybe the craftsmen those days believed that all dolls had to have a smile on their face?"

Hatsue said nothing.

"When I come here alone at night and see him sitting there in the darkness, grinning to himself, sometimes even I get the creeps."

"He's horrible."

"He has feelings, you know."

"He really does seem to," said Sasaki as he joined the others. "He's always staring at something that human beings can't see. And he has that smile of satisfaction on his face. It makes me want to follow his stare, find what it is he's watching."

"Is that how you feel? It's what I thought one time, right after this room was constructed but was still empty. He was the first thing I brought in, and I sat him down. He was staring at the wall behind me and I was sure there must be a fly or a wasp or something that had landed there. He has such a strong presence. He's a peculiar looking doll, isn't he? As if he's got some secret plot he's hatching, but his expression gives nothing away. I think that's the brilliance of whoever made him."

"Why did they make him so huge?"

"Well, he's human-sized. He was probably attached to a kind of horizontal bar like a gymnast, and part of a circus act originally. Or a kind of amusement park. If you look closely at his hands there are small holes in the palms. I think that's where he was attached to the bar. All of the joints in his legs and arms have the same range of movements as a human body's. I'm guessing he used to do a giant swing on the horizontal bar. His body is just a chunk of wood, though, with no kind of special features."

"It must have been quite a sight—a life-sized doll performing like that."

"Yes, quite a draw, I'm guessing."

"And why is he called Golem? Does it have any meaning?" asked Hatsue.

"Wasn't 'golem' a word for a kind of automaton that appeared in a story or something?" said Sasaki. "He was forced to carry a jar filled with water for eternity. I've got this image that he used to move like a robot... Or maybe that was something else."

"A golem is a man-made creature in Jewish folklore that looks like a human being. Seems the original concept of a golem was mentioned in Psalm 139:16. For generations it was believed that leading figures of the Jewish faith possessed the ability to create golems. There's supposed to be a passage that describes how Abraham, together with Noah's son Shem created a great number of them, and led them into Palestine."

"So golems have been around for thousands of years? Since the Old Testament?"

"That was their origin. But they aren't widely known. I've done a little research into their history. The golem stories came back to life around 1600 in Prague."

"Prague?"

"That's right. At the beginning of the seventeenth century, Prague was a bright centre of learning and culture. It has been referred to as the City of a Thousand Wonders and Countless Terrors. The main areas of study that it was known for were astrology, alchemy and magic; in other words, it became a flourishing centre for mysticism and the occult. The mystics and thinkers and magicians who had proclaimed that they could perform all kinds of miracles were drawn to the city in droves. And that was the environment in which golems were reincarnated. This was because Prague also had the largest Jewish population in Europe—a large ghetto community. A golem was as much part of the Jewish teachings as Yahweh. For their persecuted community, he was a ferocious protector. With superhuman strength he was considered to be invincible. There was no figure of authority, no weapon with the power to defeat him. The Jewish people had been nomadic, had suffered, and been persecuted since ancient times. Yahweh and golems were created out of imagination and hope. Well, that's the way I'm going to explain it. Yahweh is God, but a golem is a kind of man-made being or automaton that only an ascetic holy man or wise man has the power to create. Kabbalah is a branch of the Jewish religion that believes in mysticism and magic, and its practitioners studied how to become great enough to create a golem.

"Then in the twelfth and thirteenth centuries, the character of a golem began to turn up in essays published in France and Germany. A rabbi by the name of Hasid and the French mystic, Gaon, left behind written descriptions of how to form a golem from clay and water. They included precise details of required incantations and rituals. It was the secret formula that since the time of Abraham no one but the highest-ranking holy men had been privy to. And now it had finally been written down. The Golem of Prague was based on the golem of these essays."

"So the practice of creating golems in Prague came from its status as a centre of learning and from it having a Jewish community?"

"That and from the persecution of those Jews. Prague was also a centre of persecution."

"Who were the persecutors?"

"The Christians, obviously. That was why the Jewish community needed golems. They were constantly in danger. The first maker of a golem was believed to be Rabbi Loew ben Bezalel, a leader of the Jewish community. He is said to have taken clay from the banks of the Vltava River that runs through Prague to create his golem. There have been many pieces of folklore and stories about this handed down, and even, much later, a black-and-white silent film, and they all say approximately the same thing: the rabbi created the golem out of clay while reciting some kind of incantation."

"So there's a film about it?"

"Many films in fact. It was from these that the story of the Golem of Prague became well known. The German film-maker, the genius Paul Wegener, made three different films about golems."

"What kind of films?"

"All sorts. I've kind of forgotten which was which, but in one a rabbi brings his home-made golem to the royal court at the request of the king. This rabbi uses magic to create a kind of film about the history of the hardships and perpetual nomadism of the Jewish people, and shows it to the king. But right at that moment the court jester tells an ill-timed joke, and all the nobles and dancing girls fall about laughing. The Jewish God is furious and with a thunderous roar begins to tear down the palace. In exchange for a vow to end the persecution of the Jewish people, the rabbi instructs his golem to save the king's and the courtiers' lives."

"Wow."

"Another film starts the same way with a rabbi creating a golem, but unfortunately, he wasn't a very skilled holy man yet, and he's unable to control the golem he produces. It ends up being way larger than he intended, and its head breaks through the roof of his home. So he tries to destroy it."

"How does he do that?"

"The secret Kabbalah ritual involves writing the word *emet* on the golem's forehead in the Hebrew alphabet. Otherwise it won't move. If you remove one of the letters, equivalent to the 'e' from the word, it spells *met*, which means 'death', and makes the golem return to the earth from which it came."

"Huh."

"In the Jewish faith, words and letters have spiritual power. And so the important ritual and incantation for bringing a golem to life revolved around the letters written on its forehead. The rabbi ordered the golem to tie his shoelaces for him, and when the golem knelt down before the rabbi, he quickly erased the letter 'e' from his forehead. Cracks immediately began to appear in the golem's body and it crumbled to the ground."

"Wow."

"This golem here is made from wood, but if you look very carefully, you'll see very tiny Hebrew lettering on his forehead. It says *emet*."

"Does it? So if this golem starts moving, I should get rid of this letter here?"

"That'd do it."

"I've read a story about golems somewhere before," said Sasaki.

"Oh? What kind of story?"

"The well in some village dries up and the villagers have nothing to drink. They order a golem to go and fetch them a jar of water from a river far away. The loyal, hard-working golem obeys, and the next day, and the day after that, he goes back and forth between the river and the well, refilling the well with the river water. Eventually the well begins to overflow with all the water he's brought, and the village is flooded. The houses begin to disappear under the water but nobody can stop the golem. They don't know the right spell to make him stop. And that's the story."

"Terrifying," said Hatsue Kanai.

"Automata are unable to be flexible, to adapt to circumstances. That's their fatal defect. It comes across to human beings as a kind of insanity, and incites fear. Do you think dolls have the same tendency to inspire fear?" asked Kozaburo.

"That's probably true. Isn't it like the fear of nuclear warfare? Human beings press the button but once the weapon has begun to deploy, there's nothing they can do about it any more. They can beg all they like but their words are useless. The expressionless face of a doll or an automaton is similar."

Kozaburo looked impressed and nodded vigorously.

"You make a good point, Sasaki. Very well put.

"By the way, this doll originally had the perfectly ordinary name of Jack. He's Gymnastic Jack. It just so happened that the old man who ran the second-hand shop in Prague where I bought him told me that on stormy nights he goes out by himself to find wells, rivers or any other place where there's water."

"Ugh!"

"And he said that on the morning following a storm, Jack's mouth is always wet."

"Ha! That's ridiculous!"

"There were always signs that he'd been drinking water. After that, the shopkeeper gave him the nickname Golem."

"It's just a made-up story, right?"

"No, I saw it with my own eyes."

"What?"

"One morning I looked at his face and there were drops of water trickling down from the edge of his lips."

"Honestly?"

"Honest to God. But I thought nothing of it. It was just condensation. It happens a lot, doesn't it—like glass getting misted up—that a face can get beads of sweat on it? It had trickled down and followed the line of his lips."

"Oh, okay."

"Yes, well that's how I managed to explain the phenomenon."

The guests began to laugh, but were stopped by a piercing scream behind them. Everyone jumped in surprise, then turned to see Kumi, her face drained of colour, collapse to her knees. The men rushed to support her.

Kumi was pointing at Golem.

"That's him! That's the man who was looking in my window!"

224

SCENE 10

The Salon

In the end, this new piece of information did very little to advance the investigation. As always, the detectives were overly cautious; for the rest of the day they refused to believe Kumi's story. It wasn't until the morning of the 30th that they reluctantly admitted that it could be true. To them the story was beyond the bounds of common sense, but eventually after struggling with the idea for half a day, they found a loophole that made the outrageous possible—namely, that some person or persons unknown had used the doll to frighten or intimidate Kumi. This was the three detectives' classic modus operandi. But of course the moment they began to consider who, or for what reason, or why Kumi specifically had been the victim, they immediately hit a wall.

They found it difficult to imagine that the perpetrator had been trying to kill Kumi. She hadn't suffered any harm in the days since. In fact, Golem had appeared around the time a completely different victim, Ueda, had been murdered.

It was even less likely that the murderer had thought scaring Kumi would make it easier to kill Ueda. Kumi had reported seeing Golem a full thirty minutes after he had been murdered.

And then there was the sound of a man screaming. What was that? Golem was found in pieces in the snow near Room 10, so had he been taken to pieces after being used to frighten Kumi?

The detectives spent the whole morning on a sofa in the corner of the salon, looking utterly perplexed. Okuma lowered his voice so that the guests at the dinner table couldn't hear.

"I've said it many times, but I've had enough of this bizarre case. I want to step down from the investigating team, get out of here as fast as I can. It feels like they're taking the piss."

Ushikoshi dropped his voice too.

"Same here. Some kind of madman killed Ueda, then hoisted up a doll to terrify the living daylights out of Kumi Aikura, then pulled it apart and tossed it in the snow. I don't want anything to do with the kind of psycho who would do something like that."

"Kumi Aikura's room, number 1, is right above Room 3, the room where the doll was kept," Sergeant Ozaki pointed out.

"True, but there's no window below hers on that side. The south wall of the Tengu Room has no window."

"The sequence of events that you gave just now, Chief Inspector, does it make any sense?"

"How could it? Personally, I've given up on making any sense out of it."

"There is one way to bring together all of the unknown parts of this riddle and make something of it," said Okuma.

"And what's that?"

"It was the doll. It did everything—killed Ueda and Kikuoka too. And then that night after doing Ueda in, it flew up into the air and on a whim decided to peep in through Kumi's window. But it got a bit carried away, and its body fell to bits, causing it to roar in pain."

Okuma's comment was met with complete silence. Although everyone knew it was inappropriate and childish, no one felt like telling him off. On the contrary, they felt that somewhere in the fairy tale there was a grain of truth.

Okuma, for his part, thought better of it, and decided to suggest a more reasonable theory.

"Let's forget about the wild version for now and get back to the problem of Kikuoka's locked room. The knife was stuck into his body, like this, right?"

"That's right," said Ozaki. "The knife entered from diagonally above, on a downward trajectory. So we can assume the killer held it high in the air and then brought it down with force on the victim like this. The knife entered his body at a slight diagonal angle."

"We're thinking the killer stood behind him and stabbed him?"

"Yes, that's what I think. Alternatively, that the victim was bending forward slightly. That could have made it easier for the suspect to stab him."

"What you're saying, Ozaki, is that you think that it's likely the victim wasn't sleeping when he was stabbed, but that he was up and about in his room?"

"Well, I don't have enough evidence to reach a conclusion about that, but yes, I think he was hunched over. If he'd been stabbed while sleeping, he would have to have been lying on his front. And besides, if he had been lying down, it would have been more likely the knife was stuck in at a lower angle."

"If you're standing over someone sleeping like that on their front, you might bring down the arm with the knife from straight above and then it would end up perpendicular to the body."

"Well, I suppose so."

"And if Kikuoka was awake and moving around, there's something I don't understand," said Ushikoshi. "At around 10.30, or maybe more like 10.25, Kozaburo Hamamoto knocked on the door of Room 14. I know he did because I was right there with him. It was a relatively gentle knock, but there was no response from Kikuoka. If he'd still been awake he would have answered. His time of death was about thirty minutes after that, so he couldn't already have been dead at that point. He must have been asleep.

"But then, if what you say is right, thirty minutes later the victim woke up again and let his murderer into the room. So how did the killer manage to wake Kikuoka? Was there any different way of waking him from the one that Kozaburo Hamamoto tried? All he could have done was to knock on the door. There's really no other way. That night, Inspector Okuma was sleeping in the room above, and Haruo Kajiwara next door. The killer couldn't have shouted or made any other kind of noise. So how did he manage to wake Kikuoka? Or perhaps Kikuoka was just pretending to be asleep when Hamamoto knocked."

"Okay, then, so d'you still think the killer stuck a stick though that air vent?" said Okuma.

Perhaps it was the snide tone, but Ushikoshi pulled a face. He was fed up with all the puzzles.

"Hey, if Ozaki's right with his theory that the victim was stabbed when he was standing upright, can't we work out the suspect's height from the angle of the knife?" said Okuma.

"That kind of thing is surprisingly difficult. It doesn't work like it does in mystery novels. Like we said before, the victim might have been bending down. Still, it could be said that the knife is in a fairly high position. I think we could probably rule out a very short person. That's about as much as we can say at this point. In which case, we can probably eliminate the women—except for Eiko who's over 170 centimetres tall."

"There goes the dwarf theory."

"What the hell?" snapped Ushikoshi.

In an instant, the atmosphere between the guardians of the peace turned threatening.

"Well, anyway," said Ozaki hurriedly, in an attempt to break the tension, "the bigger problem is that the knife was stuck in the right side of his back."

"Because the heart isn't on the right," continued Ushikoshi. "Maybe the killer was in a hurry?"

"Maybe he didn't feel like stabbing him in the heart," said Okuma. "You never know with folks."

"Actually, I was talking about whether he was right- or left-handed."

But no matter how much Ozaki tried to revive the discussion, the other two had completely clammed up.

Abruptly, Ushikoshi got up from the sofa.

"I've had enough! I give up! I just don't get it. There'll probably be another crime committed by the time we finish talking about it. I'm going back to the station and I'm going to ask Tokyo for help. You okay with that? Any objections? At this point we're just going to have to swallow our pride."

Everyone fell silent as Ushikoshi briskly marched out of the salon.

"I s'pose it always was too much for us to handle alone, this confounded case," said Okuma.

Ozaki was the only one who looked disappointed.

The three detectives hadn't exactly been incompetent, but their years of experience were proving useless in solving this particular case.

Outside, not a single snowflake fluttered by the window. It was a gloomy, heavy morning. The rest of the residents of the mansion sat at a distance from the three police officers in the corner, holding their own private discussion. Sasaki muttered something.

"However you look at it, the detectives are the criminals here."

It was the afternoon when Ushikoshi returned to the Ice Floe Mansion.

"How did it go? Ozaki asked.

"They were quite disapproving, to tell the truth."

"What?"

"I mean they really want us to forget about saving face and agree to accept help in doing everything we can to solve this. Superintendent Nakamura, who I met when I was in Tokyo for the Yuzo Akawata case, is someone I can get along with. I explained our case in great detail and he agreed it was a very strange one, and if the killer really was one of the people here in the house, then there was no need to be in too much of a hurry.

"And I think he's got a point. If we can eventually work out who the killer is, then that's enough. I think we have to acknowledge our failings up to now, and realize that the most important thing at this moment is to make absolutely sure that no more murders are committed."

"Right."

"Anyway, I don't know about the city, but this kind of case never happens out here in the countryside. Even if it's rare, at least they're a little more used to weird stuff like this up in Tokyo."

"But, Chief, this does reflect on our standing. We really shouldn't give up too easily. We'll manage to sort it out some-how. Isn't this admitting that we are powerless?"

"Yes, it is. But have you managed to solve it yet, Ozaki?"

"Well, no, but—"

"Anyway, if Tokyo sends someone to help us, then we'll still be working the case, but staying in the background. Surely it's good to get help? It's all about protecting people's lives. That takes priority over our reputation."

"But are there likely to be any more murders?"

"As we haven't a clue about the motive, I can't answer that for sure. But I think there will be."

"You do?"

"And when I said that to Tokyo, they said together we could all work out the best way to deal with it. They said they had an idea about it."

"What do they have in mind?"

"I'm not sure, but they said they'd get in touch later."

"And how are they going to do that?"

"By telegram, apparently."

"Ugh. Now that gives me a very bad feeling. I can't help picturing some kind of Sherlock Holmes clone turning up with a pipe in his mouth. I can't stand that type."

"Ha ha. If there'd been a detective as famous as that in Tokyo, I'd have definitely requested his presence up here. If there was anyone remotely like that…"

ACT THREE

Perhaps it is the very simplicity of the thing which puts you at fault.

C. AUGUSTE DUPIN,
"The Purloined Letter", by Edgar Allan Poe

SCENE 1

The Salon

"Telegram!"

Hearing the voice in the entrance hall, Eiko got to her feet. Chief Inspector Ushikoshi immediately followed her out. He soon returned, a sheet of paper in his hand, pulled up a chair next to Sergeant Ozaki and showed him the telegram.

"You gonna let me take a look?" said Okuma moodily. Ozaki decided to read it out loud.

"This kind of… er… monstrous crime… requires the right kind of detective… no better in the whole of Japan… already on a flight… His name is Mita… um… how do you read this, Mitarai? What the hell? Shit! They really are sending some jumped-up Sherlock Holmes wannabe!"

"What? Is this Mita-whatsit person from Tokyo HQ?" asked Okuma.

Ozaki knew exactly who Mitarai was.

"He's a fortune teller."

Ushikoshi and Okuma sat there blinking in silence for a good few moments. Then Ushikoshi found his voice, albeit one of someone being choked.

"Is this some kind of joke? We're not so desperate that we need to rely on a fortune teller or a psychic or something."

Okuma began to laugh.

"Chief Inspector, that's not much of a friend you have there in Tokyo! He's taking the piss out of us. But if you think about it, this so-called fortune teller with his bunch of divining sticks

235

might guess who the murderer is and earn quite a bit out of it. Our honour will be saved, and the Tokyo lot will seem as if they tried to help. It's a good move for everybody. The best possible way. But they'd have been better off sending us a dog than some fortune teller. A police dog with a good nose would be better any day than a wizened old codger."

"But Superintendent Nakamura isn't so irresponsible... Ozaki, you know this Mitarai?" said Ushikoshi.

"Have you heard of the Umezawa family massacre?"

"Of course. It was a famous case."

"That big murder that happened back when we were kids?" Okuma asked Ushikoshi. "The one that was finally solved three or four years back?"

"Yes, that's the one."

"Well, one theory has it that Mitarai was the one who solved it," said Ozaki.

"Wasn't it some detective from HQ who solved it? At least that's what I heard."

"Yes, well, that's probably what really happened. But the fortune teller has been going around bragging that he's the one who did it."

"There are plenty of old cranks like that," said Okuma. "You can work your arse off solving a crime and the criminal turns out to be the same one they guessed, and they start thinking that they're some kind of oracle."

"No, this Mitarai isn't an old guy. He's still quite young. A real arrogant pain in the neck, by all accounts."

"There must have been some sort of misunderstanding with Nakamura..." sighed Ushikoshi. "I'm not looking forward to this meeting at all."

*

They would probably have been even more anxious if they had known what the eccentric Kiyoshi Mitarai was planning for that evening. Chief Inspector Saburo Ushikoshi would have done a lot more than sigh.

Kiyoshi and I weren't going to be arriving at the Ice Floe Mansion until late, so we took dinner at a little local eatery before heading up there. It wasn't snowing, but the whole landscape was wrapped in a kind of mist.

We were pretty sure that as far as the occupants of the Ice Floe Mansion were concerned (and especially the police detectives), we were uninvited guests, and we were soon given the opportunity to test that theory. Eiko and the three detectives came to answer the door, but no one thanked us for coming all that way to the far north, and we realized we weren't going to be welcomed with open arms. But the detectives' preconceived idea of Kiyoshi was nothing like the actual man. His friendly smile always managed to win people over— at first.

The detectives were confused as to how to deal with us so they announced to the eleven residents of the Ice Floe Mansion that we had come all the way from Tokyo to aid the investigation, and proceeded to introduce each of the residents to us. Some of them smiled in welcome, others looked very serious, and under their gaze I felt like a magician who had been hired to entertain the company. I wondered if they were waiting for me to produce a white handkerchief and start performing tricks.

But Kiyoshi wasn't so self-effacing. The moment Chief Inspector Ushikoshi said, "This is Mr Mitarai", he immediately began to address the assembled guests as if he were some kind of VIP.

"Good evening, everybody! So sorry to have kept you waiting. I'm Kiyoshi Mitarai. Consider the power of the human race… When human power fails it falls to the dolls, and then the dolls rise up instead. That is the theory of a lever or a seesaw. Jumping Jack, a one-act marionette. What a painful vision! I came all the way to this northern land to kneel and pay my respects before he is laid to rest."

As Kiyoshi gave his cryptic speech, the affable expressions on the faces of the three detectives began to cloud over, and the meagre amount of goodwill they had harboured for him immediately melted away.

"The new year is almost upon us, ladies and gentlemen. Right now in the capital it is the season of the bargain sale. As we speak, ladies clutching paper carrier bags are fighting tooth and nail. But up here it is another world. Quiet. But how unfortunate! By the time the 4th of January rolls around, everyone will have to head back to the front line. But at least you'll all be taking a great tale back home with you; the story of how I solved the case of the last few days will be quite an unusual one, I believe.

"But two dead bodies are surely enough. Fear not. Now that I have arrived, not a single one of you here will be joining the ranks of cold corpses. And why, you ask? Because I have already worked out who the murderer is!"

There was quite a commotion in the room. Even I, standing up there with Kiyoshi, was taken by surprise. Needless to say, the detectives too. But they kept silent.

"Who is it, then?" called Sasaki from the audience.

"Well, it goes without saying, doesn't it?"

Everyone present held their breath.

"The one known as Golem!"

There were snorts and snickers around the audience as they realized it was a joke, but no one looked quite as relieved as the three detectives.

"After partaking of a cup of hot tea to warm myself up after trudging here through the snow, I hope to climb the stairs and make his acquaintance."

At this point the police officers frowned.

"But there's no need to hurry. I don't imagine he's going to try to escape."

Well, that's true, I overheard Togai saying to Eiko. Other people were murmuring things like, *What the hell's this? A comedy duo?*

"Everyone here is connected to this fascinating case. I think you've already been grilled for any knowledge or information. But if any of you believes that the doll just sits there all year round in Room 3 like a wooden dummy, then I think you'd better get yourself a new pair of glasses. That's no mere lump of wood. He's a two-hundred-year-old European. He's passed through two hundred years of history and is now resident in this very house. You should all feel very honoured and privileged. A two-hundred-year-old Czech. He's a miracle. He braves blizzards to dance in the sky, peers in through glass windows, drives knives into people's hearts, right under our very noses as easily as we reach for our teacups now. By the Jewish mystical tradition of Kabbalah, he has awoken from a thousand years of slumber and has been gifted with life in order to perform in this one act. This play in which he has been cast in the leading role.

"The brilliance of the dancing doll. Only on a stormy night does he arise from his dark throne, his puppet strings gleaming white against the jet-black sky, and dance the dance of a thousand years ago. The dance of the dead. What a vivid moment! That first dead body, he was bewitched too, dancing on a string like a marionette.

"History repeats itself. Things are the same as they were a thousand years ago. Time is stuck like a broken-down bus. Without doubt, that moment he was waiting for was over in the blink of an eye.

"Progress is an illusion. We just started running faster. This morning I was in Ginza, and now I'm shivering here at the northern tip of Japan. But can we use this extra time freely? No, we most certainly cannot."

Kiyoshi seemed intoxicated by his own words, but eventually the snorts of derision from the audience began to turn into full-on laughter. The detectives, for their part, were itching to put an end to this ludicrous performance.

"Do machines really make life easier? I think we know the truth of that. By comparison, the false advertising of the real estate agent—*three minutes from the station, thirty minutes from the city centre, an ideal location with lots of green space*—is far more trustworthy. We should never feel a sense of superiority towards our creations. We get machines to do our everyday chores; it also becomes possible to reach Hokkaido from Tokyo in just one hour. I can be asked one morning to come up to Hokkaido the same night even though I had other work to do. It used to take three days to get to Hokkaido but these days I have become much busier. There's no time any more even to read a book. What a swindle! Before long policemen are going to be able to purchase their criminals from vending machines. But at the same time, those criminals will be able to drop in their own coins and buy themselves a corpse—"

"Mr Mitarai?"

The spiel was finally interrupted by Ushikoshi.

"I think that's enough for preliminary greetings. If you've nothing more specific to say, it seems the tea is ready."

"Ah, is it? Then I must introduce my companion here. This is my friend, Kazumi Ishioka."

Just the simplest of introductions for me.

The Tengu Room

After tea the indefatigable Kiyoshi Mitarai asked, "So where's Golem?"

"Do you intend to arrest him?" asked Ushikoshi.

"No, there's no need for that this evening," replied Kiyoshi, in complete earnest. "I just want to examine whether or not he's the homicidal maniac that I imagine."

"Do you really?" said Okuma, who seemed to be very impressed.

"Then please allow me to show you the way," said Kozaburo Hamamoto, getting to his feet.

When Kozaburo opened the door to the Tengu Room, we were greeted by the giant clown. This particular doll was mounted on a stand, so there was no way it could move.

"Whoa! This is the clown from *Sleuth*!" said Kiyoshi as soon as he saw it.

"Oh, you've seen that film?" said Kozaburo, clearly delighted.

"Three times. I think the critics were right about it being a B-movie, but I liked it."

"It's one of my favourites. I saw the play in England too. I think it's well done. That's partly where my interest in collecting all this junk came from. It was so colourful, and the music of Cole Porter was a perfect match. I'm so glad to know you're familiar with that film."

"Does this clown laugh and clap its hands like the one in the film?"

"Unfortunately, to borrow your words, it's just a wooden dummy. I searched all over Europe, but I couldn't find one like that. I think it must have been constructed especially for the film. Or perhaps it was just a trick of the camera."

"That's a pity… So, where is he?"

Without waiting for a reply, Kiyoshi dashed off farther into the room. Kozaburo set off after him and pointed to the corner.

"There he is… Oh, he… Well, that's shocking."

Kiyoshi's loud voice surprised everyone. (Most of the people from the salon had followed us up to Room 3.)

"That's no good at all. No you can't do that. He's naked. That can't be permitted, Mr Hamamoto!"

Kiyoshi was getting quite worked up.

"Why's that?"

"This doll is the very embodiment of warped hatred. And it's had two hundred years to accumulate. But no—it's more. He's the very incarnation of all the grudges held by the Jewish people as they've suffered persecution after persecution. To display him naked like this is an insult, humiliation. You can't do this. It's extremely dangerous. This is the cause of every tragedy that has ever occurred in this house. You have to do something. Mr Hamamoto, I can hardly believe that a man of your knowledge can have overlooked something like this!"

"B-but what can I do?"

Mr Hamamoto looked at a complete loss.

"Obviously, you have to put clothes on him. Kazumi! What about those jeans and that jacket you were saying you hardly ever wear any more? Go and fetch them!"

"Kiyoshi!"

I'd had enough of this bad joke, and was desperate to make him stop.

"I know you've got an old sweater in your bag too. Bring that too."

I wanted to try and warn him to stop, and opened my mouth to say something, but he urged me again to hurry. Reluctantly, I made my way back to the salon.

When I returned with the clothes, he gleefully dressed the doll in the jeans and the sweater. By the time he put the jeans jacket over the top, he was humming a cheerful tune. By contrast, the graduates of the police academy looked as if they were sucking on lemons as they watched my friend at work. With admirable patience, they managed not to utter a word.

"So is he the murderer?"

It was Sasaki who addressed Kiyoshi.

"No doubt about it. He's a brute."

Kiyoshi was about done dressing Golem at this point. With clothes, the doll was even creepier looking. It looked as if some kind of vagrant had sneaked into the house.

"So you're telling me," said Kozaburo, "that this doll murdered two people because I left it lying here naked?"

"We'll be lucky if we end up with only two dead," said Kiyoshi. Then he quickly added, "This won't do. There's something missing."

He folded his arms.

"He's got a jacket and a sweater, but I still don't think it's enough... A hat! He needs a hat. He needs to cover that head. It really shouldn't be left exposed. But I didn't bring a hat with me... Has anyone here got a hat? Any kind'll be fine. I'd like to borrow one. I promise I'll return it."

Kiyoshi looked over at the assembled guests. It was the chef, Haruo Kajiwara, who responded.

"Er... I've got one," he said haltingly. "It's a ten-gallon cowboy hat. Like you see in Westerns."

"A cowboy hat!?"

Kiyoshi practically screamed it. The guests had absolutely no idea what had set off the lunatic this time. They waited on tenterhooks for his next words.

"There's nothing better to protect us from violence. It's like a blessing from the gods. Quick! Go fetch it!"

"Okay, then..."

Shaking his head in wonder, Kajiwara left the room and headed down the stairs. A short while later he returned with the cowboy hat.

Kiyoshi positively radiated joy from head to toe. Taking the hat, he placed it with a flourish on the doll's head.

"Perfect! Now we'll be safe. Thank you, Mr Kajiwara. You have done great service to this case. I can't imagine a better hat than this for the job."

Kiyoshi was rubbing his hands together in glee, but to me Golem looked more ghoulish than ever. Now it looked as if a real person were sitting there on the floor.

There was still a piece of string tied around his wrist. Kiyoshi examined it, announced that they ought to remove it, and immediately snapped it off. I overheard Chief Inspector Ushikoshi mutter "Stop" but it was too late.

Everyone returned to the salon and Kiyoshi chatted with Kozaburo and the rest of the guests. He seemed to get along best with Sasaki, and they talked together late into the night on the topic of mental disorders. Viewed from afar, the two men seemed to be having a friendly heart-to-heart, but I couldn't help feeling that the medical student was interested in Kiyoshi more as a patient than a conversation partner. Still, the discussion between the psychiatrist and his patient was very calm.

The room allocated to Kiyoshi and me was the room in which Kazuya Ueda had been murdered—Room 10. I felt this made it very clear how our female host felt about us. Kohei Hayakawa was told to bring us an extra folding bed (the one in Room 10 was only a single). There was no toilet or bathroom in that room, so I used the shower in the detectives' room to try to relax after the long day's journey.

Still, to sleep in a room where a murder had been committed was a uniquely valuable experience. It wasn't something you could get on your average sightseeing tour.

I was still trying to get to sleep in that uncomfortable bed when Kiyoshi came in, just after midnight.

SCENE 3

Room 15, The Detectives' Bedroom

"What kind of mental hospital did that one escape from?"

The young Sergeant Ozaki was unable to control his anger any longer.

"I mean, what could have possessed them to send that complete idiot for us to babysit?"

That night, the detectives had assembled in Room 15. Constable Anan was there too.

"Never mind, Ozaki," said Ushikoshi soothingly. "The man is definitely not normal, but that is who Superintendent Nakamura at Tokyo HQ trusted enough to send. Let's take this opportunity to observe his skills a while."

"His skills? We've seen them already. The ability to put a pair of trousers on a doll!"

"Our job'd be a whole lot easier if we could catch a suspect by dressing up a doll," Okuma remarked.

"I've never seen such a complete and utter moron in my whole life," said Ozaki. "Letting that one loose on this case is not going to help the investigation one iota. He's going to screw the whole thing up."

"But you can't claim that putting trousers on the doll has hindered the investigation in any way, can you?"

"Right now he is so pleased with himself playing around with that doll that if there's another murder, he'll probably start spraying ketchup on the body."

Ushikoshi sat there lost in thought. Privately he also believed that Mitarai was capable of doing something that crazy.

"Anan, what do you think about that man?" he asked.

"Hmm... I don't really..."

"Have you given up billiards already?" said Ozaki.

"That other man he brought with him, what's he up to right now?"

"Taking a shower in Room 12."

"He seems like a normal bloke."

"He's some kind of chaperon for the lunatic, I reckon."

"Anyway, don't you think we should probably ask them to leave?" said Okuma.

"Yes. But let's wait and see how it goes for now. If they start getting in the way of our work, I'll ask them."

"An old man with divining sticks would have been a whole lot better than this. With his bad back he'd just have been forced to sit there quietly. It's hard to handle someone so young. That was like some kind of rain dance he was doing—taking that doll and performing his little psychic dance to proclaim it the killer. Next he's going to try and get us to light the fire for him to dance around."

SCENE 4
The Salon

The next morning was relatively clear and sunny. There was the sound of hammering coming from somewhere. The three detectives were back in their sofa cluster.

"What's that hammering noise?"

"The two women guests asked to have the ventilation holes in their rooms blocked up. They said they made them too nervous, so Togai and Sasaki are playing the knights in shining armour with hammers. Sasaki said he was going to block up the one in his own room while he was at it."

"Well, I agree it would make you feel safer. But that damned hammering is driving me crazy. Not exactly a New Year's Eve atmosphere."

"It's frantic around here."

But at that moment an even more frantic man came rushing in. Kiyoshi Mitarai was babbling something that sounded vaguely like a children's comic-book character.

"Mr Banana!"

An uncomfortable silence fell over the salon, as nobody quite knew how to respond. Kiyoshi looked puzzled, but then the young police constable stood up, sensing that the man might be trying to say his name. I was impressed that he could work that out.

"The name's Anan..."

"Sorry. Could you tell me the way to Wakkanai Police Station?"

"Yes, of course."

Kiyoshi was the kind of man who always recalled someone's date of birth, but never really made an effort to learn anyone's name. He just used whatever name occurred to him at the time. And then, he would just keep using that made-up name forever.

Right now, he rushed out of the salon again and was immediately replaced by the arrival of Kozaburo Hamamoto, smoking his pipe. He took a seat next to Inspector Okuma.

"Where's our famous investigator off to?" Ushikoshi asked him.

"He's a bit strange, that one, isn't he?"

"He's *extremely* strange. A complete nut job."

"He's removed Golem's head and said he wants to take it back to forensics for another look. He says there's something suspicious about it."

"Not again!"

"At this rate he'll be removing all our heads," said Okuma.

"We'd be better off with a department store security guard."

"I've got no intention of going down along with that moron," said Ozaki curtly.

"Looks like we're about to get the psychic dance that you predicted. When he gets back it's all going to get started."

"I'll get ready to light the fire."

"This is not the time to be making jokes," said Ozaki. He turned to Kozaburo Hamamoto, a serious expression on his face. "Did he give a reason for taking Golem's head off?"

"Not really…"

"I don't imagine there's any reason at all for it."

"It'll get in the way when he's dancing," Okuma threw in.

"Personally," said Kozaburo, "I'm not particularly thrilled that he's taken the head off again. Well, I suppose he can if he wants. Maybe he's looking for fingerprints?"

"Does he even have the wits to think of something like that?" said Okuma.

It felt a little like the pot calling the kettle black.

"We checked thoroughly for fingerprints already," said Ushikoshi.

"And what did you find?" Kozaburo asked.

"Nowadays, no criminal with any kind of knowledge about police investigative techniques leaves anything like a fingerprint behind. People watch TV programmes. And if the criminal is one of the people in this house, it'll be difficult to prove anything. It'd be perfectly normal for any of them to touch anything in the house."

"I suppose so."

It was well into the afternoon before Kiyoshi returned to the Ice Floe Mansion. His mood was buoyant as usual as he crossed the salon to sit by me.

"The forensic pathologist gave me a lift back. He said he was on his way here anyway."

"Really?"

"So I asked him to drop in and have a cup of tea."

Kiyoshi spoke as if he'd invited someone over to his own home. There was indeed a man in a white coat standing by the front door. Kiyoshi raised his voice.

"Mr Banana! Would you get Mr Kajiwara for me?"

For whatever reason, Kiyoshi had happened to remember Kajiwara's name correctly. Constable Anan, who was leaning on the wall by the kitchen, made no protest and simply disappeared to fetch Kajiwara. He'd apparently decided to answer to his new name.

As they sipped their tea, the grandfather clock in the

salon struck three. I can specify that the people in the room right then were Kiyoshi and myself, the three detectives with Constable Anan, Kozaburo Hamamoto, Mr and Mrs Kanai, Yoshihiko Hamamoto, Mr and Mrs Hayakawa. And I caught glimpses of Kajiwara too in the kitchen. In other words, the people who weren't with us in the salon were Eiko, Kumi, Togai and Sasaki—those four. The forensic pathologist, Dr Sano, was also with us at that time.

Suddenly we heard a howl, a man's voice, from somewhere far away. It was more than just a scream. I'd have described it as the cry someone would make when they came face to face with unimaginable horror.

Kiyoshi kicked his chair backwards, leapt to his feet and ran in the direction of Room 12. Reflexively, I glanced up at the grandfather clock. It wasn't even five past three: 3.04 and 30 seconds.

The three policemen rushed out shouting. They hesitated, not really knowing where they were running to, and it was annoying having to chase after Kiyoshi, so only Ushikoshi and Anan actually followed him. Ozaki and Okuma went a different way.

Everyone assumed the howl had come from either Togai or Sasaki, as they were the only men missing—the other two not present being women. But it was impossible to know which one. However, Kiyoshi had no doubt. He headed straight for Room 13 and banged on the door.

"Sasaki! Sasaki!"

He pulled out a handkerchief and turned the doorknob. But it kept sticking.

"It's locked! Mr Hamamoto, is there a spare key?"

"Kohei, quickly, go and get Eiko! She's got the spare."

Hayakawa rushed off.

"Okay, get out of the way!"

Ozaki had just arrived. He too began to bang on the door. But the result was the same.

"Should I break it down?"

"No, let's wait for the spare key," said Ushikoshi as Eiko came running. "Is this it? Let me have it."

He put the key in the lock and turned it. There was the click of a lock releasing, but when Ozaki tried to turn the knob, the door still refused to open.

"Oh, the other lock is on," said Kozaburo.

Besides the push-button lock in the centre of the doorknob, each room had a second oval-shaped lock underneath, which, if you turned it 180 degrees, would send a bar bolt across. This bolt could only be turned from inside the room.

"Break it."

At Ushikoshi's command, Ozaki and Anan threw their shoulders against the door. After a few tries, it broke.

Sasaki was lying face up in the middle of the room. On the table there was a medical textbook that he'd apparently been reading. The room looked completely undisturbed.

Straight through Sasaki's sweater, right at the level of his heart, was a hunting knife, identical to the ones used in the previous two murders, with the same white string trailing from the handle. But the biggest difference from the previous cases was that Sasaki's chest was occasionally rising and falling.

"He's still alive!" cried Kiyoshi.

Sasaki's face was drained of colour, but his eyelids seemed to be ever so slightly open.

Ozaki turned his head 360 degrees, surveying every inch of the room. I did the same and, simultaneously, we noticed on

253

the wall something which shed light on the strange nature of these serial killings. There was a small piece of paper attached with a pin. (See Fig. 8.)

"What did you see? Did you see something? Answer me!" shouted Ozaki, clutching Sasaki by the wrist. Kiyoshi put out a hand to stop him.

"Mr Banana, there's a stretcher in the van outside. Bring it here!"

"What the hell?"

Ozaki was immediately riled up.

"How dare you think that we take orders from a pain in the arse like you? Shut up, you freak, and get out of our way! Leave this to the experts."

"Of course I intend to leave it to the experts. We'll get out of your way. Doctor Sano, if you please."

The white-coated Dr Sano pushed his way through the crowd.

"It's dangerous for him to try to talk right now," he said to Ozaki. "Please don't speak to him."

The expert had given his opinion. And right then, just as Kiyoshi had instructed, the stretcher arrived. Dr Sano and Kiyoshi quickly lifted Sasaki onto it.

There was not a lot of blood, in fact Sasaki was hardly bleeding at all. But just as Dr Sano and Constable Anan picked up the stretcher to leave the room, a very unexpected thing happened. Eiko Hamamoto burst into tears and clung to the stretcher.

"Sasaki! Don't die!"

Togai, who had materialized out of nowhere, watched in grim silence.

Ozaki carefully removed the pinned scrap of paper from the wall. It looked to be something the killer had left behind.

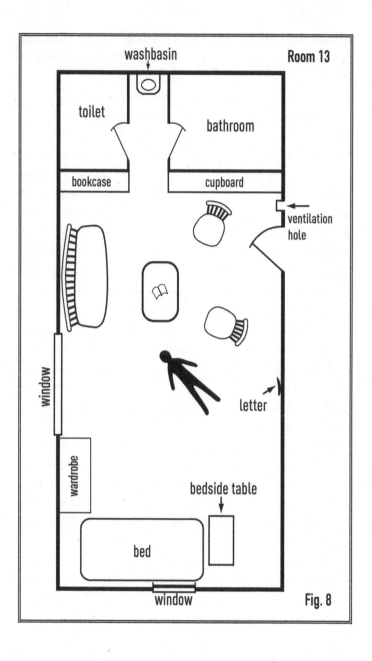

washbasin

Room 13

toilet

bathroom

bookcase

cupboard

ventilation hole

window

letter

wardrobe

bedside table

bed

window

Fig. 8

He didn't immediately tell us what was written on the paper, but he showed it to us later. In very simple lettering, it read as follows:

> *I will have revenge on Kozaburo Hamamoto. Very soon you will lose the most precious thing—your life.*

Ozaki had regained his habitual professional composure; it seemed that coming face to face with someone on the verge of death hadn't fazed him much at all. He quickly ascertained that it was not only the door of Room 13 that had been completely locked, but both of the windows had been too, and the glass was entirely intact. He immediately and thoroughly checked the built-in wardrobe and cupboard, under the bed, and the bathroom for anyone hiding. He didn't find anyone or anything that shouldn't have been there.

But the thing I really should point out here is that this time the one previous (excuse my pun) break in the case, the twenty-centimetre-square ventilation hole in the wall, was completely blocked by a thick piece of plywood. This time it really was the perfect locked room. The door frame was entirely intact, and there was no gap or crack to be seen.

What's more, the door had been broken down by two of the police officers themselves, and they had been the first to set foot in the room. And this had been witnessed by a large crowd of onlookers. There had been no time for anyone to have tried some sort of trick. Our only hope was that Sasaki himself had seen something.

Around an hour later, we were all gathered in the salon when the news came that Sasaki had passed away. The time of death was after three in the afternoon, and the cause was, of course, the knife in his chest.

"Where were you around 3 o'clock, Mr Togai?"

Chief Inspector Ushikoshi had called Togai over to the corner of the room and was questioning him in a low voice.

"I'd gone for a walk. The weather wasn't too bad and I needed space to think."

"Is there anyone who can back up that story?"

"I'm afraid not."

"No surprise. I don't like to put it this way, but you can't say you didn't have a motive to kill Sasaki."

"That's horrible! His death is more of a shock to me than anyone else."

Both Eiko and Kumi insisted that they had been alone in their separate rooms. Their testimony was nothing out of the ordinary, but the evidence given next by Haruo Kajiwara was enough to make the detectives' own hearts stop.

"I never thought it was important until now, so I never mentioned it. It's nothing to do with Mr Sasaki's murder, but the night that Mr Kikuoka was killed I was leaning on the door frame in the doorway of the kitchen when I heard a different noise mixed in with the sound of the snowstorm—a kind of rustling noise. A bit like a snake slithering. But I definitely heard it."

"A snake!"

The detectives almost jumped out of their skins.

"What time was that?"

"Well, I guess it must have been around 11."

"Right when he was killed."

"Did anyone else hear it?"

"I asked Kohei and Chikako but they said they didn't hear it. I thought I must have been hearing things, so I didn't say anything. I'm really sorry."

"Tell us more about the sound."

"I don't know. It's difficult to explain… Sort of sniff, sniff, like a woman sobbing… But very faint. I didn't hear it when Sasaki died."

"A woman sobbing?!"

The detectives exchanged glances. This sounded like some sort of ghost story.

"And when Ueda was killed?"

"I didn't hear anything. I'm sorry."

"So you only heard it with Kikuoka?"

"Yes, that's right."

The police officers individually questioned every other person about the mysterious sound, but nobody besides Kajiwara had heard it.

"What do you reckon? Do you think it's real?" Okuma asked the other two. "I've had enough of all this crap. It's driving me crazy. Blasted if I can work it out."

"I'm at my wits' end too."

"I'm beginning to believe there's some sort of evil demon living in this place. Or this house itself is the demon. It's like the place has a mind of its own and has decided to start murdering people. Especially with the murder of Sasaki—that's not the work of a human. If we're looking for a killer, then it's this house!"

"Or someone is managing to play the most extraordinary trick ever," said Ozaki. "Like some kind of mechanical thing-amajig that somehow pops up in the rooms, or a flying knife, or… something in the rooms that somehow switches around."

"Well, if it's any of those things, then the suspect can't be one of the guests. It has to be one of the hosts," muttered Ushikoshi.

Okuma continued the thought.

"But it isn't one of them. If you ask me, out of the eleven of them, it has to be Aikura. I reckon it's a load of crap that story about the doll looking through her window. No way any of that happened. Impossible. It has to be a made-up story. Those kind of women—total liars. And she doesn't have an alibi for any of the murders."

"But Inspector, if she's the killer then there's something that doesn't add up," said Ozaki. That Kumi woman couldn't have seen the face of the Golem doll before the 29th of December when she went to Room 3. But in her testimony from the night of the first murder, she described his face perfectly."

Okuma groaned.

"Well, then, there's no way our suspect is any of that lot there. They're hiding something. Very cleverly. Let's take apart the walls and ceilings. Especially the ones in Room 13 and 14. That's all that's left. Don't you agree, Chief Inspector Ushikoshi?"

"I think so. Tomorrow's New Year's Day and I hesitate to do it, but I don't think the suspect is going to take the day off just because of that. No, I think we're going to have to do it."

At that moment Kiyoshi happened to walk by. Okuma called out to him.

"So what went wrong, Mr Fortune Teller? Didn't you say that now you were here there'd be no more dead bodies?"

Kiyoshi showed no reaction, but he was clearly out of sorts too.

SCENE 5

The Library

The morning of the 1st of January 1984 saw Kiyoshi and myself holed up together in the library. Kiyoshi had completely lost face with Sasaki's murder and had been in very low spirits ever since. He refused to answer whenever I spoke. He sat there pressing his fingers together in various triangular and square shapes, and muttering under his breath.

From my seat in the far corner of the library, I had a view of the jostling ice floes on the northern sea. I sat contemplating them for quite a while until the constant racket of hammers and chisels from the downstairs floor finally succeeded in disturbing my reverie.

"*Omedeto!*" I said to Kiyoshi.

"Yeah," he replied, distracted.

"I'm congratulating you," I said again.

He finally looked up at me.

"For what?" he said with obvious irritation.

"It's what you say to one another on New Year's Day. Today is the first day of 1984."

He groaned.

"You seem very angry. I suppose it's to be expected, after all that grandstanding you did… But why aren't you down there checking how the police are getting on with ripping out the walls and ceilings of Room 13 and 14?"

Kiyoshi laughed scornfully.

"Do you think they're going to find anything? Hidden passageways, secret rooms?" I asked.

"I think I can place a bet on it," he responded finally. "Tonight the police'll be sitting there on that sofa in the salon completely exhausted, and with nothing but blisters on their hands to show for it. Especially that young one—Ozaki—I'll bet he's putting the most effort into the search right now. Tonight he'll actually be quiet for once. I can't wait."

"Room 13 and 14 don't have any hidden tricks, then?"

"Of course not."

I tried to work out how he could be so sure, but nothing came to mind. In the end I asked another question.

"You really know just about everything about everything, don't you?"

To which my friend just stared up at the ceiling and reprised his mutterings. It was very strange.

"Are you saying you've solved the whole thing?"

"Far from it. I'm very confused right now."

His voice sounded hoarse.

"Do you at least have an idea what direction you should be looking?"

Kiyoshi turned and looked very seriously into my eyes.

"Well, that's the problem, isn't it?"

I felt strangely uneasy, and then a little fearful. Eventually, I decided I should man up a little.

"Do you think I should go and talk to them? Perhaps I could be of help."

"No point. Better solve it than talk about it... But that's too difficult. There's an up and down staircase... So which one would he be standing on?... That's the problem. There may never be an answer. I'm going to be forced to gamble..."

261

"What are you talking about?"

Kiyoshi tended to ramble this way when he was close to solving a case. It often freaked people out. To me it always sounded as if he were just one step short of being completely off his rocker.

"Never mind," I said. "Right, now I've got a question for you. Why do you think Kazuya Ueda's body was arranged the way it was? Like he was dancing?"

"Ah, I think if we spend the whole day in this room, we'll find the answer."

"In this room?"

"Yes. The answer is in here."

I looked around. The room was filled with bookshelves.

"Could you be a bit less vague? Okay, how about this? Sasaki's murder yesterday—you're feeling responsible and it's made you depressed. The way I see it, you had no idea what's going on and yet you promised that there would be no more deaths—"

"That couldn't be helped!"

Kiyoshi sounded distraught.

"Besides him... but... well... I don't think that can be... anyway now..."

My friend didn't seem to have a grasp on reality at all. But whatever the case, I had never before heard him describe a murder as something that couldn't be helped.

"I've been thinking," I said. "And now, listening to what you're saying, I'm confident I'm right. I think Sasaki committed suicide."

To which Kiyoshi seemed to react with shock. He was dumbfounded for a moment, then slowly opened his mouth.

"Suicide... I see. I didn't think of that. Well, that's one way..."

His shoulders sagged.

Not to have thought of such a simple thing… I was worried about him. But then,

"That's a great idea," he continued. "If we tell them that it was suicide, it'll confuse them even more."

I suddenly felt angry.

"Kiyoshi! Have you been plotting this the whole time? Because you don't really know what's going on, you've been spending your whole time pretending to be some kind of famous detective? Wow. That's low even for you. If you don't know, then just say you don't know. The professional detectives have been racking their brains over this case, but still don't understand it. It's nothing to be ashamed of. But because you've been faking it for so long, your shame is going to be all the greater."

"I'm tired. I need to rest."

"Then please just listen to my thoughts."

He didn't respond, so I began to speak. I'd also given this case plenty of thought, and I was trying to develop a theory of my own.

"Even if we decide that Sasaki killed himself, it's still all wrong. There was that letter pinned to the wall. One which showed a definite lack of writing ability."

"Meaning?"

"That message was really poorly written, right?"

"You think?"

"And you don't?"

"I don't think that it could have been written any other way."

"For a dramatic letter that announces an intention of revenge, it was third rate. There are so many better ways it could have been said."

"For example?"

"Well, how about a more literary flavour? Let's see… 'I vow to rob you of your life', or 'I will not rest until I've exacted my revenge upon you', or 'My blood runs like fire in my veins' or something?"

"Well, that's poetic."

"There are so many other phrases like that the writer could have used, like—"

"Okay, I get it. What's your point?"

"I mean regarding this whole revenge thing, if the killer wanted to get revenge on Kozaburo Hamamoto for something, the theory that Sasaki was the killer and then took his own life doesn't work. He had no reason to take revenge on Hamamoto. He only met the man very recently and the two of them seem to have got on very well. And anyway, to kill himself before killing Hamamoto could hardly be counted as revenge… Or possibly he's set up some trick that's going to take Hamamoto's life."

"Well, the police are investigating all possibilities for that. They said they were going to thoroughly check the room in the tower as well."

"And how are the deaths of Ueda and Kikuoka a form of revenge against Hamamoto?"

"Right. They're not."

"And yet, if we drop the theory that Sasaki was the killer and look at who's left, there are the three members of staff and then the daughter, Eiko, Kumi Aikura, the Kanais, Yoshihiko and finally Togai. That's it. There doesn't seem to be anyone among them who might have a grudge against Hamamoto."

"No, nobody."

"And really when you think about it, the act of murdering Sasaki can hardly be said to exact revenge on Hamamoto."

"I agree."

"Unless of course because, as there was some sort of relationship between Eiko and Sasaki, the act of killing Sasaki would cause grief to the daughter, and therefore also grief to the father by association. A bit of a roundabout way to achieve it though.

"It's such an impossible case! Starting with that horrible grinning doll, it has so many weird elements. Like those two stakes stuck in the snow—"

At that moment the library door opened to reveal Eiko Hamamoto and Kumi Aikura. At first the two women appeared perfectly calm as they strolled over to the window, but if you looked more closely you could see there was some kind of simmering tension between them. They didn't seemed to notice the two of us.

"You're really going for it," said Eiko, as nonchalant as if she were talking about the weather.

"What do you mean?" asked Kumi carefully. I was wondering the same thing. But Eiko's next response made it clear. She was referring to the other woman's pursuit of Sasaki, Togai, Kajiwara and the other men.

"There's no point in beating about the bush," said Eiko with a sweet smile. "I think you understand what I'm talking about?"

Eiko's condescending attitude never faltered.

"I'm sorry, no. I have absolutely no idea what you're talking about," Kumi answered loftily.

I held my breath.

"Look, I can forgive you everything else. Perhaps you can't help that you're such an irresponsible fluffhead. I'm just different, that's all. I can't live the way you do. But what I can't forgive you for is Sasaki. Do you understand?"

"What do you mean by 'irresponsible fluffhead'? You say you can't live the way I do, but you certainly seem to know a lot about that way."

"So you refuse to answer my question?"

"I'm the one asking you a question."

"Look, it would be better for you just to admit it. Or do I need to spell out your relationship with President Kikuoka as his so-called secretary?"

Kumi couldn't come up with a response right away. There was a moment of chilling silence.

"What the hell do you mean by you can't forgive me for Sasaki?"

Kumi's composure was gone. She didn't have the energy any more to feign politeness.

"Oh, I think you know." Eiko's voice turned dangerously soft. "How you employed that professional box of tricks of yours to seduce that innocent young man."

"Just a minute! 'Professional box of tricks'?"

"Isn't sleeping with men your profession?"

Kumi was sensible enough not to lose it at this point. She was clearly fighting back the urge to yell something. Instead, she laughed defiantly.

"Now you mention it, I did notice you throwing yourself at Sasaki's stretcher. Kind of embarrassing, really. Reminded me of a bar girl fawning all over her patron. Very impressive."

It was Eiko's turn to be lost for words.

"But that's the irony, isn't it? You forbid other women to go near your darling Sasaki, but you never even slept with him? What century are you from? You'll never get anywhere with that kind of thinking. If you thought of him as your man, why didn't you just put a leash on him?"

Both women were on the point of exploding in fury. Kiyoshi and I felt in physical danger. We were on the point of getting up and running for our lives, but Eiko's pride stopped her from going too far.

"It's impossible to keep my dignity around someone like you."

Kumi laughed scornfully.

"You call yourself dignified? Try losing a bit of weight. That'd give you more dignity."

Eiko took her time before responding.

"I'm going to ask you straight. Was it you who killed Sasaki?"

Kumi was dumbfounded.

"What the...?"

The two women glared at each other.

"Are you crazy? How could I have killed Sasaki? What motive could I have had?"

"I don't know how, but I know you had a motive."

"What?"

"To stop me getting him."

Kumi laughed again, this time more shrilly. But her eyes didn't join in. They stayed fully focused on Eiko's face and showed no sign of amusement.

"Please stop making me laugh! Why would you imagine I'd need to kill Sasaki? I liked him, but he was madly in love with you? Is that it? Oh, that's priceless! I didn't care about him at all, and he didn't care about you at all either. Why would I want to kill him? In fact, the one who might want to kill him is you! Isn't that right? Because he was attracted to me."

"Don't talk rubbish."

Finally, the situation had reached its most frightening point.

"I can't believe a dirty whore like you would even dare to set foot in this house. Get out! Get out of my house now!"

"Believe me, there's nothing I'd like better. If only I could get permission from the police to leave. I've had more than enough of this house with its serial murders and a woman constantly stomping around like a sumo wrestler. And that hideous piercing voice."

For quite a time after that the two women exchanged a barrage of insults that I couldn't possibly write down here. Kiyoshi and I kept perfectly still and tried to merge into the scenery.

Eventually, the door was slammed so hard the whole wall shook, and Eiko was left alone. For a while she stood there shell-shocked, but then finally summoned the presence of mind to scan the room. And, of course, her eye fell upon the two accidental spectators. The blood drained from her face and her lips began to tremble.

"Good afternoon," said Kiyoshi boldly.

"Have you been there the whole time?"

She seemed to be feigning calm, even as she knew the answer to her question. Or perhaps she really did think that we had somehow crept in through the window while she'd been engaged in her battle.

"Could you not have let me know you were there?"

"Well, we… we were too afraid to say anything."

This was not the sensible thing to say on the part of Kiyoshi, but we were lucky. Eiko barely seemed to lose her cool at all. It was almost as if she hadn't understood Kiyoshi's meaning.

"It's quite unforgivable that you didn't say a thing. So you just sat there and listened?"

Kiyoshi glanced at me as if to say, *Don't just sit there. Help me out.*

"We didn't mean to listen," he said.

268

"But we were worried," I said, ignoring Kiyoshi.

"Yes, about the outcome," Kiyoshi quickly added.

"The outcome? What did you think might happen?" she snapped.

My shoulders began to tremble.

"Why were you lurking there listening to our conversation?"

Privately I objected to the word "conversation".

But Eiko's voice was getting shriller. I was frantically preparing a pretty good excuse that I hoped might help to improve the atmosphere in the room. I felt confident that I could do something. Had I been alone, I might have succeeded.

But it's no good when your friend has no common sense whatsoever. Right then the man sitting next to me decided to say the most inappropriate thing that any human being could possibly have come up with, negating all of the effort that I'd made up to that point.

"So... which one of you do you think won?"

Eiko's shoulders immediately stopped trembling, and she summoned up a deep voice from deep in her belly.

"You despicable man! You've no manners at all."

"Yes, I'm very used to being called that," said Kiyoshi with a smile. "And my manners are so lacking that until just now I was under the impression that a library was a place to read books."

I elbowed him in the ribs and whispered urgently to him to shut up. But it was too late and things could not have got any worse. Eiko didn't speak another word—she just glared at Kiyoshi, then headed towards the door. As she opened it, she turned to face us as if she were searching for the wickedest curse to put on us. But then, as if she had been unable to find the words, she left, closing the door behind her.

I let out a long groan. It was a while before I could speak.

"You're outrageous, you know that? You have absolutely no common sense whatsoever."

"I've heard it a thousand times."

"And I'm sick of saying it! What a great New Year this is turning out to be."

"It's okay to be outrageous once in a while, don't you think?"

"Once in a while?! So you're saying that I just happen always to be with you on those 'once in a while' occasions? Are there any times you leave the house and don't cause trouble? I don't think I can think of a single one! Just put yourself in my shoes for once. Imagine how I feel. Every time I try my hardest to keep a situation from getting out of hand, you manage to wreck everything, just for fun, for your own amusement."

"Understood. I'll be more careful next time."

"Next time? Ha! Next time! If it happens again, I know what I'm going to do."

"What's that?"

"It'll be the end of our friendship."

There was an uncomfortable silence. But then I decided we'd better focus on the case again.

"Anyway, forget about that for now. How about this case? Are you going to solve it?"

"About that…" he murmured.

"Pull it together!" I said. "And if you decide to do a runner in the night, I'm not going with you. I don't want to freeze to death. But anyway, we've found out something this afternoon. We can more or less rule out those two women."

The hammering downstairs had stopped by now.

"There's one more thing that's perfectly clear to me now," said Kiyoshi.

"What?" I asked, hopefully.

"It's going to be a while before our hostess lets us move out of that freezing cold storeroom of a bedroom."

I couldn't help wishing he'd thought of that before opening his mouth.

SCENE 6

The Salon

That evening, despite my doubts, we were provided with dinner.

The guests had now been cooped up in the Ice Floe Mansion for a whole week, and they couldn't hide any longer how exhausted they were. What's more, among them (or in someone's case, inside themself) was a homicidal maniac, and they were constantly living with the fear that the knife with the white string attached might end up in their own heart next.

Tonight, however, it was the police officers who were having the hardest time hiding their exhaustion. They looked at least ten times more haggard than even Kiyoshi had predicted, and anyone seeing the way their shoulders sagged couldn't help but feel sorry for them. All the way through dinner, and even when it was over, not one of them spoke a word. If any one of them had opened his mouth to speak, doubtless he would have simply repeated the same phrases that they had said a hundred times already. I had to be constantly vigilant to make sure that Kiyoshi didn't turn to them and ask them if they'd found so much as a rat's nest in their search.

"What in God's name is going on in this place?" said Okuma, making it one hundred and one times.

Nobody had a response. Ozaki and the others had put so much into the search that they could barely lift a hand to drink their tea. If Ozaki had opened his mouth right then, nothing good would have come out.

"We know nothing," said Ushikoshi, his voice barely a whisper. "We have to accept it. Why was there a metre of string attached to those hunting knives? Why were there two stakes out in the snow the night of the first murder? As for the three locked rooms, especially the second two, we have no idea how it was done. And they only get more impossible as the murders go on. It's just not feasible to commit a murder in such a perfectly impenetrable room! It's impossible! So we stripped away the walls, the ceilings and the floors. And found nothing! Even the heating pipes were untouched.

"We know absolutely nothing. We've gained nothing. I'm left believing it was all done by some sort of evil spirit. My daily reports to HQ are torture for me to make. If there is anyone at all who thinks they can give me any sort of explanation that makes any sense at all of this freak case, then I will bow deeply and listen to whatever he has to say. If such a person exists."

"I don't think they do," said Ozaki, massaging his own right shoulder.

And those were the only words he spoke all evening.

Kiyoshi and I were in conversation with Kozaburo. In the very short time that we had been guests at the Ice Floe Mansion, Kozaburo Hamamoto appeared to have aged about ten years. He wasn't usually very talkative, but he did enjoy talking about music and art, and on these topics he seemed to have regained a little of his vitality. Kiyoshi must have taken note of my earlier complaints, or perhaps it was because of his own loss of confidence, but he had stopped baiting the detectives and was relatively subdued.

When it came to music it seemed that Kiyoshi and Kozaburo had surprisingly similar tastes. They'd been discussing Richard Wagner's brash theatricality for close on an hour.

"Wagner was really ahead of his time. His music broke through the norms of the age, upset its harmony," said Kozaburo. "A true revolutionary."

"Right, right. At the time his music was considered truly avant-garde in England and other European countries. Even now he's treated as something modern."

"I agree. But he could only make it because he was under the patronage of Ludwig II."

"I suppose you could see it that way. Wagner was demanding impressive sums of money from him. Without Ludwig II as a patron, after *The Ring* none of his greatest masterpieces would have been possible. He was deeply in debt, constantly being forced to flee different countries. If he hadn't been rescued by Ludwig, he would probably have rotted away in some village in the middle of nowhere."

"Well, that's possible, I admit. But he still would have written his scores."

"Just now you said something about harmony?…" Kiyoshi asked.

"The situation at that time in European cities just before the appearance of Ludwig II or Wagner, had reached a certain state of harmony, I believe. For example, the perfect architectural balance between the use of stone and glass and wood."

"Aha. I see."

"The layout and concept of the ideal cities of the day resembled a giant stage setting. In other words, a city was like a theatre, in which the common people were to go about their daily lives as if it were one great performance."

"Huh."

"In that environment, the technological development of glass as a new building material was the most important facet of this theatrical construction and one that added to its beauty. But you couldn't make anything substantial with it. The leaning tower that I've built here couldn't have been made in those days. And wouldn't have been. Not only the architects and city planners, but also painters and musicians created their work with an implicit understanding of preserving harmony.

"And then, along came technological advancements that included the construction of strong steel frames and huge plates of glass, as well as the invention of trains. And that was when the giant that was Wagner made his appearance in Bavaria."

"Interesting. You say he arrived to destroy the perfection of the Gothic period."

"Right. And ever since, Europe has been racked with troubles. They're still suffering today."

"And what was the role of Ludwig II, the pure-hearted boy king, in all this? He copied King Louis of France and he took Wagner in. Was he just a frivolous airhead?"

"No, I think it was just the tendency of Bavarian people at the time. Society wanted to make Ludwig II appear a lunatic so they changed the definition of normal. It wasn't only Ludwig II who liked to mimic France. Ludwig I had already created his own version of the Arc de Triomphe in Munich."

"But what interests me most right now is you, Mr Hamamoto."

"Me?"

"You don't seem like Ludwig II. This mansion is no Herrenchiemsee Castle. A man of your intelligence doesn't build a house on the farthest tip of the northernmost island of Japan for no reason whatsoever."

"Aren't you overestimating me? Or perhaps you are over-estimating Japanese people in general. There are monstrosities like Herrenchiemsee Castle in Tokyo. How about the State Guest House—Akasaka Palace?"

"Are you saying this mansion is a kind of Akasaka Palace?"

"Yes, I suppose it is."

"Well, it doesn't look like it to me."

"I guess that it's the same way that you don't look like a frivolous airhead to me."

The two men lapsed into silence for a while. Eventually Kozaburo spoke.

"Mr Mitarai, you're a mysterious man. I have absolutely no idea what you're thinking."

"Oh, really? Well, I suppose I am a little more difficult to comprehend than those police officers over there."

"Do you think the police have comprehended anything?"

"Their minds haven't changed since they arrived at this mansion. They're like a Gothic façade. The house won't collapse without them."

"And how about you?"

"How about me in what way?"

"Have you seen the truth of this case? Do you know the name of the killer?"

"The killer's identity is quite plain for all to see."

"Oh! And who is it?"

"Didn't I already say? It's the doll."

"I can't believe that you mean that seriously."

"Ah, you too? At any rate, this is a very elaborate crime. And it seems that the game is already underway. To bring it to anything but an extraordinary climax would be insulting to the artist who created it."

ENTR'ACTE

Because of the threatening letter he'd received, from the night of the 1st of January onwards, the decision was made that it was too dangerous for Kozaburo to sleep alone in his isolated room in the tower. Instead, he was to sleep in Room 12 with Sergeant Okuma and Constable Anan as his bodyguards. This was not a decision easily reached, but to write here in detail about all the fuss it caused would be too much trouble, so I'm leaving it at that.

The next day, the 2nd of January, there was no sign of any crime having been committed. The police officers spent the whole day unsuccessfully trying to put the rooms they'd pulled apart back to their original condition.

Kiyoshi and the detectives didn't appear to be speaking to each other at all, but Chief Inspector Ushikoshi came to ask my opinion. Not being able to rely on Kiyoshi, I had given the case some thought and come up with four issues that had to be resolved.

The first was the strange twisted shape of Kazuya Ueda's body with arms in the V-formation above his head.

Second, the knife in Eikichi Kikuoka's back—the fact that it wasn't in the left side where his heart was, but in the right. Was there any significance to that?

Third, the fact that Ueda and Kikuoka's deaths were on consecutive nights. I found that extremely strange. The killer could have taken as much time as he or she needed, but it seemed as if he'd been in a rush. If he'd left an interval after murdering Ueda, he'd have been more likely to find a moment to catch the detectives off guard. Waiting for that moment would have been the more logical thing to do.

In fact, because a murder had just been committed, there had been four police officers staying the night at the mansion. If the murderer had waited two or three nights more, at least Constable Anan would have been gone. Why didn't he wait? Why attack when the police were at their most vigilant? It was surely important to work out the reason the killer committed a crime at the most dangerous moment.

And then the final issue: number four. This house has a unique layout with two staircases—one in each of the east and west wings. In theory, if you wanted to get from Room 1 or 2 to Room 13 or 14, you'd have to go through the salon on the ground floor—but is that correct? Many people had escaped suspicion because of this theory. But were we missing something…?

These were the four topics I brought up in my conversation with Ushikoshi. I didn't tell him, but there was one more outrageous theory going through my mind about the locked rooms. In the cases of Room 14 and Room 13, in particular, a murder seemed to have been ruled out. So instead, was it somehow possible that the victims had seen something through the hole in the wall, something that had terrified them enough to stick a knife in themselves—some kind of projected image—or perhaps they might even have heard a sound…

But this theory seemed hardly possible. The walls of the rooms had been torn apart and searched. There were no film projectors or speakers concealed inside. In fact, there was no kind of electronic or computerized device anywhere in the house.

On the 3rd of January, a team of five or six workmen arrived to fix the mess that the detectives had made of the walls and ceilings. The door of Room 10 had already been mended, but now the doors of 13 and 14 were also restored. This meant that Kiyoshi and I were finally permitted to move out of Room 10 and into Room 13.

It was almost midday on the 3rd. Uniformed police officers arrived with Golem's head. The forensics lab had apparently completed their analysis. Kiyoshi took delivery of the head and carried it up to Room 3 to reunite it with its body. He even replaced the cowboy hat.

Okuma and Ushikoshi were anxious to hear the reports of the latest forensic investigations, but there was no good news. The hunting knives, the string, the cord were nothing special. Any of them could have been purchased at any shop anywhere in the country.

By the afternoon of the 3rd, the weather suddenly took a turn for the worse and heavy snow began to fall. By 2 p.m. it was so dark and gloomy inside the house that it felt like evening. Another blizzard was surely on its way. The murder mystery that was playing out at the eccentric mansion on the northern tip of Japan appeared to be heading towards its climactic scene.

Before we reach the climax, I should record two things. One is that around sunset on the 3rd, Kumi Aikura insisted that she could hear the sound of someone breathing somewhere in the ceiling of her room. And a half-crazed Hatsue Kanai reported seeing the vague outline of a dead body standing outside in the swirling snow.

Both of these occurrences could be explained the same way—the occupants of the Ice Floe Mansion had reached the limits of their terror and their patience.

And now a report of a more obviously tangible kind. At dinner on the evening of the 3rd, a very disturbing thing happened. From the beginning, everyone who gathered at the dining table looked a little green around the gills. No one had any appetite at all. The women left their knives and forks untouched on the table and sat there listening to the sound of the raging storm. Eiko placed her left hand over the right of Togai, her neighbour, and said quietly, "I'm scared." Togai gently reached across and covered her left hand with his own.

Including the four police officers, all of the surviving occupants of the house were in attendance. But then a small puff of white smoke floated into the room from the direction of the staircase. Kiyoshi was the first to notice it.

"There's a fire!" he shouted.

The police all dropped their forks and rushed up the stairs. Kozaburo, fearing for his precious collection, followed right behind.

In the end, the fire was extinguished before it could develop into anything serious. The source was Eiko's bed in Room 2 which had been sprinkled with paraffin and set alight. But as always, no one had any idea why or by whom this fire had been set. I have already said it, but absolutely everybody had been sitting at the dining table when it happened.

At this point, everyone was convinced that besides the regular occupants there was someone else in the mansion.

Some person or some other mysterious entity with homicidal intentions was clearly lurking. But no matter how many times they searched, the police continued to come up with nothing.

On this particular occasion, however, Room 2 hadn't been locked, nor had the window on the east staircase landing, so for once this strange case of arson wasn't in the realm of the impossible. But the who and the why still required a great deal of thought.

The storm grabbed hold of the window frames and shook them with all its might and the noise resounded through the mansion. The dozen or so helpless humans cowered in fear inside.

Everything was in place for the final act.

Before we get to that final act, there is one more thing I should write down. Perhaps the reader is already familiar with it, but those of you who are hearing this phrase for the first time might be confused. However, this writer cannot resist including these famous words.

CHALLENGE TO THE READER

The clues are all there. Can you solve this case?

FINAL ACT

*Mysterious being, crouching there in the dark
of night, stand up and shine the light of truth
so that I might know the answer.*

The Ground Floor Landing of the West Wing Staircase, or By the Door of Room 12

Yoshihiko Hamamoto came down the stairs from Room 8, his bedroom.

Chief Inspector Ushikoshi was with Kiyoshi in Room 13 discussing something or other, but everyone else was in the salon. The wind was howling outside, and just like the night that Kikuoka was murdered, no one was in a hurry to go to their own room. If Yoshihiko looked straight ahead of him as he descended the stairs from Room 3 on the middle floor, all there was before him was a huge towering wall like a barricade. This was in fact the walls of Room 10 and Room 12, one above the other.

Because there were no windows or other openings in the wall besides the door to Room 12 down at the bottom, the wall was sheer and felt oppressive. There were of course the two ventilation holes, one for each room, and lined up vertically, but that was all. The lighting on the staircase was rather dim.

Yoshihiko had almost reached the ground floor when for some reason he glanced up. The vent to Room 10, the room in which Kazuya Ueda had been murdered, was way above him in the wall, facing the open space above the staircase.

Yoshihiko had no idea why he had happened to look up at the hole at this moment, but at the same time, he hadn't just glanced up for no particular reason. He was standing right alongside this great cliff of a wall, and turned his gaze upwards. He caught his breath. Way above his head, a small square-shaped light had just gone out. The after-image stayed imprinted in Yoshihiko's retinas.

He found himself frozen to the spot. For a moment it felt as if the wind, which had an eerie way of echoing in his head, had come blowing into the interior of the house and was now dancing wildly around the high ceiling space above.

He had the illusion that he was standing alone in the wilderness. The howls and screams of the wind became the moaning of the ghosts of all the people who had died in this house. Well, not only those three, but a whole multitude of spirits. All the souls who had been here in this northern land forever.

He came back to himself. And now he realized what he had seen. It was a reality that was hard to fathom. He knew that he ought to call someone right away, because as nobody was using Room 10 any more, there was no reason for anyone to be in there. Mitarai and Chief Inspector Ushikoshi were in Room 13 and everyone else in the salon. So why had there been a light shining from the vent in Room 10? He had definitely seen it. There was something or someone in there.

He ran to the salon and flung open the door.

"Could somebody come?" he shouted.

Everyone turned to look, and most jumped to their feet. Kozaburo, Eiko, Mr and Mrs Kanai, Togai, Kumi Aikura, Mr and Mrs Hayakawa, Kajiwara; also Inspector Okuma, Sergeant Ozaki and Constable Anan and myself—all of us moved towards Yoshihiko. He checked quickly—yes, everyone was there besides Mitarai and Ushikoshi.

"What's up?" asked Ozaki.

"This way!"

Yoshihiko led everyone to the foot of the stairs and pointed up at the wall.

"I could see light coming from that vent in Room 10."

There was general commotion.

"No way!" said Okuma.

"What's going on?"

Ushikoshi and Kiyoshi had heard the commotion and came out into the corridor.

"Chief, were either of you in Room 10 just now?" asked Ozaki.

"Room 10?"

Ushikoshi was clearly surprised by the question.

"Why? No. We were both in Room 13 the whole time."

It was clear from his tone and facial expression that he was telling the truth.

"Seems there was light coming from that ventilation hole just now."

"Impossible! All sixteen of us are standing here right now," said Ushikoshi.

"It was just for a moment. I'm sure I saw it—a light going out."

"Has some sort of animal got in this damned house?" said Okuma. "An orang-utan or something?"

"You mean like 'The Murders in the Rue Morgue'?" said Kozaburo.

Everyone looked dubious. But then the normally taciturn Kajiwara spoke up.

"Er, actually…"

"What? Go on."

"The refrigerator… well, it seems there's some ham missing."

"Ham?"

More than a few people repeated the word.

"Yes. Some ham and a little bit of bread—"

"Has this happened before?" asked Okuma.

"Um, I don't think so… Well, I don't think it has…"

"You don't think?"

"I'm not really sure. I'm sorry."

There were a few moments of heavy silence.

"Anyway, let's go and check it out, Room 10," said Ozaki. "There's no point in just standing around here."

"No point in checking either," said Kiyoshi, without enthusiasm. "There'll be nothing there."

Nevertheless, the police set out into the snow. Kiyoshi and I, the women, Kozaburo, as well as Kanai and Yoshihiko stayed where we were. After a while, a light came on behind the ventilation hole.

"Yes, that's it! That's the light I saw!" cried Yoshihiko.

But of course, the search was fruitless yet again. According to Ozaki's report, the padlock was still on the door; in fact there was even fresh snow covering it, and the room itself was freezing cold inside with no signs of life. He concluded that Yoshihiko had seen some sort of illusion.

"How about the spare key to the padlock?" asked Ozaki.

"I've got it," said Hayakawa. "I haven't lent it to anyone else. But I did leave the padlock itself by the entrance to the kitchen for a while."

"You mean while guests were staying in the room?"

"Yes, that's right."

Just in case, the detectives proceeded to search the main building of the house, the garden shed and Kozaburo's room at the top of the tower one more time. But there was nothing unusual anywhere.

"I don't get it. What could have made that light?"

The detectives had drawn their usual blank.

About an hour after that incident, the door from the salon opened and Hatsue Kanai came out. She made her way towards the west wing stairs with the intention of fetching something from her room.

The wind was getting louder. As she climbed the stairs, Hatsue happened to glance over the banister down to the basement corridor. She normally bragged about having psychic powers, and what happened next might well have been because of her special abilities.

The basement corridor was poorly lit, and looking down felt like lifting a tombstone and peering down into a crypt. In one corner Hatsue could see a faint light, which gradually took on a human form.

All of the living human beings were currently in the salon. Hatsue knew because she had just left them there.

A numbing terror took hold of her, and her gaze fixed on the form as if held there by a powerful magnetic force. It was the hazy figure of a person (or what appeared to be a person) who made no sound, not even so much as the slight rustle of paper that falls to the floor, as it glided along the corridor. It was heading towards Room 14, where Kikuoka had been murdered, as if headed for a meeting of all the spirits of the house.

As if by some prearranged signal, the door to Room 14 opened, and the glowing figure continued inside. Right at that moment, it turned its head to the side. And the head continued to turn until it faced backwards, and Hatsue caught a glimpse of its face. For a moment her eyes and those of the mysterious being met. That face! It was definitely the smirking face of the Golem doll!

Hatsue felt her hair begin to stand on end and her whole body turned to goose pimples. She realized that she was screaming, but the voice didn't seem like her own. Like the raging storm outside it went on and on, as if propelled by a will that wasn't hers, gushing forth. Eventually out of fatigue and exhaustion, she fell into a faint. Her screams became distant to her own ears until finally they were merely an echo on a distant mountain.

The next thing Hatsue knew was that she was in her husband's arms and surrounded by anxious faces. It seemed that not much time had passed. Everyone was there. Her husband's normally feeble arms had for once proved sturdy.

For the next few minutes, Hatsue answered the questions thrown at her by the bystanders, and explained the terrifying scene she had just witnessed. In her own mind she felt that she was describing everything clearly, but it seemed that nobody around her could grasp what she was saying.

How can they all be so useless? she was cursing inside. *That's it, I've had enough of this house of horrors*, as she babbled on like a deranged lunatic.

"Bring her some water!" somebody shouted. She didn't want anything like that, but when it arrived and she put the glass to her lips, the sensation of the water on her throat was strangely soothing.

"Do you want to lie down on the sofa in the salon?" her husband asked, his voice full of concern. She nodded weakly.

However, as soon as she was safely on the sofa and began to explain again exactly what she had just seen, infuriatingly her husband returned to his usual obstinate, petty bureaucratic self.

"Dolls can't walk."

No one was surprised that this was Michio Kanai's opinion.

"You must have dreamt it."

And as she feared, this was his final conclusion.

"Those stairs aren't normal," she insisted. "There's something there!"

"There's definitely something wrong with you," continued her husband, ignoring her protests.

"Now, now," said the detectives, quickly inserting themselves between husband and wife. They suggested checking on the doll in Room 3 and the status of Room 14 right away, but it was clear from their attitudes that they didn't believe a word of Hatsue's story either.

Kozaburo opened the door to Room 3, and Ozaki flipped the light switch. Golem was sitting in his usual spot, leaning against the window-side wall, just by the south Tengu mask wall.

Ozaki marched briskly up to the feet of the doll.

"Was this the face you saw?"

Hatsue, who was hovering in the doorway, couldn't bring herself to look at the doll. And anyway, there was no need for her to look.

"There is absolutely no doubt about it. It was him!"

"Please take a close look. Was it definitely this face?"

There was an almost sarcastic smile on Ozaki's face.

"Absolutely, definitely!"

"But the doll is right here."

"Don't ask me how that's possible!"

"Was it wearing that hat and those clothes?" asked Ushikoshi.

"Huh… I'm not sure about that. But it was that face. That sneering, grinning, creepy face. But now that you mention it… I don't think he was wearing that hat."

"He didn't have the hat on?"

"No, I can't say. I don't remember that clearly."

"That's what I'm saying. There's something wrong with you," said Kanai again.

"You can shut up!" said Hatsue. "After going through what I've just been through, anybody would forget the minor details!"

The detectives didn't interrupt. She had a point. But nobody had a clue what they ought to say next. That is, except for my friend.

"Well, I told you all so!"

Kiyoshi was absolutely elated. Ozaki and the other detectives immediately rolled their eyes.

"He's the killer. He looks like a doll, but he's been deceiving us all. He's been perfectly capable of walking around by himself all this time. If he undoes his joints, he can get in and out through tiny openings. And he can kill without feeling remorse. He's a brutal murderer. You were about to check Room 14, weren't you? Go ahead. And when we get there, I'm going to tell you the whole story, all about his evil deeds. Officers, it's better not to touch him, if you value your lives."

Oozing confidence, Kiyoshi turned to face the detectives.

"Mr Kajiwara, you were just about to pour some tea, weren't you? Please get Mr Hayakawa to help you to bring it to Room 14. I think that will be the ideal location for the big reveal."

SCENE 2

Room 14

The clock on the wall of Room 14 showed exactly midnight. Kajiwara and Hayakawa had brought trays of tea and were currently circulating and making sure that everyone was served.

Kiyoshi grabbed two cups from the tray and handed one to me. He politely offered the other to Eiko beside him, after quickly grabbing a saucer and placing her cup on it first. Then he finally served himself. His behaviour was rather untypically gallant.

"The service is unusually good tonight," I remarked to him.

"This way there will no grounds for complaint from her ladyship," he replied.

"Hurry up and reveal the trick behind this bloody case. If you really can, that is," said Togai, who was standing drinking his tea. He was expressing what everyone felt, and all eyes were immediately on Kiyoshi.

"The trick?" Kiyoshi looked puzzled. "There's no trick here. Just as I've been saying all along, this is a series of murders committed by the doll Golem, who has been possessed by the vengeful ghosts of the dead."

Kiyoshi's performance was painful for me to watch. His habitual teasing tone was back and I was sure he wasn't being honest.

"I have discovered from my own research that before this mansion was built, this area was a large, open plain. One evening long, long ago, a young Ainu man threw himself off the very cliff that this house is built on."

That's how Kiyoshi's story began, but it was clear to me that he was making it up as he went along. I had no idea what his true intentions were. It felt to me as if he were trying to play for time.

"This Ainu boy had a young lover by the name of Pirika, who out of sorrow jumped off the cliff after him."

Kiyoshi was clearly retelling some tale he'd heard somewhere or other.

"Every spring since then, on that very spot, a blood-red iris is said to bloom."

I remembered that Pirika had been the name of the restaurant in the village where we'd eaten the day we arrived at the Ice Floe Mansion. There'd been a photograph of irises on the wall, and a printed poem about the flowers. Still, these irises had been the regular purple shade. I'd never seen or heard of a red iris.

"The young lovers had been kept apart by the selfishness of the other villagers. The son of the most powerful clan in the village wanted to marry Pirika himself. If Pirika agreed to marry him, the boy's father had promised to give everyone in the village a wheelbarrow. Despairing of ever being free to be together, the lovers took their own lives. Since then, the grudge that the two lovers held against the rest of the village has been roaming this land. With the construction of this mansion their souls have found a kind of base from which to act. Their spirits—"

"Ah!"

He was interrupted by the voice of someone in distress. I realized it was Eiko, who had just sunk to her knees, her hand pressed to her forehead.

"Please… my cup…"

I reached out to grab her teacup right as she slumped to the floor. Togai and Kozaburo came rushing over.

"Get her to the bed!" said Ushikoshi.

"Looks like some kind of sleeping drug," said Kiyoshi, as he examined her. "If we leave her to sleep, she'll wake up just fine in the morning."

"Are you sure it's just sleeping pills?" Kozaburo asked him.

"I'm positive. Look how peacefully she's breathing."

"Who could have done this?" said Kozaburo, looking at the household staff.

"No idea." The three of them shook their heads.

"The criminal is in this room!"

When angry, Kozaburo had the energy of a much a younger man.

"Anyway," he continued, "it's dangerous for Eiko to stay here. Let's get her up to her room."

His tone made it clear that there was no room for discussion. Right now it was easy to picture what he'd been like back in his youth.

"But the bed in Ms Hamamoto's room got burnt," said Ozaki.

Kozaburo looked for a moment as if he'd had an electric shock.

"If she's been drugged, then I think we should let her sleep it off right here," said Ushikoshi.

"All right then, but that hole! That hole needs to be blocked up!"

"But to do that we need to stand on the bed…"

"Then do it from the outside!"

"But truly, to start hammering right by the head of someone

sleeping after a dose of pills like that, well, tomorrow morning she's going to wake up with a terrible headache," said Kiyoshi.

"But this room is dangerous!"

"Why? Room 10 or Room 13 are exactly the same as this one."

Kiyoshi hadn't said it, but in Room 13 where Sasaki had died, the ventilation hole had been completely blocked up. What would be the point of blocking Room 14's vent too? Everyone was thinking the same thing.

Kozaburo stood still, his fists clenched and his head hanging down.

"If you're worried about your daughter, I can have a guard put on this room all night. Of course, it'd be inappropriate to have him actually sleep in here with her, but we can lock the door and set a chair outside in the corridor. He can keep watch until morning. How does that sound?"

Ushikoshi turned to Constable Anan.

"Anan, how about it? If you think it would be too hard to stay awake, I can get Ozaki to take over halfway through the night.

"This room doesn't have a spare key, does it?" he continued. "So I suggest that you keep hold of the key yourself, Mr Hamamoto.

"Anan, I don't know who the killer is, but he or she is probably one of us. Therefore, if someone comes, you don't let them in. Even if it's me or Okuma. Not until everyone has got up tomorrow morning and checked in. Is that acceptable to you, Mr Hamamoto?

"Right, everybody, you've heard the plan. As for me, I'm feeling a bit sleepy after listening to our learned fortune teller's fascinating bit of folklore. I'm dying to hear the rest but I'm afraid it's really going to send me to sleep. And it wouldn't do to make too much noise while our lady hostess is trying to rest. So how about going to bed now, everybody? It's already late. Let's hear the rest tomorrow."

Everyone seemed pretty much in agreement, except for Kozaburo. He couldn't help thinking of how many people had already been murdered in completely locked rooms.

"I'm not completely comfortable with this," he mumbled.

SCENE 3

The Tengu Room

Everyone had settled down to sleep. The dark corridors and spaces of the Ice Floe Mansion were deserted, and the only sound was the wind raging to itself.

The lock on the door of Room 3 made a faint noise as it turned, ever so gently, and the door very slowly opened. The pale light that filtered in from the corridor brushed the faces of the dolls, vaguely illuminating them. Among them, Golem's grinning face.

Someone tiptoed into the room, as cautiously as if they'd been crossing a thin layer of ice, and approached Golem. When they reached the window, the light from the corridor revealed their face in profile.

It was Kozaburo Hamamoto. Well, he was, of course, the only person who had a key to that room.

Kozaburo never even glanced at Golem, sprawled in his usual position on the floor. Instead, he turned his attention to the southern wall of Tengu masks and began to do something quite mysterious. He set about removing the masks from the wall, one by one.

Each time he had gathered about ten or so in his arms, he would lay them down on the floor, and gradually, the gently sloping middle section of the room's south wall was revealed for the first time.

But then something astounding happened. Golem's feet twitched, and then his wooden joints began to creak as his legs were gradually pulled in towards his body. The painted grin on his face never changed.

The doll got slowly to its feet, and with the clumsy, jerky movements of a puppet, took a step towards Kozaburo.

Slowly, but steadily as the second hand on a clock, Golem lifted both his arms and drew his palms closer together in a circular formation as if to place them around Kozaburo's neck.

Kozaburo, still absorbed in his work, had now cleared the major part of the south wall. Several masks still clutched in his hands, he took a couple of steps over to the corner of the room, to fetch some bricks that were lying there. He had turned his back and was bending down to pick up a brick when he sensed something. With the brick in his right hand he turned slowly around. And there was Golem, standing right behind him.

The shock sent Kozaburo's body into convulsions and his face froze in an expression of terror. The wind howled, and at the same time he somehow managed to call out. The masks in his hands fell and scattered on the floor, and the brick followed with a dull thud.

Right then there was a flash of lightning and suddenly the room was lit with a fluorescent glow as bright as daylight. Automatically, Kozaburo looked towards the doorway. All the detectives stood there.

"Secure the scene!"

The voice didn't belong to one of the detectives heading towards Golem, but came from Golem himself!

"Why are you taking the Tengu masks down from the wall, Mr Hamamoto?" Golem asked. "There can only be one explanation. You are the only person who knows that these Tengus killed Eikichi Kikuoka."

Golem reached up and removed his hat, then put his hands up to his grinning face. As he lowered his hands again, the ghoulish grinning face disappeared and was replaced by Kiyoshi Mitarai's.

"You forgot to erase the letters on his forehead, Mr Hamamoto," said Kiyoshi. "How do you like my mask? It's pretty good, isn't it?"

In his hands, he held a mask identical to the face of the Golem doll.

"Forgive my tricks. But they were all learnt from you."

"Aha!" said Kozaburo. "So that's why you dressed the doll. I see now! An excellent move. Nicely played, Mr Mitarai, I have to admit defeat. I've always believed in good sportsmanship. I give up. It was me. I killed Ueda and Kikuoka."

The Salon

"If you think about it…" said Kozaburo Hamamoto, taking a puff on his pipe. We were sitting around the dining table— Hamamoto, Ushikoshi, Okuma, Ozaki, Kiyoshi and myself.

"…this is the perfect night for me to make my bizarre confession. The person I'd prefer didn't hear what I have to say is fast asleep under the influence of sleeping drugs."

Sensing something was afoot, the other occupants of the Ice Floe Mansion began to turn up in the salon. Eventually everyone was assembled, except for Constable Anan and Eiko. The storm was still raging outside, and it seemed no one had been able to sleep. The grandfather clock in the corner read 2.50 in the morning.

"Would you prefer to have more privacy? We could move to a different location," Kiyoshi suggested.

"No, it doesn't matter. I'm in no position to make demands. All of these people have been living in fear because of me. They have a right to hear what I have to say. Could you just allow me one selfish request? Make sure my daughter…"

He faltered for a moment.

"We wouldn't be able to wake Ms Hamamoto even if we wanted to," said Kiyoshi. "The sleeping drugs she took are incredibly strong."

"I get it now! It was you who drugged her, and you who set fire to her bed. How did you manage it? You were with us the whole time."

305

"All in good time. I'm going to start at the beginning," said Kiyoshi. "If I go wrong or leave anything out, let me know."

Everyone began to gather at the table, hoping that the string of murders had finally come to an end and the case had been solved.

"Understood. I doubt, though, that it'll be necessary."

"I had a really hard time figuring out your motive for killing Ueda," began Kiyoshi almost impatiently. He seemed to be in a hurry to get the story out.

"Well, actually that's not quite accurate. To tell the truth I had a hard time figuring out the motive for the whole thing. But with Ueda in particular, you don't seem to have any reason for killing him.

"However, I got it right away with the murder of Kikuoka. I realized the only person you actually wanted to kill was Kikuoka, at least at the beginning. For that reason you spent so much time and money building this eccentric mansion. Its sole purpose was for murdering Eikichi Kikuoka. But in the end you had the desire to kill both Ueda and Kikuoka. You'd refined and polished your plan, but Ueda got in the way. That was it, wasn't it?"

"It was important that I was the one to kill Kikuoka. If I didn't, I would have failed in my duty," said Kozaburo. "The other day, I noticed something strange about Kohei and Chikako when they returned from their daughter's funeral. I questioned them about it and they eventually broke down and confessed that they had hired Ueda to kill Kikuoka.

"I panicked. I told them I would pay them back the money they'd used, but they had to withdraw their request. I trusted them, and I'm sure Kohei did as I asked. But Ueda refused to stand down. He was stubborn but also had a streak of chivalry

306

in him. He had his own intense personal hatred of Kikuoka. It seems that he had had some kind of run-in with the man too."

It turned out that Kikuoka was almost universally despised.

"What kind of run-in?"

"To us, it may seem insignificant. Ueda took something that Kikuoka said as an insult to his mother. It seems there was a dispute between his mother and her neighbour over land. The neighbouring house had suffered a fire and the fence that divided the properties had been burnt. Ever since, the exact location of the boundary between the two properties had been unclear. Ueda's mother let neighbourhood cars park on the disputed land for a fee, and her neighbour had taken her to court over it. His mother was obstinate too. She was involved in a fight that could only end by one side or the other moving out, and needed money for that. Kikuoka called her a 'stubborn old bag' and other pretty awful things, which really awoke Ueda's fury. But I don't suppose it'd have come to murder until Kohei Hayakawa offered to pay him to do it. Well, whatever, it's not my place to make judgements on the motives of others…"

"And so you decided to kill Ueda. You thought if you were going to kill him anyway, why not use his murder as a kind of foreshadowing of the carefully prepared murder of Kikuoka? In a way that would cause so much confusion in the investigation. That's what the string tied to the handle of the knife was about, wasn't it?"

"Yes, it was."

I glanced at the Hayakawa couple. Chikako was staring down at the floor, and Kohei hadn't taken his eyes off his employer.

"That's because in the subsequent murder of Mr Kikuoka, you were planning to use a knife with string attached, or rather you *needed* to attach string to the handle of that second knife to accomplish the crime. So you decided to foreshadow the crime by tying string to the knife used to murder Mr Ueda, when in fact there was no need for any string on it at all. But there's one thing I still don't understand. Why did you tie Ueda's wrist to the bed with that piece of cord?"

"I'm not really sure myself. I was in quite a state and not thinking properly. I'd never killed anyone with a knife before. I couldn't imagine what would happen. I suppose I was afraid that he might go wandering outside half dead or something."

"How did you manage to take down a great big ex-military type like that all by yourself?" said Okuma.

"Yes, well, I had to employ some shameful tactics. I talked to him numerous times about the Self-Defence Forces so that he came to trust me, but still, no matter how much his guard might be down, there was no chance I'd overpower him in a fight. I'm sure he'd even had training to deal with that kind of sneak attack.

"There was a chance that I might bump into someone so I wore a jacket to hide any blood spatter. Part of my plan was to take it off to kill him and then put it back on to hide any blood that might have got on my sweater. The jacket had one more use too. When I went to his room—"

"How did you get in?" Ushikoshi asked.

"I just knocked on his door, announced myself, and he let me in. It was as simple as that. He had no reason to believe that I was going to murder him or Kikuoka. Kohei had never told him I had anything to do with his request not to kill Kikuoka after all."

"Hmm. Go on."

308

"I entered his room, took off my jacket and observed Ueda. If I could have done it, I would have stabbed him right there and then, but it wasn't possible. He was too big, and I was particularly afraid of how strong his right arm looked. I really wasn't thinking straight. I had the knife in my jacket pocket and all I could think was if I could just get his right wrist tied to the bed, it would be so much easier to do the job. And then after thinking about it for a while, I executed my plan.

"I held out my jacket telling him it was a little too big for me and if it happened to fit him I would let him have it. I told him to try it on. He put it on and fastened the buttons, but of course it was too small for him. While I was pretending to check the fit, I took the knife from the pocket and concealed it in the sleeve of my sweater, then announced that the jacket seemed too small for him after all. I undid the buttons and took hold of both sides of the collar, pulling it simultaneously downwards on both sides, as if to take it off for him. He stood quietly and let me do it. After getting the collar past his shoulders, I suddenly tugged downwards as hard as I could, and because the jacket was so small on him, it got stuck tight, temporarily disabling both his arms. Even then, he had no idea what I was up to. I pulled the knife out from my sleeve and plunged it as hard as I could into the left side of his chest. He must have thought the knife was going to come out through his back. Even now I can't get his bewildered expression out of my head.

"Then I took my jacket off him and put it back on myself. My sweater was a dark colour so the blood spatter didn't show up at all. I was lucky too that there wasn't too much blood on my hands. I hid the sweater in the bottom of the wardrobe in my room. You detectives were very polite when you went through my room, and you stopped at digging through all my clothing. That saved me, but in fact, when I look at it now, there aren't really any obvious traces of blood.

"After I'd committed the murder, my mind was a bit crazy, and when I came to, I realized that I was tying Ueda's right wrist to the bed frame, even though he was already dead."

There was a shocked reaction from the listeners at this.

"I guess that even after sticking a knife in a victim's heart a murderer feels anxious. They can't know whether the victim is really dead. There was no time for me to set up the snow-under-the-lock trick. I wanted to get out as quickly as possible."

"So when you set up the locked room, did you use the shot-put like that student said the other day?" Ushikoshi asked.

"That's right."

Kiyoshi took up the story again.

"But even if you say it's because you'd lost your mind, by tying that cord around the victim's wrist, it made it quite obvious that the killer had been inside the locked room. But you didn't go into the next locked room at all, did you? That managed to create all kinds of confusion for the detectives.

"Anyway, as he was dying, Ueda realized that he could move his wrist and tried to leave a message. If he lifted both hands up over his head in a V-shape, he could make the Japanese semaphore signal for 'ha'. In Japanese semaphore most syllables require two separate placings of the flags, but 'ha' just happens to need only one.

"But the problem with 'ha' alone, is that it might not only signify Hamamoto. It could just as easily have meant Hayakawa. So he needed to signal 'ma' as well to make it clear who he

310

meant. Unfortunately, it takes two placements of the flags to make a 'ma'—the right arm horizontally out to the side with the left arm placed thirty to forty degrees below it, or pointing diagonally downwards; followed by a dot where you cross the flags above your head. However, it was impossible to recreate these two separate placements in one single move, not to mention that he was already signalling 'ha' with his arms.

"But of course he had his legs. Semaphore is created using flags which are held in both hands, but Ueda decided to use his legs to create a 'ma'. That's why his legs are pointing at that strange angle, and the circular spot of blood on the floor beside him is the dot. That was the meaning of the blood spot and the 'dancing corpse'. I checked out semaphore signals in the encyclopaedia in the library yesterday evening.

"And then we come to the murder of Eikichi Kikuoka—"

"Hold on a minute!" I said. "There are still so many questions about the first murder."

I wasn't the only one who felt that way. Several other people began calling out. It was typical of Kiyoshi to skimp on the details when he'd already worked everything out for himself.

"What about those two stakes stuck in the snow?"

"And the doll that looked in through my window?"

"And the scream that came thirty minutes after the murder? What was that?"

"Ah, yes, those things. Where to begin? Well, they're all connected. Kazumi, you've worked out the meaning of the stakes by now, surely? So as not to leave footprints in the snow you could walk backwards in a crouching position, erasing them with your hands as you went. As long as you took the exact same path going back as the one you took when you came. But that method isn't perfect and too easy to spot. So what's

311

an alternative? The easiest is to make it snow again, just in the area where your footprints are."

"And how do you do that? Beg it to snow? And only where you've been walking?"

"You do it the opposite way around. You only walk in the places where you can get it to snow."

"What? I'm still asking you how you get it to snow."

"From the roof. You make it snow from the roof. And as luck would have it, that night it was covered in powder snow. Normally, as long as it isn't blown off by the wind, when snow falls off a roof it lands directly under the eaves. But this house is built on a slant and leans to the south. When the snow falls off this roof it lands about two metres away from the eaves."

"Aha!" said Ushikoshi.

"Mr Hamamoto had to be careful. The snow would only land in a parallel line to the roof, so that was the only place he could step. The best thing was for him to mark the line and go and return along that exact same route. But drawing the line in the snow would be way too much trouble. And if it happened to snow that evening, the line would disappear. So that's the reason. You get it now?"

"I still don't get it. Why put stakes in the ground?"

"As markers! Instead of drawing a line. The imaginary line between those two stakes was the exact position of the edge of the roof. In other words, the route that he needed to walk. It would be hard to see your own footprints at night, but on his way there he could aim for the stake at the west end of the house, and on his return the east one. On the way back he would have tried to erase his footprints a little bit I assume. Of course, he would also have pulled out the stakes and taken them with him, then burned them in the fire.

"Of course, he wouldn't have had to bother with all that if it had been snowing when he killed Ueda, but it was a precaution in case the snow stopped falling—and it had stopped that night, so he made use of his trick."

"So you are saying that after killing Ueda he climbed on the roof and knocked the snow off it?"

"Yes. He made it snow."

"I see."

"Next—"

"Just a minute! What about the doll that was found in pieces near Room 10? Why was it there? Was it used for something?"

"It's obvious, isn't it? That was the place where he couldn't make it snow. He could only make the snow fall by the edge of the roof."

"Huh? So that means... Er, what does that mean? Something to do with the problem of the footprints..."

"When he climbed the steps to Room 10 he could walk along the edge where the handrail overhangs and not leave any footprints. The problem was the bit between the west corner of the house and the bottom of the steps. There was no way of hiding prints. So he put the doll down in the snow and walked over it."

"Aha!"

"But if he just placed it there as it was, it wouldn't be enough to cover the distance between the edge of the roof and the stairs, so he disassembled it and spread the pieces across the space. Then he walked across it like stepping stones."

"Ah!"

"That's why he chose a doll that could be taken apart."

"Why didn't we think of something so simple? But... The doll looked in through Ms Aikura's window. Was that before...? Or...?"

"Yes, well, that was only the head. Now as to why he had to do that—"

"I think perhaps I should explain this part," said Kozaburo, noticing that Kiyoshi was getting a little impatient.

"It's just as Mr Mitarai said. I walked over the doll's body, used the stakes in the ground as landmarks and roughly levelled out the snow to cover my footprints as I went back inside the house to head up to the roof. But I was still carrying Golem's head at that point. I planned to return the head to Room 3 and then quietly wait for morning, hiding either in Room 3 or in the library next door.

"Because everyone thought I had gone to bed in my room in the tower, I couldn't risk making all the noise of lowering the drawbridge until it was a believable hour in the morning for me to be getting up. I planned to wait until around 7 and then open it, pretending I had just woken up.

"I was still carrying the head because I didn't want it to get damaged from lying out in the snow overnight. I had thought about dropping off the head in Room 3 first, but then I decided as I was going there later to wait out the night anyway, it was probably best not to go back and forth too many times and increase the possibility of being seen. So I was carrying it when I climbed the ladder on the side of the main building up to the roof. Earlier I had left the door end of the drawbridge slightly ajar, just enough for me to slip out through and then later get back in.

"I scraped the snow off the roof and climbed down, thinking I was now almost home and dry. But I discovered to my dismay that Eiko had woken up and closed the drawbridge door completely. The door doesn't open from the outside and if I were to try to force it, the noise would probably alert

314

somebody and I'd be seen, and without doubt be suspected of the crime. I'd already killed Ueda and there was no taking that back. And I didn't want to be arrested before I'd had my chance to kill Kikuoka.

"Locked out and stuck on a windswept roof, I racked my brain for an idea. There was a short rope about three metres long attached to the water tank that a workman had used to climb up the side of the tank. But obviously it was way too short for me to lower myself to the ground. The ladder was only between the level of the drawbridge and the roof. Even if I'd tied the rope to the bottom rung of the ladder, it still wouldn't have reached the ground. And besides, I'd locked the salon door from the inside earlier, so I wouldn't have been able to get back into the main building—or into my own room in the tower, again making me an obvious suspect in the killing. Then I realized I still had Golem's head. I wondered if by using the doll's head and the three-metre piece of rope, I could find a way into the house. And then I came up with an idea.

"First I tied the rope to the railing that runs around the roof and used it to lower myself to Ms Aikura's window. I thought if I could make Golem's head appear to be looking in, and wake her up, she'd be bound to scream. I knew that Eiko had only just closed the drawbridge door so she must still have been awake. If she heard Ms Aikura screaming I knew she'd get up. I would estimate the timing and climb back up to the roof, untie the rope and reattach it to the railing by Eiko's room window. Then I would make a loud noise right above Eiko's room, making her get up and come over to the window. I hoped she'd open the window to take a look outside. She's not afraid of much, that girl, so I thought the chances were pretty good.

"When she didn't see anything outside, what would she do next? I guessed she'd head to Ms Aikura's room to find out why she was screaming. If I were lucky, she'd be in a hurry and forget to close and lock the window properly first, and I'd be able to come down the rope and enter through Eiko's window. Before that I would dispose of Golem's head from the western edge of the roof as far as I could throw it.

"If Eiko were to go completely into Room 1, I would be able to slip out of Room 2 next door and hurry to let down the drawbridge, pretending that I was rushing across from the tower because I'd heard screaming.

"But if Eiko simply stood talking in the doorway of Room 1, and didn't go right inside the room, I'd have no other choice but to hide in her wardrobe until morning. Likewise, if she did enter Room 1 but came out again to find me standing on the main building side, lowering the drawbridge, that would be very hard to explain away. Not to mention the possibility that she might not even have opened her window in the first place, or that I could have been spotted climbing in through her window by the Kanais. It was all or nothing, really. My advantage was that I knew my daughter's personality so well that I felt the likelihood of success was rather good. And then, in the end, it went as smoothly as I could have dared to hope for."

"Incredible. What a brilliant plan!" said Ushikoshi. "If it had been me, I'd have knocked on my daughter's window and begged her to let me in."

"Of course I thought of that too. But I still had so much left to do."

"Yes, you still had to kill Kikuoka," said Kiyoshi. "Mr Ushikoshi, if this part of the story has amazed you, just wait

316

until you hear the rest. The planning that went into it is stunning. You'll be in awe."

"The murder of Kikuoka… But that happened while I was with Mr Hamamoto. We were definitely together at the time of death, drinking Louis XIII cognac. How on earth did—"

"He used an icicle. When I first arrived at this mansion, and looked up at the tower, it was as I had expected—there were so many huge icicles."

"An icicle!?"

The detectives looked flabbergasted.

"But it was a knife," said Okuma. "It was definitely a knife that killed Kikuoka!"

"A knife *inside an icicle*. He hung a knife from a string under the eaves of the tower roof, and it created an icicle with a knife at the tip. Isn't that right, Mr Hamamoto?"

"You got it, nicely done! This far north, the icicles are gigantic. Some of them grow longer than a metre. When I'd made my knife-cicles I dipped the tips in warm water to expose the blade of the knife. Then I kept them in the freezer."

"Ah, so that's why there was string attached to the knife. Great trick! But…" Okuma broke off.

"Yes, that's right. But theory and practice turned out to be very different. It wasn't that easy to turn a hanging icicle with a knife into a weapon. It took me a very long time to perfect it."

"But why did it have to be an icicle? Or rather, why did you need to attach an icicle to a knife?"

This was the same thing that I was wondering.

"I suppose what I really want to know is, I understand how you made a weapon, but how did you manage to—"

"Well, obviously by sliding it."

317

"Sliding it where?"

"On what?"

Several people began clamouring at once.

"Down the stairs of course! As you recall, this mansion has two staircases, one in the east and one in the west wing. If you lower the drawbridge, then there's a straight line from the window of the kitchen in the tower down to the ventilation hole in Room 14. It becomes one long, steep slide. That's the whole plan behind the eccentric arrangement of the divided staircases in this mansion."

"J… Just a minute!"

I couldn't help interrupting. There was something that was bothering me.

"So you say you slid an icicle with a knife inside down the stairs… But wouldn't it get stuck on the landings?"

"Why would it? There are twenty-centimetre gaps between the walls and the south end of each of the landings."

"So you could be sure that the icicle would pass through those gaps at the end of each landing? But the staircases are pretty wide. Surely you couldn't predict the exact course the knife would take? What if it had slid down the centre of the staircase? How could you make sure it stayed over… to the… side… Oh, I get it!"

"That's right. That's the only reason that I built this house on a slant. If the house is sloping to one side, then it follows that the stairs are too. This long staircase slide, to exaggerate a little, becomes a kind of V shape between the staircase and the wall. The house leans towards the south, so the knife-cicle was sure to travel down the southern edge of the stairs." (See Fig. 9.)

"Wow!"

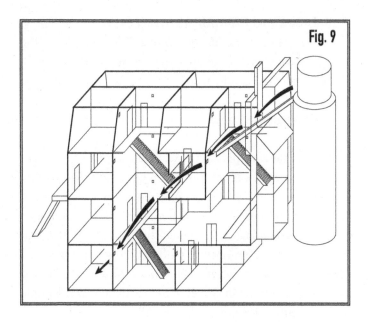

Fig. 9

I wasn't the only one lost in admiration. If Eiko had been here too, what kind of praise would she have been heaping on her beloved father right now?

Ushikoshi took over the questioning.

"So the icicle would have definitely slid through that twenty-centimetre space at the end of the corridors... I would never ever have imagined that someone could build a whole house with the sole purpose of killing another human being. Especially one so crooked... And then, Mr Hamamoto, you are saying that the icicle entered Room 14 through the ventilation hole?"

From here, Ushikoshi began to sound a little pained.

"You experimented over and over to make sure the hole was in the exact right position, so that you could place the icicle at the top of the drawbridge and have it fall without any extra force straight down into Room 14."

I realized what Ushikoshi was trying to say.

"But right in the middle of the long slide was Room 3, the Tengu Room. There's no slide in there to support an icicle!"

"But there is," said Kiyoshi.

"Where?"

"The Tengu mask noses!"

"Oh!"

I wasn't the only person to exclaim in surprise.

"The southern wall is covered in Tengu masks. The window in that room was always kept open about thirty centimetres, supposedly for ventilation. Didn't you think that was strange?"

"Of course! Somewhere among those hundreds of Tengu masks there must have been a pattern of noses arranged in a diagonal line, acting as an extension of the staircase. But it was concealed by all the other masks that filled up the whole wall. Camouflage! Now that was clever!"

"You must have practised for ages, Mr Hamamoto," said Kiyoshi.

"Yes. It took a long time to get the position of the masks just right. It all depended on the speed of the icicle. There were so many other points I had to take into consideration, I don't want to sound as if I'm bragging…"

"No, we'd like to hear it all," said Ushikoshi.

"Anyhow, I had plenty of time. I made excuses to get Mr and Mrs Hayakawa and my daughter out of the house and kept practising. I was worried that the icicle might snap in two on the way down, or because I was sliding it over quite a distance, whether the heat produced by friction would melt it. It was easy to make sure the icicles I prepared in advance were long and thick, but if too much ice remained when it arrived in Room 14, no matter how high the heating was turned up,

I was afraid that it might not have completely melted by the morning. Likewise, too much water remaining after the icicle melted would also pose a problem. Therefore, I had to make the icicle as short and thin as possible, but still strong enough to reach its target in Room 14 before melting. Luckily, it turned out that the icicles always slid so quickly that they reached the bottom in an instant, and friction caused a surprisingly small amount of melting."

"But weren't you still worried about the amount of water it produced as it melted?"

"Indeed. At times I gave serious thought to creating them out of dry ice. But I'd have to purchase the dry ice from somewhere, and that might mean I could be traced. So I gave up on that plan, and that's why in the end, to avoid suspicion, I had to spill water over Kikuoka's body from the flower vase.

"Actually, the water created other problems too. First of all, there was always a small amount of water remaining on the stairs. And then as the icicle entered Room 14, it always dripped a slight amount of water into the basement corridor and down the wall below the ventilation hole. It was always possible that somebody might notice. However, the corridor down in the basement was dimly lit, and the heating would be on all night, so I figured it should evaporate completely by the morning. There wasn't much of it."

"But it's the Tengu noses that surprised me the most," said Kiyoshi. "I remember the discussion about the export of Tengu masks."

"What was that?" I asked.

"In the past, Japan received an order from the United States for a large number of Tengu masks. The mask manufacturers made a huge profit from these sales. So they went on to manufacture great numbers of *Okame* and *Hyottoko*, the comic man and woman masks, and exported those too, but they failed to sell at all."

"Why was that?"

"Apparently, Americans were using the Tengu masks to hang hats and other stuff on. Perhaps it's only Japanese people who failed to see those noses as something useful."

"But there was nothing to support the icicle between the stairs and the ventilation holes either," Okuma pointed out.

"Yes, just outside the ventilation hole to Room 14. That's true. But by that point it was travelling so fast there was no need for anything. Outside the ventilation hole into Room 3, there's a decorative wall carving, part of which juts out at just the right level to support the icicle.

(On this point, the author feels he may have been unfair to the reader. However, he believes that it will not cause any lasting damage to those with a vivid imagination.)

"I see. After leaving the noses in the Tengu Room, the second staircase would take care of the rest," I said.

"And that's why there was such a narrow bed in Room 14 with feet that couldn't be moved…"

This was the first time that Sergeant Ozaki had spoken since leaving the Tengu Room.

"It was so the victim's heart would be in the right location," continued Kiyoshi. "And that's why he only had a thin electric blanket to cover him—so he could be killed while he was in bed. If he'd had a thick duvet or a blanket, it would have made it difficult for the knife to penetrate his body.

"But reality is stranger than fiction. At this point Mr Hamamoto had an unforeseen stroke of luck along with another similar piece of bad luck."

"What was that?" asked Ushikoshi and Okuma in accidental unison.

"The brilliance of this whole trick was that the icicle would melt, leaving just the knife stuck in the corpse, so it would look like a stabbing. To add to the illusion, just one night earlier Kazuya Ueda had in fact been stabbed to death, making it even more likely that everyone would believe that the same method was used in both murders."

"Yes, I see."

"And to make sure that the ice did melt, Mr Hamamoto instructed that the heating that night be turned up. The good stroke of luck was that Mr Kikuoka was so warm that he had taken off the electric blanket, and was sleeping with nothing over him. And so the knife went straight into his body unimpeded. The bad luck was that he was sleeping on his stomach.

"This whole trick was devised to pierce the heart of someone sleeping face up on that bed. But it seems that Mr Kikuoka was in the habit of sleeping face down. And so the knife ended up going into the right side of his back.

"But then, ironically, that one piece of bad luck was followed by another unexpected stroke of good luck. Mr Kikuoka had—how should I say it—a cowardly side to his character. His chauffeur had just been murdered, and he was so terrified that he wasn't satisfied with setting all three of the locks on the door; he had also dragged the sofa over to block it, and even put the coffee table on top of that. And that's why when, severely injured and on the point of death, he wasn't able to get out of the room and get help.

"As the knife hadn't reached his heart, if he hadn't built that barricade, he might have got out of his room and maybe even staggered up to the salon and got help. Instead, he ended up using his last ounce of strength to push over the table and sofa before collapsing. And so the crime scene ended up with another similarity to Mr Ueda's, which Mr Hamamoto had never intended: traces of the murderer having been in the room."

"It's true. I was very lucky. There was only the one bit of bad luck—that a talented investigator like you came along to solve the crime."

Kozaburo Hamamoto didn't seem particularly upset by his misfortune.

"Hang on! I just remembered!" cried Ushikoshi. "Right at 11 o'clock, the time of Mr Kikuoka's death, when we were drinking cognac together in the tower, you played that piece of music. It was—"

"It was 'Chanson de l'adieu'—Farewell."

"Yes, of course. That's what it was."

"I told you my daughter hated it, but for me it was the very first piece by Chopin that I ever heard."

"Me too," said Ushikoshi. "But in my case, I still don't know anything else of his."

"Because that one's in the school textbook," offered Okuma.

"If only I'd remembered its title that night," said Ushikoshi regretfully.

But I couldn't help thinking that if Chief Inspector Ushikoshi had guessed the truth that night from the title of a tune, the outcome would have been so much less satisfying.

"I guessed the truth," said Kiyoshi, getting to his feet, "when I heard that Golem had peeped in through Ms Aikura's window; I guessed immediately that it had to be the work of someone used to passing to and fro across that drawbridge. Nobody else would have come up with a plan that involved leaving the door to the drawbridge open—to what was essentially Mr Hamamoto's domain.

"But when I thought about it, the only way of establishing proof of the crime was to establish proof of the identity of the criminal. By experimenting, I could easily explain *how* the killer had managed to commit the crimes, but as to the *who*—well, there were other people besides Kozaburo Hamamoto who could have done it."

Everyone pondered the meaning of his words.

"To cut a long story short, the occupants of Rooms 1 and 2 could have done it, and if Chikako Hayakawa had been in the room in the tower around the time of death, she could have done it too.

"Right then, the hypothesis was that the icicle was sent all the way down the slide from the very top. But imagine the point on the slide just beyond Room 3, in other words, the staircase that you have to climb to get up to Room 3 from the ground floor. I couldn't completely rule out the possibility that someone quite different might have sent the icicle from that much lower point with a very strong push. As long as the motive for this murder remained so vague, I had to assume that anyone could have prepared a similar icicle under the eaves outside their own bedroom window. Outdoors is the perfect freezer.

"So I decided that the only way to be sure was to hear an explanation from the killer himself. In other words, to corner him so that he would be encouraged to confess everything in his own words. I'm not personally into tying someone up and forcing it out of them. That's not the way I work."

Kiyoshi threw Sergeant Ozaki a sideways glance.

"Obviously, I had already guessed the identity of the killer, but the method I devised to flush him out was by using the thing most beloved to him, that is, the life of his daughter. I made him fear that someone was planning to kill her in the exact same manner as Mr Kikuoka had been murdered. The only way to do that was to have her sleep on the bed in Room 14.

"But her father wasn't able to confide in the police why he was anxious for her life without explaining his own part in Kikuoka's murder, so he made up his mind to protect her by himself. He was a murderer himself. And the conditions were perfect—there was a blizzard outside. Oh… it seems to have stopped."

It was true—the noise of the wind had become much softer.

"For Kikuoka's murder there needed to be something loud like that storm. The icicle made quite a noise at it slid down the stairs."

"I see. So that's why Kikuoka's murder came so close after Ueda's!" I said.

"That's right. He couldn't squander the chance of using a stormy night like that one. There was no way of knowing when the next blizzard would blow in. However, anyone with their ear close to a door frame or a pillar could hear the sound of the icicle slithering down the stairs. That was—"

"The snake!"

"The sound like a woman sobbing!"

"And as it was an icicle the conditions needed to be full-on winter. But in my case, it wouldn't matter if the night outside was silent as a cemetery, I planned to go ahead with the trick I was going to play on Mr Hamamoto. I had everything set up.

"Of course Mr Hamamoto didn't know for sure that some-one planned to kill his daughter. And he couldn't confide in anyone. But he knew the exact way Mr Kikuoka had been murdered, and feared that someone was going to try to take their revenge the same way. Perhaps he thought that Kikuoka's employee was the one who was going to do it.

"This is what he decided. If the door to the drawbridge was shut, it would be practically impossible for whoever it was to open it and lower the bridge without making a lot of noise. So he figured the theoretical killer would probably push the icicle from the point on the east wing staircase just below the drawbridge.

"It was more difficult for me to imagine what he would decide next. What would be his next course of action? I couldn't read him with a hundred per cent accuracy. Would he go to the east wing staircase? That would mean coming face to face with the person planning to kill his daughter. Would Kozaburo Hamamoto choose this route? Or would he go to the west wing staircase and try his best to stop the icicle as it came sliding down? No, that would be difficult to achieve. There were several courses of action he might have taken. He could have placed bricks on the west staircase and then headed up to the east one. But in the end I was convinced that he was going to try something completely different. And that was to go to Room 3 and take down the Tengu masks from the wall."

For the umpteenth time that evening, the "aahs" could be heard around the room.

"Obviously I couldn't be a hundred per cent sure about that either. He might have left the masks intact and used another method to stop the icicle. It was a gamble, but a good one. There was a long time until morning, and Mr Hamamoto had no idea what time the killer would strike. It was better for him not to be seen. Putting bricks on the stairs might not succeed in stopping the icicle, and he really didn't want to hang out on the stairs all night waiting for the killer to arrive.

"But the position of the Tengu masks was crucial. If he took some down, burned them or just bent the noses of a few of them, the attack from the east wing was almost sure to be blocked. I believed he'd go for it.

"Thus I figured that if Mr Hamamoto could be caught red-handed removing the masks from the wall, then he wouldn't be able to talk his way out of it. By this point I was sure that Mr Hamamoto was the killer. His own daughter was in danger, but he didn't ask the police for help, because this would have revealed his knowledge of the method used to kill Kikuoka.

"But how to catch him red-handed? That was still a major problem. Hide in the library next door and wait for him? But what if Mr Hamamoto checked the library before going into Room 3?

"Anyway, as the house's designer he would know all the places that I could possibly find to hide. I was bound to lose if I tried that kind of game with him. And if I were simply to go up there shortly after Mr Hamamoto and catch him with the masks in his hand, well, that wouldn't have much impact. He could have just claimed he was unable to sleep, came to check out the room, and found that someone had broken in and destroyed his Tengu mask display. He would be intelligent enough to use the policemen who had come running with me; he'd have quickly regrouped and gone with that strategy.

"So I had to catch him in the process of removing the masks from the wall. And in addition, to avoid any kind of confusion afterwards, make it crystal clear to him that he had been seen. In order to do that I had to find the perfect place to conceal myself. And as you know, Mr Hamamoto, I found myself the best seat in the house."

"Brilliant! A truly excellent plan."

Kozaburo was full of genuine admiration.

"But how did you make that mask of Golem's face? And in such a short time? How on earth did you manage that?"

"I did it when I took his head to the forensics lab. I got in touch with an artist friend of mine and had him make it."

"Could I take a look?"

Kiyoshi handed Kozaburo the mask.

"Ah! Excellent workmanship. I'm surprised to hear of such a craftsman living in Hokkaido."

"Actually, I don't think there are any outside Kyoto. This was done by a mutual friend of mine and Kazumi's. He's quite a famous doll maker in Kyoto."

"Oh!"

I was surprised to hear of my friend's involvement.

"Did you go all the way to Kyoto in that short time?"

"I set out the evening of the 31st and called him from a phone in the village. He told me he could have it ready by the morning of the 3rd. That was why the conclusion of this case had to take place tonight, the night of the 3rd."

"A full two days' work…" said Kozaburo, deeply impressed. "You've got a great friend there."

"Did you get one of the police officers to fetch it from Kyoto?" I asked.

"No. It's not my place to get the police running errands for me."

"But I never noticed you getting any delivery of a Golem mask."

"Who cares how some mask was delivered?" said Okuma irritably. "I want to hear about the murder of Sasaki in Room 13!"

Personally, I had no objection to moving on.

"But, Mr Hamamoto, there's still one thing I don't understand," said Kiyoshi. "It's the motive. It's the one thing I can't work out. I can't imagine someone of your standing killing someone just for fun. I can't see any reason for you to kill Eikichi Kikuoka, who you don't even really know that well. I'd like to hear it from your own mouth."

"Hey, before that can we please hear about the other locked-room murder?" I begged. "There's so much more that we still need an explanation for."

"There's no need for any explanation!" Kiyoshi rudely interrupted me.

"I'll explain," said Kozaburo in a much calmer voice.

"Then should I call the other person who deserves to hear this?" asked Kiyoshi.

"You mean Anan?" said Okuma. "Right, I'll go get him."

Okuma got up and started to head off to Room 14.

"Mr Okuma?" called Kiyoshi. "If you don't mind, could you also, er…"

The Inspector stopped and turned around.

"Could you also fetch Mr Sasaki from Room 13?"

Gobsmacked would not be strong enough a word to describe the look on Okuma's face at that moment. Even if a UFO had landed right in front of him and a two-headed alien had stepped out, he could not have been more stunned.

But nobody was laughing at him. Myself included, everyone at the dining table wore pretty much the identical expression.

When Sasaki arrived in the salon along with Constable Anan, everybody was so delighted by the one single piece of good news among all the depressing events of the past few days that a small cheer went up.

"Here's Mr Sasaki returned from Heaven," announced Kiyoshi.

"So he's the one who went to Kyoto for you," I cried. "And the Golem ghost that Mrs Kanai saw, and the person who set fire to Ms Hamamoto's bed."

"He's also the one who ate the bread and ham," said Kiyoshi with a grin. "He was the perfect person to play the role of a dying man. As he was a real medical student, we didn't need to use ketchup for blood. And he knew the exact amount that would have resulted from the injury."

"I've been pretty much fasting these past few days, hiding away in Room 10 or hanging around outside. For a while I was hiding in the large wardrobe in Room 1. I almost became a real corpse!"

Sasaki seemed rather cheerful about it. It was easy to imagine why Kiyoshi had picked him for this important role.

"I see now. The most inexplicable locked-room murder was inexplicable because it never happened," I said.

"You have to trust logic," said Kiyoshi.

"But I could have gone to Kyoto for you," I said.

"That's very true. But to be perfectly honest, you're not a very good actor. You'd probably not convince anyone the knife was really in your heart. Someone would have told you to get up and stop pretending. It was important for Mr Hamamoto to feel the pressure of one of his guests being murdered."

It seemed to me as if Kozaburo had felt greater pressure when he thought his daughter was in danger.

"Did you write that threatening letter too?" Ushikoshi asked. "It's a good thing I didn't decide to run an analysis of everyone's handwriting."

"This one is about to tell me he'd have liked to write that for me too," said Kiyoshi, slapping me on the shoulder.

331

"You didn't need to trick us too," said Ozaki, clearly annoyed.

"Really? So if I'd confided my plan to you, you'd have agreed at once to go along with it?"

"It looks like you got the straight-laced lot back at my station to play along," said Okuma, with a touch of admiration.

"Yes, I have to admit that was the most difficult part of this whole case."

"Must've been."

"But I got Superintendent Nakamura from Tokyo HQ to keep on at them until they gave in."

"That Nakamura has a discerning eye all right," murmured Ushikoshi, loud enough only for me to overhear.

"Right, I don't think there's any more to add about that. Now—"

He was cut off by Ushikoshi.

"I just realized! That's why that night you insisted so strongly that Yoshihiko and Eiko stay all night at the billiard table. You wanted them to be with a police officer to give them the perfect alibi for Mr Kikuoka's murder."

Kozaburo nodded. A father's love for his daughter—the fatal weakness that had caused him to fall into the trap set by my friend.

"Chief Inspector Ushikoshi, had you heard from this man any part of what he planned to do?" said Ozaki quietly.

"Yes. The name of the suspect and the general outline. I told him to do as he liked."

"And you kept quiet about it?"

"Well, yes. But do you think that was the wrong decision? He's got an extraordinary mind, that one."

"Has he? I'm not so sure about that, personally. Seems all swagger to me."

332

Ozaki was venting his frustration.

"He behaves differently depending who he's with."

"Oh… I just remembered—the hair I put on the door of Room 14. When you went with Mr Hamamoto, and rattled the doorknob, you must have knocked it off then."

"Ah, yes, I suppose so… And I've just realized myself about the blood on the string when Ueda was killed. The string had absorbed some of the red blood then, but in the case of Kikuoka there was nothing. Even though in both cases the string ought to have touched the blood. I should have noticed."

"Right, then. If there are no more points that need explaining, let's get to the thing I want to hear the most. I'm ready to ask the big question."

I felt that Kiyoshi's emotionless, businesslike way of talking was particularly cruel right now. It felt like a punch to the guts. This was his usual way of doing things. Except that, unlike the police, he never seemed to look down on the criminals that he caught. Kozaburo Hamamoto had been a worthy opponent, and he had treated him with respect to the very end.

"Yes, of course. Where to begin…?"

Kozaburo seemed to find it hard to speak. It was clear he had a heavy heart.

"Everyone is no doubt wondering why I wanted to kill Eikichi Kikuoka, a man with whom I had no close relationship. Well, that's a reasonable question. We hadn't grown up together, we hadn't even met when we were young men. I had absolutely no personal grudge against him. But I feel no remorse—I had a perfectly good reason to kill him. My only regret is that I killed Mr Ueda. I really didn't need to. That was my own selfishness.

"I'll tell you the story of why I had to kill Kikuoka. It won't be moving, or beautiful, or just, nor for some admirable cause.

333

It was the atonement for a mistake that I made back in my youth."

He broke off there, as if trying to deal with some unbearable pain. It was the face of a man tortured by his own conscience.

"The story begins almost forty years ago, when Hama Diesel was still Murata Engines. I'll keep it short. Back then Murata Engines was just a simple office—nothing but a row of desks in the dirt-floor entrance way of a hut hastily constructed in the ruins of burnt-out Tokyo. Nothing but a backstreet work-shop, really. Anyway, I had confidence in my own abilities and was promoted from apprentice up to head clerk. The boss had great trust in me, and although I say so myself, the company wouldn't have run as smoothly without me.

"The company president had a daughter—his only child. He'd once had a son too, but the young man was killed in the war. This daughter and I got on very well. Back in those days I couldn't say we were going out together, but she made it clear that she liked me and it seemed that I had her father's approval. I can't deny that I had ambitions to marry the boss's daughter and inherit the business, but my intentions towards her were always pure. While I'd been away fighting, my parents had been killed in an air raid, so there would be no objections from my family to taking my wife's name.

"And then a man by the name of Yamada turned up. He was the second son of a certain politician, and had been at school with Tomiko. (That was the name of my boss's daughter.) It seemed that he'd had an eye for Tomiko for a while.

"I can attest that this man was a fully fledged member of the *yakuza*. At that time he was already living with a woman of dodgy repute. All I wanted was for Tomiko to be happy, and if he'd been a good man, I would have been able to deal with the rejection. If by marrying this man from a good family, the small company could have profited and done well, then I would have been happy to step aside. But this Yamada was just a worthless punk, and totally unworthy of Tomiko. Unfortunately, her father was into the idea of his daughter marrying a politician's son.

"I couldn't understand my boss's attitude at all, and worried day and night. But now that I'm a father myself, I understand him much better. A father doesn't want his daughter to marry purely from love. There are other considerations.

"Anyway, I wanted to save Tomiko from the misery of becoming this man's wife. I swear that I didn't only have the ulterior motive of making her my own. Back then, it never even occurred to me.

"Around that time I bumped into an old childhood friend of mine by the name of Noma. I'd thought he'd been killed on the front line in Burma. It was a joyous reunion, we went out drinking and caught up. Noma was in a bad way—nothing but skin and bones, sick and weak.

"I'll get to the point. Noma had turned up in Tokyo at that time because he was hunting down a man. This man was a few years younger than him, but had been his commanding officer in the army—an unspeakably cruel man. Noma had managed to survive but he couldn't forget the suffering he had endured at the hands of this officer.

"I heard the story of what happened to him many times over. But what was slightly different in his case was that to him this officer was a double murderer—he'd been directly responsible for the death of one of Noma's comrades-in-arms and also the woman Noma loved. In time of war, this officer had got kicks out of inflicting private punishment on his subordinates. It was an everyday occurrence with him. In fact, there were some

335

of Noma's fellow soldiers who ended up permanently scarred from his cruelty.

"Noma had become involved with a local Burmese girl, an extremely beautiful young woman. He'd decided that once the war was ended, if he managed to survive, he would marry her and remain in Burma.

"But with the misfortune that comes in wartime, his commanding officer captured this woman, accusing her of being a spy. Noma knew it wasn't true, desperately tried to stop him, but the officer merely replied that 'All beautiful women are spies.' Utterly ridiculous reasoning. He made her a prisoner of war, and proceeded to subject her to worse abuse than any human being could possibly imagine.

"Finally, when the order to retreat came, the officer ordered all of the prisoners to be shot. And later, when Japan surrendered, he threatened all of his men to keep quiet about it—I mean the fact that he had had all the prisoners of war killed. As a result, one of Noma's fellow soldiers ended up being executed for having carried out those orders, while the officer, after a brief detainment, went scot-free.

"Noma was an academic type, not physically strong at all. The way he was living his life, constantly plotting revenge on his commanding officer, was destroying him. He had started coughing up blood. It was clear to me that he didn't have long to live. Noma told me he wasn't afraid to die, but that if he did he would die with regret in his heart, because just a few days earlier he had finally managed to find that commanding officer.

"Noma used to carry a concealed pistol around with him at all times. But it only contained one bullet. He used to say that it was impossible to get bullets any more, but he was ready for the day when he faced off with his enemy. He wouldn't hesitate.

"After being demobilized, this commanding officer had apparently lost everything he ever owned, and spent his days drinking. He used to hold his bottle of cheap sake and look Noma in the eyes, telling him, 'Oh, it's you. Make sure you shoot me right in the heart.' If Noma hesitated, he'd say, 'I've got nothing left to lose. I don't care if I die. Death would be a release.'

"Noma used to tell me, with tears pouring down his face, that because of all the pain this man had inflicted on him, his fellow soldiers and the woman he'd loved, he didn't want to give him such an easy death.

"There are probably many stories like this one, but this is one of the worst I've ever heard. I was furious, and even thought of getting revenge on his behalf. Noma then asked how I was doing and I told him about my own troubles, all the while aware that mine were nothing in comparison to his.

"I finished talking, Noma's eyes were glistening. 'Let me use my final bullet on this Yamada,' he said. 'Then you'll be able to marry that woman. I don't have long on this earth, but in return, promise me that when that bastard finally has something worth losing, you will get rid of him for me.' It was a heartbreaking appeal from a close friend.

"I didn't know what to do. If I got rid of Yamada, then I would be free to marry Tomiko and eventually take over Murata Engines. And however I looked at it, it wouldn't only be beneficial to me, but to my boss and to Tomiko too. I was young and hard-working, and I believed I had a lot of talent. I thought it would be crazy for me not to be given the opportunity to work the way I knew I could. I was sure I could expand the company—I had already developed concrete plans as to how I would achieve this.

"It would get tedious for me to describe every single bit of my thought processes back then. Suffice it to say, Yamada died, and together with my beloved Tomiko, I was eventually able to run Murata Engines.

"It was a time where demobilized soldiers wandered around in the ashes of post-war Japan, where children starved to death every day, and often no one could help.

"I worked like a dog to build up the little backstreet workshop into the Hama Diesel you know today. And I'm very proud of all the work I've done. But in the breast pocket of every jacket I've ever worn, I've kept the old photo that Noma gave me of his commanding officer, along with his address on a scrap of paper. I'm sure I don't need to tell you that the officer in question was Eikichi Kikuoka."

Kozaburo stopped for a while. I stole a glance at Kumi Aikura. Her expression didn't reveal anything.

"I heard through the grapevine that Kikuoka's company's fortunes were improving, but I had no intention of contacting him. My own company was doing really well, my overseas investments were succeeding and the time spent with Noma back in my youth began to feel like a distant bad dream. I wore expensive clothes and sat in my president's office, and the path I walked, the chair I sat in, were so different from back when I was poor that I felt as if I now lived in a completely different world. I never wanted to go back to having nothing. I almost got away with telling myself that my current status had been earned by my hard work alone. But the truth is, if Yamada hadn't died, Murata Engines would still be a backstreet workshop, and I would still be a humble factory worker. It took the death of my wife for me to admit this to myself.

"But bad things do happen to those who do bad things. My wife didn't die of old age... She died of an illness, much too young. The cause remains unclear. But with her death I felt Noma's demand that I should hurry up and keep my promise.

At that time, Kikuoka's company was doing rather well. I got in contact with him in a perfectly normal way. For him, to hear from me must have felt like a sudden windfall.

"And after that I think you all know what happened. I retired, and built this eccentric mansion. I suppose you all thought that it was the whim of a crazy old man, but in fact I designed it with a very specific purpose.

"I committed a crime, but something good came out of it. I realized yesterday when I was listening to Wagner. I've spent my whole life keeping that secret inside, while around me the lies have been building up and hardening until it was as if I'd been fixed in cement. There have been 'yes-men' jostling for position around me, and all the flattery they've heaped on me has set my teeth on edge. But now I've managed to smash through that false protective layer I'd built up, and I'm feeling like I did back in my youth—finally, truth and honesty have returned to me. You said something about Jumping Jack the other day?"

"Yes, the doll," said Kiyoshi.

"That's not Golem. It's me. The last twenty years of my life I've been nothing but a kind of doll. I was only creative right in the beginning, after that I was nothing but a snowman. Long ago people were impressed by my work, but I haven't done anything creative for years.

"Just for a moment, I believed I could be my old self again. Pure-hearted, honest, with close friends, that brilliant young

339

man of long ago. That's why I kept my promise. It was a promise made forty years ago, by a version of me that I admired."

Nobody spoke. Perhaps they were contemplating the true meaning of success.

"If it were me, I wouldn't have done it."

It was Michio Kanai who spoke. I saw his wife poke him in the ribs to try to make him stop, but he ignored her. Perhaps he thought this was his opportunity to show what he was made of.

"I don't think I would have been so faithful to my old friend. Society is full of deceit. I mean that people deceive each other all the time. I don't mean this entirely in a bad way. Cheating is a kind of art, particularly in the working world. A salaryman has to spend half his working life lying. I mean this in all seriousness.

"Take, for example, a doctor. He has a patient with stomach cancer, but he tells him that it's an ulcer. Can you blame him? The patient will die in the end, but he'll believe it's because the ulcer got worse. He'll die relieved that he never was unlucky enough to suffer from a terrifying cancer.

"It was the same with Mr Hamamoto's friend. He was able to believe that his good friend would destroy the evil brute for him, and so he died a peaceful death. What's the difference between Mr Noma and the cancer patient? Mr Hamamoto had to become the president of Hama Diesel and so he did. There were no losers in this scenario.

"I was forced to show respect to Kikuoka. How many times did I dream of strangling that dirty, lecherous old man? But, as I said before, society is full of deceit. And in Kikuoka's case, I planned to use him, profit from him, suck him dry before he died. That was to my benefit. That's what you should have done. Anyway, that's my opinion."

"Mr Kanai," Kozaburo replied, "this evening, I am sensing everyone is... how should I put it...? Lacking in outrage. In fact, sympathetic to me. It's something I never used to feel back there in my company president's office. You may well be right. However, I should emphasize that Noma didn't pass away peacefully in hospital. He died in a prison cell, wrapped in a flimsy blanket. When I think of that, I can't bear the thought of spending the rest of my life sleeping alone in a luxurious bed."

Night had somehow slipped away and the sun was already up. The wind had died down and outside was completely quiet. There were no more snowflakes tumbling from the sky, and the section of deep blue sky outside the salon window hadn't a single cloud.

The guests sat for a while, then gradually, in groups of two and three, got to their feet, bowed to Kozaburo, and went off to their various rooms to prepare to put an end to this extraordinary winter holiday.

"Mr Mitarai, I just remembered," said Kozaburo.

"Hmm?" said Kiyoshi, in his habitual flat tone.

"Did you work that one out too? The flower bed puzzle I set for Togai and the others? Did they tell you about it?"

"Oh, yes, that."

"Did you solve it?"

Kiyoshi folded his arms.

"That one... No, I didn't get it."

"Oh, that's not like you! Well, if you didn't work that one out, then I wasn't totally defeated after all."

"Isn't it better that way?"

"If it's just some misplaced sense of sympathy on your part

SCENE 5

The Hill

We reached the top of the hill, exhaling white clouds into the frigid air, just as the morning sunshine reached the ice floes out on the northern sea. The house we had been staying in was wrapped in a cottony blanket of morning mist.

Everyone turned to the north to face the Ice Floe Mansion and its tower, which from this direction stood to the right of the main building. The glass at the top of the tower picked up the rising sun and for a moment shone with a dazzling, yellow light. Kiyoshi shaded his eyes with both hands, stood and watched the spectacle. I thought he was appreciating the aesthetics, but I was wrong. He was waiting for the sun to move off the glass. Finally, the moment arrived and he opened his mouth to speak.

"Is that a chrysanthemum?"

"Yes, it is," said Kozaburo. "A chrysanthemum with its head hanging down."

I had no idea what they were talking about.

"Where?" I asked.

"That glass tower. The chrysanthemum's wilted, right?"

I finally saw it. And then there was a murmur of recognition from the three detectives.

In the glass cylinder of the tower, there was a chrysanthemum with a hanging neck. The effect was like a magnificent painted scroll. The curiously shaped flower bed around the base of the tower was reflected in the cylinder, and the whole thing was the exact image of a chrysanthemum. A colourless chrysanthemum.

"If we were in a flat place, we'd have to use a helicopter to be able to enjoy that view. If you look up at the tower from the middle of the flower bed itself, you can't see the reflection. You have to be at a distance and diagonally above to be able to see it."

"It was extremely fortuitous that this hill happened to be here, wasn't it?" said Kiyoshi. "But I can see that as you were building you realized that even the very top of this hill wasn't high enough. And so you constructed the tower so it leant very slightly in this direction. And now we can see it perfectly. That's the real reason you built that tower at an angle, isn't it?"

Kozaburo nodded. And in that moment the solution to the puzzle was clear even to me.

"I see! The chrysanthemum is Kikuoka! The hanging flower head is your vow to kill him."

"I never meant to break that promise. I always intended to end up in jail one day. I hated leading that false life. But I always hoped that someone just once would be clever enough to see through that layer that surrounded me, through to the guilt of my past. So I built this tower that reflected my thoughts.

"There's another meaning behind this design. Noma's parents ran a flower shop. His father was famous for cultivating chrysanthemums. Before the war, he used to display dolls made entirely from chrysanthemum blooms. Noma's plan after returning from the war was to take over from his father and grow chrysanthemums. As you know, to people of our generation the chrysanthemum was a flower that symbolized so much. At the very least this is a tribute to my friend.

"I suppose if I'm honest I would have liked to forget my promise to Noma. Perhaps if I'd been surrounded by a different kind of people, I would have been able to…"

Kozaburo broke off and gave a bitter laugh.

"Mr Mitarai, I'd like to ask you one last question. Why did you always pretend to clown around so much?"

Kiyoshi looked puzzled.

"I wasn't pretending. That's just my personality."

I nodded my agreement.

"I don't think that's true," said Kozaburo. "I think you were trying to get me to let my guard down. If you'd revealed right away what a sharp mind you have, I'd have been much more cautious and you'd never have been able to fool me.

"I did have a slight suspicion about you last night when Eiko began to get sleepy. I wondered for a moment whether you'd set some kind of trap. I know it sounds as if I'm talking with the benefit of hindsight, but I was suspicious. But just in case Eiko was in real danger, I couldn't assume anything at the time."

Kozaburo Hamamoto stopped and regarded Kiyoshi quietly.

"By the way, what do you think of my daughter, Eiko?"

Kiyoshi considered for a moment.

"She's a great pianist; a very well-educated young lady," he said carefully.

"Hmm. And…?"

"She's also very self-centred and egotistical. Rather too much like me, I'm afraid."

Kozaburo looked away from Kiyoshi.

"Well, you and I do have a lot in common," he said with a wry smile. "But in some ways we are completely different. And as I see it now, your way is probably right. Mr Mitarai, I am

345

very glad to have met you. I had hoped to ask you to explain the current situation to my daughter for me, but I won't be so selfish as to insist."

He held out his right hand.

"There will be a much better person for her," said Kiyoshi, shaking Kozaburo's hand.

"You mean someone who loves money more than you do?"

"Maybe someone who will put it to a better purpose. You were one such person too, I believe?"

The brief handshake done, the two men stepped apart, never to come together again.

"You have a very soft hand. You've never done much in the way of hard work?"

Kiyoshi grinned.

"If you have no money to hold on to, your palm never gets rough."

EPILOGUE

Throughout my lifetime I've seen weak and
cowardly men, without a single exception
commit all kinds of stupid acts, reduce
their allies to the level of beasts, pervert
their souls by any means possible. And all
this in the name of "glory".

LE COMTE DE LAUTRÉAMONT,
Les Chants de Maldoror

Standing in the exact same spot on the exact same hill it feels as if it happened yesterday.

Right now it's late summer, or rather up here in the northern tip of Japan, it's already more like autumn. The wind blows through the dry grass, which has not yet been hidden by the first snowfall of winter; the indigo-blue sea is not yet covered in ice.

That house of horrors that once had us in panic has now fallen into ruin; now home to nothing more than a few shed snakeskins and a whole lot of dust. Nobody visits, and nobody wants to live there.

No news ever reached us that Sasaki, or even Togai, was to be married to Eiko Hamamoto. Nor did we ever hear from Michio Kanai again. A note came in the mail addressed to Kiyoshi and myself to let us know that Kumi Aikura had opened a bar in Aoyama somewhere, but to this day neither one of us has dropped by.

In the end, Kiyoshi let on about a major aspect of the case. I feel it's my duty to write it down here.

"Do you think it was purely to avenge his daughter's death that Kohei Hayakawa hired Kazuya Ueda to kill Kikuoka?" he asked me one day out of the blue.

"Do you think there was some other reason?"

"I do."

"What makes you think that?"

"Simple. If Kozaburo Hamamoto wanted to practise sliding icicles down the stairs, there's no way he could have done it alone. For example, while he was in Room 3 adjusting the position of the noses on those Tengu masks, he'd have needed someone at the top of the stairs to let the icicle go. And who do you think used to help him?"

"Kohei Hayakawa?"

"Yes. There's no one else it could have been. And so Hayakawa knew about his employer's plan to kill Kikuoka. But he—"

"He wanted to stop him, so he hired Ueda to do it before Hamamoto could!"

"I think so.

"You mean that he tried to rescue the one person he believed to be honourable from the dishonour of being a murderer."

"Right… But it went wrong. Hamamoto was too determined."

"Mr Hamamoto probably went to prison without ever knowing just how loyal his trusted servant had been. But typically of him, he insisted to the end that he had carried out the whole operation entirely unassisted. And Hayakawa too, never told anyone what he'd done."

"Why do you think that was? Why did Hayakawa never confess that he had helped his respected employer to practise sliding icicles?"

"I'm guessing because of Eiko. He knew how Hamamoto felt about her. He was guilty of aiding and abetting a murder, but the seriousness of the offence was much less than Hamamoto's. I think he knew that a daughter who lost both parents would be in need of someone to watch over her."

"Possibly so."

*

As the Ice Floe Mansion slowly rots away, its tilted angle is even more symbolic. Having played its role, and living out its very short life, it is trying to return to the ground from whence it came. Or with the northern sea as its backdrop, it appears to be sinking slowly, like some giant ship.

I had this opportunity to travel up to the north, and I found myself drawn to this hill and the site I spent that unforgettable New Year.

The sun is setting, and somehow I feel uneasy. The grass rustles at my feet. It doesn't have long to live free either, before being imprisoned itself under a dense layer of snow.

THE END

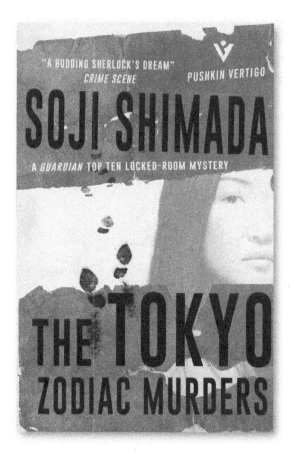

'The solution is one of the most original that I've ever read'
Anthony Horowitz, author of *The House of Silk*